"Who is willing to watch over the human?"

"I am." The two roughly spoken words resounded through the clearing with the force of a cannon blast, and Michaela instantly stilled, stiffening against Brody as all eyes turned toward them. "Until this is over," Brody growled, "the human is *mine.*"

The unbelievable words echoed through Michaela's head, the evocative warmth of Brody's breath against the sensitive shell of her ear enough to make her tremble with something more visceral than shock or fear. She struggled for the source of her reaction—then realized it was hunger, urgent and sweet, spreading hypnotically through her system. A craving that moved like warm, thick honey in her veins, settling deep within her like an intimate, pulsing glow of heat that she wanted to curl around herself. And it centered on the Bloodrunner who held her in his hard-muscled arms, the resonating beat of his heart banging out a powerful rhythm against her back.

Oh God, this can't be happening.

Books by Rhyannon Byrd

Silhouette Nocturne

Last Wolf Standing #35
Last Wolf Hunting #38
Last Wolf Watching #39

*Bloodrunners

RHYANNON BYRD

fell in love with a Brit whose accent was just too sexy to resist. Lucky for her, he turned out to be a keeper, so she married him, and they now have two precocious children, who constantly keep her on her toes. Living in the Southwest, Rhyannon spends her days creating provocative romances with her favorite kinds of hero—intense alpha males who cherish their women. When not writing, she loves to travel, lose herself in books and watch as much football as humanly possible with her loud, fun-loving family.

For information on Rhyannon's books and the latest news, you can visit her Web site at www.rhyannonbyrd.com.

LAST WOLF WATCHING

RHYANNON BYRD

Silhouette Books

nocturne™

To Debbie Hopkins Smart, for all the laughter and the
smiles, and for always being there.
With lots of love,
Rhyannon

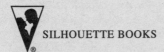

SILHOUETTE BOOKS

ISBN-13: 978-0-373-61786-9
ISBN-10:   0-373-61786-0

LAST WOLF WATCHING

Copyright © 2008 by Tabitha Byrd

www.silhouettenocturne.com

Printed in U.S.A.

Dear Reader,

I've been looking forward to sharing Brody Carter's story with you since the beginning of the BLOODRUNNERS trilogy, when the scarred, brooding Runner was first introduced. Believing himself unworthy of love and his own happily-ever-after, Brody is one of those characters you can't help but pull for, who reaches in and takes hold of your heart. Of course, like his fellow Bloodrunners, the heroic half-breed also possesses his own special brand of sex appeal. There's just something so wonderfully alluring about a powerful, love-wary warrior who's determined to fight his primal hungers, denying himself the thing he wants most in this world. And what Brody wants most is the one woman he believes he can never have— Michaela Doucet.

In *Last Wolf Watching*, the third installment of the trilogy, Brody finally finds his match in Michaela, the fiery Cajun whose beauty steals his breath and whose passionate nature thaws his guarded heart. Theirs is a deeply emotional, sensual romance about finding faith in those we hold dear and the realization that we're all worthy of love, no matter what we've been conditioned to believe. Together, Brody and Michaela discover that putting their trust in their hearts and in one another leads not to their greatest mistake, but to their ultimate triumph, as they learn to overcome the demons from their past in order to embrace the promise of their future.

Writing the BLOODRUNNERS trilogy has been a most amazing experience for me, and I hope you'll look forward to future stories from this dark, seductive world.

All the best!

Rhyannon

Last Wolf Watching
A BLOODRUNNERS Novel

The Bloodrunners Law

When offspring are conceived of a union between human and Lycan, the resulting creations may only gain acceptance within their rightful pack by the act of Bloodrunning: the hunting and extermination of rogue Lycans who have taken a desire for human flesh. Thus they prove not only their strength, but also their willingness to kill for those they will swear to protect to the death.

The League of Elders will predetermine the Bloodrunners' required number of kills.

Once said number of kills are efficiently accomplished, the Bloodrunners may assume a place among their kin, complete with full rights and privileges.

Prologue

The Bloodrunner stood on the sidewalk, staring through narrowed eyes at the silent house nestled among a bevy of trees at the end of the picturesque neighborhood street. His mood was dark, edged with impatience, muscles coiled with tension that wound tighter…and tighter with each passing second.

"Just get in, tell her and get the hell out," he muttered in a husky rasp, the nearly silent words lost in the gusting Maryland breeze, the heavy chill of autumn wrapping its arms around his shoulders like a coldhearted lover.

It was a simple enough plan—and yet, Brody Carter knew there would be nothing *simple* about it. With any other woman, yes. But not with this one.

Letting out a slow, measured breath, he stepped beneath the ivy-laden trellis sheltering the front porch. The golden glow of an old-fashioned streetlamp softly illuminated the deep shadows of the night, heavy storm clouds smothering the silvery rays of the moon, until only a few, pale streams of ethereal light filtered through. He concentrated on forcing the aggressive blend of rage and hunger that coursed steadily through his blood beneath a cool, untouched surface of indifference, and finally lifted his hand. With a sharp movement, he rapped his knuckles against the front door, his tanned skin dark against the antique white finish of the wood.

With the rational part of his mind, Brody accepted the fact that he'd rather be anywhere in the world than standing there, on Michaela Doucet's doorstep.

Unfortunately, the dangerous, animal side of his nature had other ideas, relishing the thought of being near the provocative Cajun once again. He'd had his first look at the mysterious human nearly two weeks ago, at the wedding of a fellow Bloodrunner, Mason Dillinger. And though Brody could appreciate physical beauty as much as the next guy, it seemed this woman was almost *too* beautiful, with that lush body, long black hair that fell in soft curls to the middle of her back, perfect features and dark blue eyes so big a man could get lost in them.

Still, a pretty face he could have forgotten—but it was her scent that wouldn't leave him in peace.

The autumn winds surged with a vicious fury, bitterly cold in the dead of night—and his nostrils flared as he caught a trace of that warm, peaches-and-cream fragrance that no store-bought product could duplicate. Suddenly, the cool air of indifference he'd struggled to maintain bled away like the last flecks of snow down the sides of a mountain, replaced by a blistering wave of heat. He imagined his features must look twisted with the madness of his emotions, his expression one of equal parts hunger and disgust for his weakness—and knew he'd be lucky if she didn't run screaming in the other direction the second she set eyes on him.

"Not that I'd blame her," he grunted under his breath. While his partner Cian was most often described as the pretty boy of their group, Brody figured he was the equivalent of the intimidating guard dog. Big, mean and scary-as-hell were the adjectives most suited to his appearance, and he'd learned to live with them. He'd never wished to be anything different than what he was—he only wished he'd never set eyes on the sexy Cajun with a siren's smile, who was perfect enough to have any man that she wanted.

Look, there's no need to make it complicated. Just get in, deliver the news and get the hell away from her before that scent has time to screw with your head.

He rubbed uneasily at the back of his neck, and a scowl twisted the scarred corner of his mouth, while he wondered what was taking her so long to answer the door. A dog barked down the street, and his gaze slid across the row of neighboring houses, his frown deepening with unease. This pristine world of white picket fences and quaint, family homes was as alien to him as any make-believe landscape, making him feel like the horrifying monster trespassing within a storybook fantasyland. The uncomfortable feeling had Brody struggling for calm, and he locked his jaw, just wanting to get back to the peaceful quiet of the forest.

Being in the city always set him on edge. The man in him hated the constant grind of the noise and crowds and irritating stares, preferring the isolation of the mountains where he and the other Bloodrunners lived. The wolf in him found the endless sensory overload a constant source of frustration. It felt constrained, tethered, when all it wanted to do was throw off his human mantle and howl beneath the comforting, seductive pull of the moon. The continual fight against his primal, instinctual urges whenever a hunt took him into civilization made him restless, wearing him thin.

And now he had to deal with Michaela. Not good. Not good at all.

"You're tempting fate, just like your old man," he quietly grunted to himself. "The last thing in the world you need is to be close to her."

As if to confirm what he already knew, his beast lifted its nose to search for a deeper source of that heady, mouthwatering scent that seemed to destroy him a little more with each breath. He wanted to moan, it was so good. Wanted to claw his way into her house, take her beneath his body and pretend that he'd forgotten the reasons why he couldn't touch her. Claim her. Search out her delicate pulse and *bite her.* He wanted to sink his fangs into her slender throat, her warm flesh damp and deliciously tender beneath his mouth, and lose himself in the hot, carnal rush of her blood at the same time as he buried himself hard and thick and deep between her silken thighs. His hands fisted at the dizzying thought, muscles locked in a paroxysm of agony, while he choked back a low, rumbling growl of frustration.

He was a Bloodrunner, the offspring of his human mother and Lycan father. A hunter of rogue werewolves. A protector of the Lycan way of life for the Silvercrest pack. But unlike his fellow Runners, Brody knew that in some ways he was more monster than man. He walked a delicate balance between the two opposing worlds, and the woman inside this house upped the stakes to a dangerous, deadly level. For too many months, his beast had been denied the physical pleasures that fed its soul, not unlike the way a wild kill fed his animal appetites. By the time he'd understood the dangerous effects of his self-imposed celibacy—it was too late. He hadn't dared to seek out a woman, even a Lycan one, because he didn't trust his human half to be able to master the savage urges of his beast.

Then Michaela Doucet had walked into his life, and Brody discovered what it was like to live in true fear—what it was like to live in hell. Every moment spent in her company took him one step closer to the crumbling edge of his control, until he could all but feel the fires of damnation licking at his skin.

"You need to go home, grab a bottle of Jack and find a way to forget she even exists," he muttered to himself, squeezing his eyes tight as he lifted his fist and knocked harder, all but shaking the sturdy door within its frame, nearly cracking the wood. The wind grew savage, riffling through his hair, pulling the dark auburn strands across his face until he had to swipe at them with his hand. Drawing in another deep, ragged breath, Brody hammered at the door again…and again, feeling every bit the part of the Big Bad Wolf getting ready to huff, and puff and blow her picture-perfect world to pieces.

Finally, the lock on the front door clicked, the handle turning, and Brody shoved his shaky hands deep in the pockets of his jeans, steeling himself to get what needed to be said over and done with as fast as possible. After all, he'd come tonight to tell the woman who'd become his secret obsession that she'd lost her brother—or rather, the brother she'd always known.

The boy she'd raised was gone. Forever.

"And you get to be the lucky bastard who tells her," he snarled, the whispered words so guttural, they barely sounded human.

Brody muttered a foul word under his breath, and with the rasping ease of an old, comfortable house, the front door quietly opened...

Chapter 1

Eighteen hours later...

Fear sat on the tip on Michaela Doucet's tongue, as bitter as an aspirin waiting to be swallowed. It possessed a sharp, acidic flavor that made her mouth water in the way that it does when you're about to be sick, while her eyes burned with a stinging wash of gathering tears. She willed them back with the sheer stubborn force of her will, reminding herself again and again that Doucets weren't ones to cower. Raised in the superstition-rich environment of the Louisiana Bayou, she'd grown up on whispered tales of ghosts and goblins, vampires and werewolves.

Yes, she'd always been a believer, even if she'd never seen proof of the paranormal creatures most humans consigned to the realm of fantasy and fiction. But now the veil between the two worlds had been lifted. Two weeks ago, she and her brother Max had learned the truth about the secret that resided in the eastern mountains just a few hours' drive west of their home in Covington, Maryland. Werewolves did indeed live among us. Some good. Some bad. Some so evil, they were more monsters than men.

And then there were others who were truly heroes. Dark, dangerous and tortured ones, yes—but undoubtedly heroic.

Michaela's best friend, Torrance Watson, had fallen in love with one such hero: Mason Dillinger, a man who was half human–half Lycan. Mason was one of a select breed of hunters known as Bloodrunners who were committed to hunting down and exterminating the rogue Lycans who'd begun murdering humans. Because of their half-human bloodlines, the Runners lived separately from the Silvercrest werewolf pack they protected, in a place named Bloodrunner Alley.

The Doucets had been under Bloodrunner protection ever since a rogue werewolf had made a move on Torrance's life. And while Michaela didn't care for the lack of privacy, Wyatt Pallaton and Carla Reyes—the Bloodrunning team assigned to their protection—had become friends to both her and Max. She had been thankful for their watchful eye, especially for her brother's sake.

Yes, she could accept the existence of werewolves. She'd even begun to embrace a few of them as part of her family. But tonight, terror consumed her.

Beneath the wraithlike streams of silvery moonlight, the autumn wind whistled past her ears, reminding her of a specter imparting secrets, the cool frost of its voice chilling against her skin. Shivering, she inhaled deeply through her nose, searching for the fresh scents of the surrounding forest, for pinesap and juniper and the moist smell of the soil. Like a frightened child grasping at a frayed security blanket, she needed the familiarity of those things to ground her in a world that had tilted on its axis, knocking her off balance—but all she could find was the acrid stench of aggression. Feral and thick, the heavy scent closed around her like a physical vise, banding her chest, making it difficult to draw enough air into her lungs.

Even as an outsider in this ominous setting, she understood instinctively what the menacing energy permeating the night signified. They were ready—the Silvercrest pack's anticipation ripe for the ceremony that would soon begin.

Hold it together, she silently scolded. *Do not fall apart.*

Willing her backbone to keep her upright, Michaela focused on the towering blaze of a roaring bonfire that rose from the far side of the clearing, its orange flames burning with maniacal zeal against the ink-black curtain of night. Not even the stars shone in the eastern sky. Only the moon burned in the stygian darkness of the heavens, its yellowed mass seeming to reflect the fiery glow of the sinister flames.

The mountains were silent but for the low, nearby noises that filled her ears, more animal-like than human. This was Silvercrest pack land, and the werewolves were tired of waiting. Michaela kept her gaze fixed on the fire, aware that many of the Lycans had already shifted into their preternatural shapes, their fur-covered bodies standing like monstrous shadows at the edges of the forest as they waited with restless expectancy.

If not for her friends, she'd have thought she was in hell. But she wasn't alone, thank God. Mason stood on her left, while Torrance moved in closer to her right side and grabbed her hand, squeezing her icy fingers in support as the wind surged around them, rattling the autumn leaves upon the gnarled branches of the trees, scattering others in the ravaging gusts. It still seemed astonishing that her best friend, who'd always been wary of the supernatural, had married a man who could howl at the moon, but Michaela liked Mason, as well as respected him. And there was no denying that the gorgeous half-breed was head over heels in love with his red-headed wife.

"Everything's going to be okay," Torrance murmured, the tone of her voice soothing, as if gentling a cornered animal. "Mason won't let anything happen to Max, I promise."

Okay? she thought, blinking rapidly as tears threatened to spill once more from her raw, swollen eyes. How was that even possible? Her nineteen-year-old brother had been attacked by a rogue werewolf—a Lycan who preyed upon humans for food. Max had been bitten in the attack, which meant he was no longer human, but a breed of creature that existed between the two worlds of man and beast, much like the Bloodrunners themselves.

Last night, it had been Carla Reyes's turn to wait at the hospital while Max worked his shift as a security guard. Michaela had been enjoying a relaxing evening at home after a long day at her store, when Reyes called to let her and Wyatt know that Max had taken his car and disappeared in the middle of making his rounds. Michaela couldn't think of any possible reason that Max would do such a thing—unless it had something to do with Sophia Dawson. And she'd been right.

Sophia was an eighteen-year-old Lycan who'd discovered the gruesome murder of a human female the week before. She'd spent a few days at their home, before returning to her parents' house in Shadow Peak, the mountaintop town that was home to the Silvercrest pack. Max and Sophia had become fast friends, despite Michaela's warnings that her brother should be cautious. Sophia was mixed up with a wild party crowd down in Covington, and the last thing Michaela had wanted was to see her brother become involved in an unhealthy relationship. She didn't care that Sophia was a werewolf—but she *did* care that the teenager was heavily involved in the local drug scene.

In fact, she suspected it was Sophia's troubled lifestyle that had drawn Max to her in the first place. He'd always been a champion of the underdog, willing to take on everyone's worries as his own. Michaela loved that his heart was so generous, but she'd also worried that it would eventually land him in trouble—which was exactly what had happened.

After Carla's call, Wyatt had contacted the other Runners and a search of the city had been immediately set into action. Then Brody Carter had arrived on her doorstep with his heartbreaking news.

"Max is still alive," the Bloodrunner had explained to her and Wyatt in gritty, clipped tones. *"Sophia Dawson showed up in Shadow Peak with him about a half hour ago. They're trying to get the story out of her, but she's pretty hysterical. Seems she'd called Max from a concert, scared that she and her girlfriends were being followed. Says Max told her he knew Reyes wouldn't let him into that part of town, so he slipped out a back entrance at the hospital, grabbed his car and met up with them. He talked Sophia into coming back home with him, but before they could make it back to his car, they were attacked. The only thing that saved their lives was an accident that happened up the street. When he heard the*

approaching sirens, the rogue fled and the girls were able to get Max in his car. Sophia panicked and drove him straight to her parents' house. They notified the Elders and he was taken into custody."

Michaela had stood there feeling dead inside, a great roaring wave of pain ripping through her body, while Wyatt had talked with the scowling Runner. Then Brody had left as quickly as he'd come, leaving Wyatt to explain that Max would be kept in a holding cell in Shadow Peak, where he would be watched by guards until his first shift into a werewolf, which usually came the second night after an attack. Once the signs of impending change were noted, a *Novitiates* ceremony would be called.

Wyatt had driven her up to Bloodrunner Alley, a picturesque glade that sat several miles south of Shadow Peak on the mountain. The Alley held cabins where the Runners lived, and she'd spent the rest of the night with Torrance and Mason.

The wait for nightfall during the long, torturous day had been a living hell—but the call warning them that the ceremony would soon begin had finally come. They'd immediately set off for the clearing, which sat equidistant between Shadow Peak and the Alley.

And now it was time.

The muscles in her throat quivered, and Michaela wondered if she was about to lose the tea Torrance had forced into her before they'd left. The fear threatened to overtake her, too huge and monstrous to evade, swallowing her like Jonah in his story of the whale. The kind of fear that covered your skin after a nightmare, sticky and cold and wet. She knew they could scent it. From the shadowed edges of the clearing, the Lycans' glowing eyes burned like embers as they watched her through the moonlit darkness.

They're waiting for you to show your weakness, but right now you have to be strong for Max's sake.

At the thought of her brother, a devastating sense of help-lessness pierced through her, making her flinch—and it was at that moment that Michaela felt his gaze. Her breath caught, and without realizing it, she found herself search-ing the nightmarish scene for the man, the Bloodrunner, who sparked an uncomfortable awareness in her every time she saw him.

Brody. Her mouth formed the words, though she didn't make a sound.

He watched her from the corner of his eye, as if he didn't want her to know. But there was no way she could have missed him. All he had to do was enter a room, and her senses kicked into high alert, her equilibrium taking a spin that left her reeling, same as it had last night. He had the scarred body of a warrior, but in Michaela's opinion, he was one of the most magnificent men she'd ever known. Not pretty, but so utterly hard and masculine that he all but bled testosterone. Every-thing about the rugged Bloodrunner screamed dark, intense intrigue, and despite her efforts, she'd been unable to stop thinking about him. The effect was even worse when he was near, like being struck by lightning, her nerves left revving and raw. A total and complete meltdown. Not even Ross Holland had affected her like that—and she'd thought she loved her ex-boyfriend…until the day he'd ripped her heart out.

Hah! Shows how much you know. When it comes to love, you're as blind as a hawk beneath its hood.

Sad, but true.

Now Ross was nothing more than a first-class pain—and one she couldn't get rid of. No matter how many different

ways she explained it, he could *not* get it through his head that
she never wanted to see him again.

It was strange, but with Brody near, she could barely recall
what Ross even looked like. The Runner stood to her left, no
more than a yard away from Mason, and her stare snagged on
his powerful form, unable to look away. Though his muscular
frame had been wrapped in a stylish tuxedo the first time
she'd met him at Torrance and Mason's wedding, tonight he
wore his standard dark jeans, black boots and black T-shirt.
The soft cotton of the shirt molded itself to the broad width
of his shoulders and that beautifully carved chest, his thighs
rigid beneath the worn denim of his jeans. His auburn hair
burned a deep, dark red before the flames of the fire, lying soft
and thick on his shoulders. Against the darkness of his skin,
his scars shone like silvery pale rivers of pain, echoing the
mysteries of his past as they slashed across his face in three
thin diagonal lines.

After the *"I can't get out of here fast enough"* way that he'd
acted the night before, when he'd brought her and Wyatt the
news of what had happened to Max, she hadn't thought he'd
even show for the ceremony. But here he was. His normally
brooding expression burned with a cold, calculating fury—a
charged energy buzzing around him that suggested the rigid
control he always held over himself could crack at any
moment. Though the calmest, quietest of the Runners, he
struggled to master, even hide, an underlying violence. But it
was always there, lying in wait of its escape, and she experienced a flutter of relief in her belly that he was on their side.

Brody Carter was not a man you wanted for an enemy.

She ran her tongue over her bottom lip, aware that it
quivered, and found herself fighting a physical urge to move

closer to him, wanting to soothe that angry burn of pain he carried inside—when suddenly the restless movements of the pack ceased. Mason lifted his face, sniffing at the cool, brisk air. "The Elders are almost here," he announced in a quiet rasp.

Across the clearing, the eerie, demonic glow of torches could be seen drawing nearer, and Michaela stared unblinkingly at the shadow-thick edge of the forest.

The light grew brighter, burning against her eyes as she watched a dark-haired Lycan with distinctive golden eyes walk forward, bearing one of the torches, his lip curled in a belligerent sneer. Then the first Elder stepped from the shadows, into the clearing, his stature one of blunt, stocky strength; light brown hair shot with silver at his temples; deep-set eyes sharp beneath bushy silver brows.

"That's Graham Fuller," Torrance whispered. "He's the Lead Elder and Mason's father's best friend." Another figure stepped out of the trees, this one considerably younger than Fuller, his rich brown hair and dark eyes familiar. "You know that one," Torrance told her. "You met Dylan at our wedding."

Despite the fact that he was a member of the League, Dylan Riggs had always been a friend, as well as a supporter of the Bloodrunners. In fact, it had been Dylan who walked Torrance down the aisle at her wedding. Though his friendship with the Runners was strong, the past few weeks had put Dylan in a difficult position, as tension between the Bloodrunners and the pack increased.

More Elders entered the clearing, alternately taking their places on either side of Fuller, until the last one emerged. Michaela had yet to meet the notorious Lycan known for his purist views and hatred of humans and Bloodrunners alike, but she recognized him immediately from the description she'd been given. Stefan Drake, the one whom the Runners believed was responsible for the growing number of rogue werewolves and other horrifying crimes, and the reason she and Max had remained under Bloodrunner protection, even after the death of Anthony Simmons, the rogue who had threatened Torrance's life. Mason and the others had believed that if afforded the opportunity, Drake would use the Doucets as a way to strike out against the Runners, and they'd been right.

Drake stood tall and lean, with sharp, aristocratic features made severe by the burning light of the torches and bonfire. Deep grooves of discontent lined the raw-boned features of his face, as if hate itself had worn him down. At one time, he had probably shared the same arresting looks as his children, until years of bitterness had finally left its destructive mark. His sharp, pewter-colored eyes found her and held, staring with a burning contempt that made Michaela recoil, despite her earlier determination to conceal her fear.

In the next moment, the Elders parted, and two hulking shapes emerged from the trees. In their wolf forms, the Lycans stood over seven feet tall, their legs bent at an odd angle as they stalked forward. Each held a thick chain that had been wound around their inside wrist, the twin lengths leading back into the shadows. Michaela's throat constricted the second she realized what was happening.

She swayed. Her vision blurred. "Oh God, they haven't."

"Be strong, Michaela," Mason grunted. "Max is going to need your strength."

Strength! She didn't have any left. Her knees sagged, and both Mason and Torrance caught at her waist as the Lycans walked forward. They had taken no more than a few steps, when they jerked on the chains and her brother appeared, emerging from the thick line of trees.

Bound like an animal.

Fury roared through her, jerking her upright as if she'd been jolted with an electric current, every muscle in her body screaming for movement while she watched Max stumble into the clearing, his long, lanky body dressed in nothing more than tattered boxer shorts, his dark skin smeared with blood and grime. His thick, ebony hair hung over his brow, obscuring his eyes, his battered hands fisted around the two lengths of chain that looped his neck like a collar. His chest and legs were bloodied with deep, raw-looking wounds, which she knew had come from painful claw swipes; his left shoulder was a mangled, bloodied mess from where a rogue werewolf had latched on with its jaws, ripping into the skin and muscles with its lethally sharp fangs.

Oh God, Max. This can't be happening.

The sheer depth of her horror paralyzed her, freezing her muscles until not even her lungs were moving. "I swear it's going to be *okay,* Mic," her best friend promised in an urgent whisper. "Look around you. We have enough support to demand that they let him live, no matter the outcome of the ceremony."

Support? Biting at her trembling lower lip, she glanced left, then right, surprised to see that others had joined them. She hadn't noticed anyone beyond Brody. But Jeremy Burns, Mason's partner, and his fiancée, Jillian, had moved to Torrance's other side, and she watched as Jillian's father stepped forward to the place beside his daughter, his wife there with her arm around his waist. Michaela turned her head to the left and blinked in surprise to see Eric and Elise Drake, the Elder's children, standing next to Mason, as well as two other couples she couldn't identify standing just behind Brody.

To the Bloodrunner's left stood his partner, Cian Hennessey, his dark head angled toward Brody, lips moving as he spoke. Michaela struggled to hear what he said, but the wind carried away his words like smoke. While they talked, Carla Reyes and Wyatt Pallaton came to stand beside Cian. There was no denying that the dark-eyed, loose-limbed Wyatt was certainly attractive, but Michaela shared an easy friendship with the Runner and nothing more, her private desires obstinately focused on the man who seemed determined to keep his distance.

Now the Bloodrunners and their family and friends stood as a united force against the Silvercrest pack that had yet to accept the fact that something sinister was eating away at its foundation, rotting it from the inside out, like a cancer. Something that would rip down the protective walls that separated their world from the humans. In the back of her mind, it occurred to Michaela that loyalties were being announced tonight—a separation made between those who would stand with the Runners in their fight against the rogues and those who blindly supported the pack's refusal to face reality and see Drake for what he really was—but all she could focus on was Max. He looked so hurt…so terrified.

When one of the guards jerked on his end of the chain, sending Max stumbling forward so fast that he fell hard on his knees, she snapped. One second she was holding Torrance's hand, all but squeezing the life out of her fingers, and in the next she was flying forward.

"Leave him alone!" she screamed, her soft-soled, black satin slip-ons struggling for purchase in the damp earth as she rushed toward Max, only to find herself lifted off the ground when a hard, heavily muscled arm clamped around her waist from behind, pulling her clear off her feet. "Damn it, let me down!" she snarled, unable to take her eyes off her brother as the golden-eyed Lycan who'd first entered the clearing kicked him, yelling for Max to get back on his feet. On his hands and knees, Max's head hung forward, the gaping wound in his shoulder seeping fresh blood until a pool began to form beneath him.

Mindless with heartache and rage, Michaela clawed at the arm holding her, kicking her heels against whatever part of her captor's legs she could reach. "Stop it," a deep, husky voice grunted in her ear. "You're not helping him by losing it. I give you my word he'll survive the ceremony, but you have to keep it together."

"Nooooo!" she screamed, too hysterical to listen to reason. "You're monsters! All of you! Look what you've done to him! How dare you! *How dare you!*"

The arm tightened with a powerful flex of muscle, cinching her waist, and her breath sucked in on a sharp, wailing gasp. "Shut up before you get both yourself *and* your brother killed. I will *not* let that happen. Do you understand me?" he growled, shaking her so hard that her teeth clicked together. "Do you understand me, Doucet?"

"Damn it!" she cried, stricken as she watched one of the guards grab Max by his hair and jerk him to his feet. Around them, Lycans huffed and growled as they watched the spectacle, while others outright howled for the show to begin. "Put me down! I'm going to kill them for touching him!"

"That's enough!" the voice seethed in her ear. "They'll tear you apart before you even reach him, and I'll be damned if I'm going to stand here and watch you die."

Suddenly, through the haze of fear and agony and outrage in her mind, she finally recognized who'd caught her. *Brody.*

He held her in his arms, her body locked against his powerful form, her back to the burning heat of his chest. Held her so high that her toes didn't even touch the ground. A low, keening sound of anguish tore through her, and her head dropped forward as hoarse sobs of pain ripped from her throat. "Let me go. I have to help him. *Please,*" she begged brokenly, knowing only that she needed to get to Max. "Let me go, Brody."

He muttered something against her hair, his breath warm against her scalp, and Michaela could have sworn it was a single word...but she must have heard wrong. She was too upset. Too furious. Too terrified. She must be out of her mind.

Because it had sounded as if he'd quietly snarled the word *never.*

Chapter 2

Silently cursing his lack of control where this particular woman was concerned, Brody wondered just what he was doing. He'd sworn to himself that he'd stay home tonight—and yet, when Cian had come knocking at his door, on his way to the ceremony, he couldn't do it. His fear over what might happen to her had been too great, and he'd found himself following his partner up to the clearing where the Silvercrest pack conducted its business—business that was better suited to the wild than the civilized streets of its town.

He hadn't been able to stay away from her—he hadn't even lasted a day.

But nothing had changed, because the facts remained the same. It didn't matter what *he* wanted. The truth of the matter was that women like Michaela Doucet *never* took interest in guys like him—ones who were scarred and used and bitter enough not to care what the world thought about them. Sure, they may have used him for a raunchy one-night stand. One of those *"look at brave little me making it with the big scary guy"* situations, turned on by his scars because of the violence they represented. But even then, they still feared him because of his sheer physical size and power. And they got off on that fear, using it as a twisted means of sharpening the thrill when they found themselves beneath a man who could too easily break them if he wanted.

Users, each and every one of them, and they'd used him until Brody had just grown tired of it all and said to hell with it—to hell with women—no matter how badly his body ached for one.

And you're being an asshole. Michaela isn't like that, and you damn well know it.

He ground his jaw down until his teeth ached, soaking in the pain, knowing he deserved it. He was being an idiot, because truth be told, Michaela Doucet scared the ever-loving hell out of him. Despite his determination to stay away from her, he'd known, deep down, that he'd come tonight. Known, instinctively, that it was where he belonged.

He hated it—but there was no sense denying that he needed to be here to protect her. The entire time he'd hiked through the woods, he'd sworn to himself that he'd watch from the sidelines. Simply ensure she didn't get herself into more trouble than she could handle, and he had no doubt she could cause trouble. The woman lived up to her fiery Cajun heritage like a pro, whipping men into a frenzy of lust wherever she went.

Even now, when she was an emotional wreck, he could sense the unmated males' interest as the Lycans watched her with a dark, feral hunger, the edgy scent of their lust thick on the air, making him want to snap at them with his jaws.

She was just too beautiful for her own good. And too damn fearless! He still couldn't believe the depth of her anger toward the pack, or her willingness to confront them over the treatment of her brother. He wondered if the Doucet kid knew how lucky he was to have someone who cared that much about him, who was willing to risk her life because she wanted to keep him safe.

There was obviously a lot more to Michaela Doucet than a pretty face and a body most men would die for the chance to cover—and the uncomfortable knowledge made Brody want to let go of her, turn around and never come within a God-given mile of her again.

But his arms wouldn't cooperate. If anything, his grip tightened, the sensation of her soft curves plastered down the front of his body enough to make his teeth gnash. He'd known she'd feel incredible if he ever had the chance to be this close to her, to touch her, burying his face in her hair and letting her rich, seductive scent sink into him—but he hadn't realized her effect would actually make his knees shake…or his mouth water for a slow, deep, intimate taste of her.

He wanted her on his tongue. All of her. Everywhere. His face lowered, lips rubbing against the smooth silk of her hair, and he was a breath away from sliding lower, nuzzling behind her ear, when he suddenly realized where they were…and what he was doing.

Goddamn it! He'd worked so hard to master control of himself—there was no damned way he planned on letting her strip it away so easily. But holding her…it was even more dangerous than he'd imagined. Richer. Sweeter. Every cell of his body ached with the need to claim, to accept the dark truth he refused to even consider.

"Brody?" The sound of his name jerked him out of his internal hell, and he realized Mason was standing just a little to his left, a few feet behind him. He could hear his friend's confusion, as well as his surprise that Brody had been the one to grab hold of Michaela. Around them, the pack's energy grew sharper with the promise of confrontation between the Elders and the indomitable human he held in his arms, and Brody understood the need to retreat back to the safety of the other Runners.

"It's okay, Mase," he grated under his breath, carrying her with him as he backed up a few steps until flanked by their supporters. "We're under control here. I've got her."

She'd grown quiet, but trembled in his arms even as she lifted her head high, too fragile for such strength, a contradiction that set his teeth on edge at the same time she sent his pulse rate soaring. He gently lowered her body until her feet touched the ground, but didn't release his hold on her—and she didn't try to pull away. She just stood there, pressed against his length, and stared soundlessly at her brother, the rapid panting of her breath making a quiet rasp through her parted lips.

With a knot in his gut, Brody wondered if they had explained to her exactly what the *Novitiate's* ceremony entailed. Any moment now, Max Doucet would experience his first shift as a Lycan. Under close watch, his guards would have alerted the Elders when it was time to begin, recognizing the signs. Fever. Sweating. Cramping. The initial change was always the hardest, both mentally and physically, and only the strongest humans survived. Brody hoped the kid had it in him, because if his body failed to completely accept the shape of his wolf, yet he still lived, the rules of the ceremony were that he'd be killed—and then he and the others would have a battle on their hands, with Drake inciting the pack into a vicious frenzy.

With a cruel smile, the Elder's cold gray stare traveled over their united force, lingering with bitter disapproval on his offspring, Eric and Elise, before cutting to Jillian Murphy. "It's clear where your loyalties now lie," he sneered, curling his lip as he addressed the pack's Spirit Walker. Through her maternal bloodline, Jillian held the sacred position of holy woman, or witch, for the Silvercrest pack. She was also the mate and fiancée of Brody's fellow Bloodrunner, Jeremy Burns. Beneath Drake's scornful stare, Jillian didn't so much as bat a lash, but beside her, Jeremy bristled with outrage.

"Rest assured, Jillian, that I'll be demanding your resignation," Drake continued with malicious pleasure. "Silvercrest will no doubt be better off without you. We can't have you marring the purity of our young through your association with ones who are so repulsively impure. To be honest, I'm surprised you have the gall to face us."

"And after last week, I'm surprised you don't know any better than to watch what you say to my mate," Jeremy snarled as he took an aggressive step forward, looking more than ready to knock the racist Elder on his ass. Brody knew just how badly Jeremy wanted to take Drake apart, piece by satisfying piece, and he didn't blame him. Under the Elder's orchestration, an attempt had been made on Jillian's life the previous week, and it was only by some clever thinking on the part of Eric Drake that Jeremy hadn't killed the bastard in a murderous rage. If he had, the Silvercrest penalty would have been death, and Brody and the Runners would have lost a man who was more like a brother to them than a mere friend.

"Are you threatening me?" the Elder demanded of Jeremy, the sinister gleam of triumph in his chilling gaze revealing his ploy. He wanted Jeremy to make a move on him tonight, so that he could retaliate with the full force of the pack, using his position to strike out against the Runners.

Before Jeremy could react, Mason placed a cautioning hand on his partner's shoulder and Jillian stepped into his side, putting her arms around his waist. The group held their collective breath as they waited to see what he would do. Finally, Jeremy shook his fisted hands out at his sides, and draped his arm around his fiancée's shoulders. "I don't make threats," he said in a quiet drawl, flashing the Elder a contemptuous smile. "I make promises. I'd tell you to speak to my mate with respect, but the truth is that you're not good enough to speak to her at all."

Drake looked round at the pack. "Are you going to allow him to address his betters with such lack of respect?"

"Stefan," Dylan Riggs softly muttered, speaking for the first time, while the other Elders remained silent, their expressions tight with concern.

"The pack knows who deals with its trash so that it can sleep in peace at night," Cian called out, his words crisp with the lilting notes of his Irish accent. He pulled a pack of cigarettes from the pocket of his black leather jacket, placed one between his lips, and cupped his hand over the tip as he flicked open a silver butane lighter. After the first long drag, he lifted his head and sent the Elder a lazy grin. "If I were you, I'd worry about keeping on our good side, Drake."

"You're not a member of this pack," the Elder spat, glaring at Brody's partner. "None of you are."

"By choice," Mason rasped in a low slide of words, which

were true. Nearly all of the Bloodrunners had achieved their required number of kills to rejoin the Silvercrest pack, though they chose not to. "It'd be wise of you to remember that."

"It's time now," Fuller announced, stepping forward, sending an apologetic look in their direction. Graham Fuller may have been the best friend of Mason's father, Robert, but he still held the position of Lead Elder among the Silvercrest League. As such, he carefully walked the line of neutrality when dealing with the ancient bad blood that existed between the purists, like Drake, and the crossbreeds. Even Dylan, who Brody personally didn't like, but was a close friend of the other Runners, had his hands tied when dealing with his fellow Elders. If he showed too much support for the Bloodrunners, Drake would demand a vote on his removal—and there was too much prejudice among the Silvercrest leaders to think Dylan's position was secure.

Which meant the Runners were left on their own, same as always.

Wishing like hell that there was something he could do, Brody watched the guards pull Max to the center of the clearing. The boy stood silent and still, his head bent toward the ground, but Brody could see the thick sheen of sweat covering the young man's skin. The veins in Max's arms thickened with the heavy flow of his blood, the tendons at the side of his neck, leading into his shoulders, rigid with strain, while his hands fisted at his sides, his chest rising and falling as he took each breath harder…and harder.

"Do you know what's happening?" he asked in a rough whisper, brushing his lips against Michaela's ear. The enthralling scent of her skin filled his head, and he clenched his jaw, determined to ignore its devastating effect. "Did Wyatt or Mason explain to you what will happen?"

She nodded mutely, and then quietly whispered, "He's terrified."

Taking his gaze from Max, Brody looked down to see her pulse rushing beneath the fragile column of her throat, so slender and pale and delicate. His tongue felt thick against the roof of his mouth, and in his head, he could hear the beating of her heart in perfect tempo with that wild rush beneath her milky-white skin. Then suddenly, like a blast hitting from out of nowhere, her words sank in…and he remembered a crucial element that had somehow slipped his mind during the chaos of the evening.

Michaela Doucet was *not* your average, everyday human female. No, she held powers, talents that had yet to be completely explained to him, but which suddenly seemed like a massive tactical error on his part to have forgotten. She could *read* people she was physically close to, he recalled Torrance telling them one night over dinner. Like peering through a window, she could sense their emotions, their feelings.

He was a goddamn idiot! The last thing in the world he needed was to be here, holding her, giving her the opportunity to nose around inside his head! His fingers released their hold on her hip, the muscles in his arm flexing, ready to pull away from her—when in the next instant Max Doucet threw back his head and let out a bloodcurdling scream of horror that echoed through the quiet night like a sound torn straight from the bowels of hell.

"It hurts," she gasped, her voice cracking, and with a surge of fury at his inability to help, Brody realized it wasn't *his* head she was in. No, it was Max's. She was sharing her brother's terror…his pain!

"He…he feels like something's trying to claw its way out

of him," she stammered, the words husky and broken, while her body arched against him, her lean muscles rigid as agony tore through her. "Like it's going to—"

"Stop it," he growled in her ear, gripping onto her side with his free hand, his other arm still wrapped across her front. "Get out of his head, Doucet! I don't want you in there. Get out of it!"

She jerked, her head shooting back to slam against his collarbone, and Max fell to the ground, his expression ravaged, a broken scream pouring from his throat as his body contorted, seizing, spasm after torturous spasm clenching his strained muscles. The change rolled through him, rippling beneath the dark gleam of his skin, while blood pooled beneath his hands and razor-sharp claws pierced their way through the tips of his fingers. He threw back his head, his back arching as a throaty chuffing sound surged up from his thickening chest, through the muzzled shape of his mouth.

In Brody's arms, Michaela trembled, silent tears streaming down her face, and something sharp and agonizing slashed through him like remembered pain, making him grimace.

Son of a bitch. He couldn't stand watching her cry.

The night had turned brutal, the wind angry and vicious as it ripped through the trees with a snarling vengeance, lashing against the flames of the fires. Her long hair whipped across his face, and he couldn't hold it—the devastating combination of her scent and those tears screwing with his head.

Against his better judgment, knowing it was going to land him in hell, Brody found himself wrapping his other arm across her middle, until he was cradling her against his chest, his body pulled around her as if he could shield her from the world. She turned her head to the side and buried her face in the warm hollow between his shoulder and neck, her damp breaths panting against his throat, and he couldn't stop the heavy surge of blood rushing to his groin, making him feel like a sick bastard, considering the circumstances. She went strangely still the second she felt his rigid erection pressing against her spine, and he bit back the guttural groan that rumbled deep in his chest.

Flicking his gaze away from the dangerous terrain of her body, he looked up and experienced an overwhelming wave of relief when he saw that Max Doucet's change was complete. "It's over now," he whispered.

Despite the softness of his words, she flinched, her body trembling with an excess of emotion. She let out a slow, shaky exhalation of air, then turned her face back toward the clearing, her breath catching on a hoarse cry the instant she saw her brother.

The newly formed wolf rose on his hind legs, his massive chest rising and falling as he panted through parted jaws that revealed long, sinister fangs. Glowing blue eyes that burned like the center of a flame searched the crowd of spectators, until he found the one he was looking for. Brody's hold tightened as the wolf made a sluggish move toward Michaela, but the Lycan guards were already yanking on the thick chains that wrapped his throat, keeping him in place.

"The change has been taken and the human breed has survived," Fuller announced, his brown hair whipping around his face as the wind surged, playing havoc with the towering flames of the fire as they licked at the darkness of the sky. "Who will take responsibility for the *Novitiate's* training?"

"The honor will be mine," a deep voice called out from behind them, and Brody turned his head to see Eric Drake step forward to stand beside Cian. A collective rumble of shock reverberated through the pack at this blatant, stunning show of support for the Runners from the Elder's son.

"Eric?" Drake's silver brows pulled together in a deep-seated scowl, his sharp cheekbones slashed with a vivid streak of ruddy color.

Crossing his brawny arms across his chest, the youngest son of the most pure-blooded line in the Silvercrest pack repeated his intention. "For too long this pack has benefited from the courage and sacrifice of the Runners, giving nothing in return except the offer to join a community that treats them as inferiors. Enough's enough. It's time we make things right and give something back. The boy will pass his *Novitiate's* training, and when he does, he'll become a Runner and hold a position that demands our respect. To see that it happens, I'm taking on the training of Max Doucet as my own."

"Like hell you are," his father hissed, baring his teeth as he jabbed one long finger in his son's direction. "It's bad enough that you and your sister have actually befriended them, but I will not allow my son to disgrace our family by aligning with these aberrations and taking responsibility for a human breed, the foulest creature of all!"

"You can't stop him," Elise Drake argued, stepping forward to stand by her brother's side in a show of support against their father, though her nerves revealed themselves in the tremor of her husky voice and the violent trembling of her hands. Not that Brody blamed her. Elise had been through a hell of her own the week before when her father had used her in the attack on Jillian's life, and now she had to deal with this.

For a moment, the misogynistic Drake stood rigid with fury in the face of his daughter's defiance, and then a soft gleam slowly began to burn in the wintry depths of his eyes. "You're right," he murmured, straightening his cuffs in a purposeful act of indolence. "I can't stop Eric should he choose to malign his honor in such a fashion. But I *can* enjoy his failure." He all but purred with malicious satisfaction. "Fate has a way of righting all wrongs. It's been many years since we've taken the responsibility for a *Novitiate* in this pack, but the rules remain the same. If the human breed fails to pass judgment at the end of his training, which I've no doubt he will, the punishment still stands and Max Doucet *will* be executed."

"You bastard!" Michaela hissed, suddenly jerking forward, but Brody was already tightening his hold on her. She strained against his arms, but couldn't break away as she shouted at the Elder, the horror she'd just endured pouring out of her in an uncontrollable flash of fury and pain. "If you hurt my brother, I'll see that each and every one of you dies. Your town, your way of life. I'll bring the entire world breathing down your neck. Just see if I don't! And I'll be damned if he's staying here! I'll do whatever it takes to get him away from you! I'll get the goddamn army up here, and we'll see how power—"

Cursing foully under his breath, Brody pressed his palm over her mouth, silencing the words he knew were only going to land her in deeper trouble. Muffled sounds of outrage vibrated in her throat, but it was already too late. The damage had been done. Drake hated all humans with a passion that went beyond obsessive—and because of their close association with the Runners, they'd known the Doucets would garner special attention from the unstable Elder and his followers. And now that Michaela had openly challenged him, Drake wouldn't stop until he made her pay for the insult.

"The human is too unstable to be allowed her freedom,"

Stefan Drake announced with a gloating smile, spreading his arms in a gesture of entreaty. "Surely the pack realizes what must be done. She cannot be allowed to interfere with our dealings."

"Your so-called dealings sought out her family," Mason growled, "not the other way around. We know you're the one behind the rogues, Drake, and it won't be long before we've caught you—along with the bastard working with you—and brought the both of you down."

"Despite the slanderous accusations you and your kind have been tossing around like confetti," the Elder argued, his hateful stare burning with maniacal triumph while whispered words traveled among the members of the pack, "my guilt remains unproven. The truth is that you have no evidence to back your claims. They're all based on nothing more than hearsay and conjecture. And regardless of how it happened, her brother is now here and the fact remains that she *is* a threat to our well-being. I call for an—"

"There's no need to call for anything," Dylan growled, cutting Drake off. "She can be assigned a guard and the problem is solved."

"I agree," Fuller called out before Drake could argue, the Lead Elder's relief to have ended the disagreement without bloodshed obvious in the softened lines of his expression. "The only question is who. Who is willing to accept accountability for her actions and watch over the human while her brother completes his training?"

Brody narrowed his eyes, his chest aching as he prepared to say the words he knew were going to change his entire life. It was insanity. Madness. The action of a fool. And yet, he didn't have any other choice. He never had.

"I am." The two roughly spoken words echoed through the

clearing with the force of a cannon blast, and Michaela instantly stilled, stiffening against him as all eyes turned toward them. "Until this is over," he growled, "the human is *mine*."

Chapter 3

The human is mine...

The unbelievable words echoed through Michaela's head, the evocative warmth of Brody's breath against the sensitive shell of her ear enough to make her tremble with something sharper, darker, more visceral than shock or fear. She struggled for the source of her reaction to the possessive words—then realized it was hunger, urgent and sweet, spreading hypnotically through her system. A craving—a primal, instinctive need—that moved like warm, thick honey in her veins, settling deep within her like an intimate, pulsing glow of heat that she wanted to curl herself around. And it centered on the Bloodrunner who held her in his hard-muscled arms, the resonating beat of his heart banging out a powerful rhythm against her back.

Oh God, this can't be happening.

"If you promise to behave," he whispered in a low, husky rumble, his lips moving against her hair, "I'll take my hand away from your mouth. Do you promise, Doucet?"

She gave a jerky nod, and sensation pierced through her like a physical jolt as her lips rubbed against the masculine roughness of his palm; the musky, outdoors scent of his skin filling her head.

Shocked murmurs continued to work their way through the surrounding pack, marked by low snarls and grumblings of disapproval, but a strange buzzing noise, like static, started to fill her ears as everything she'd experienced in the last few moments crashed down on her. She shook her head, trying to clear the confusion, but couldn't escape the growing feeling of unreality. Through a hot sheen of tears, she watched as the Elders huddled into a tight circle. Only Dylan Riggs cast a sharp glance in her direction, before lowering his head and joining the other Elders in a heated conversation while the pack clustered together in groups of their own. She could see a few human mouths, as well as Lycan jaws moving, but couldn't hear the words they produced over the frenzied noise thudding against her skull.

When a nearby group of Lycans suddenly stepped toward them, Brody moved with whipcord strength, shoving her behind his back before she even knew what was happening. "Mason, get her back to the Alley," he grated, and she almost sighed with relief as the words sank into her system, the static whir slowly fading away. "The others can help me deal with things here. We'll meet back up with you at the cabin when we're done."

Vaguely aware of Torrance grabbing on to her wrist and pulling her away, Michaela stumbled, looking back over her shoulder toward the clearing, watching as Eric Drake walked toward the incredible creature her brother had become, his dark fur gleaming like black satin in the moonlight. Eric began talking with Max's guards, reaching for the chains that bound him, when his father broke away from the Elders and advanced on them. She struggled to see what was happening, but everyone was moving around and too many bodies blocked her view.

Looking back to the spot where Brody had stood, her muscles clenched with panic when she found him gone, lost somewhere in that swarming chaos of activity. What if something happened to him? It would be her fault, wouldn't it? Male voices, raised in anger, reached her, and she knew instantly that it was Brody arguing with Stefan Drake. They both sounded furious, but she knew the Runner would win. And then he'd come to the Alley, where he expected to find her waiting.

Michaela had never considered herself a coward, but after the crushing experience with her last relationship, she'd grown wary of putting her trust in the opposite sex. And more importantly, she no longer trusted her judgment—or her body's physical desires. And God only knew the powerful way she reacted to Brody Carter was enough to make any sane woman cautious. It was too much. Too…everything.

No, she wasn't a coward, but she sent a sharp look toward the trees, wondering…

"Don't even think about it," Mason warned her with a gruff chuckle, the corner of his mouth edging up into a strained grin. "You wouldn't make it more than ten feet before he had you down."

Had her down? A hazy image of being trapped beneath

Brody's long, hard, muscular body flashed through her mind, and she trembled. God, talk about emotional overload. She was shaking so hard she could barely see straight.

"I don't understand," she whispered, turning a dazed stare toward her best friend. "What just happened, Torry?"

Arching one slim red brow, Torrance shot a questioning look toward her husband. "If I had to guess, I'd say you'd just been given a personal bodyguard."

Mason nodded, his handsome face carved into a cautious expression of concern. With a strange bubble of emotion in her throat that felt as if it could end in either laughter or tears, Michaela wondered who that concern was for. Was he worried how well she'd deal with his brooding friend? Or was that hard expression that looked as if it'd been chiseled from granite for Brody? Did he think she'd lead a reign of terror over the quiet Runner's life?

"And I get *him?*" she groaned, knowing it couldn't be true. There was no way in hell Brody Carter had just volunteered himself…to what? The job had sounded more like a watchdog than a bodyguard. "When he said that I'm his, he meant his to *watch over,* right?"

Mason snorted a low, purely male sound under his breath, and led them deeper into the forest.

It took an hour of sitting there in the Dillingers' cozy kitchen, with Torrance pouring another pot of herbal tea into her system, before Brody finally came to collect her. Michaela heard the commotion at the front door as he and his partner arrived. For a moment, she felt torn between the strangely opposing urges of running into the living room and demanding he comfort her, and sneaking out through the cabin's back door, disappearing into the darkness…as if she could run away from the ugly reality of the night.

But she couldn't move.

She waited, her breath held tight in her chest, until his broad-shouldered body filled the archway that led into the kitchen. His shadowed, dark green gaze trapped her the second he set eyes on her, refusing to let her look away, holding her with the sheer force of his will. The lines around his mouth were tight with strain, and at his sides, his hands were fisted, his knuckles bruised and a little swollen. His auburn hair was damp at the temples, his shirt torn at the shoulder and the sharp line of his left cheekbone had been scraped raw. Her brows pulled together in a tight frown as she added the details together and came to an unsettling conclusion. "You…you didn't fight after I left, did you?"

"Are you kidding?" Cian snorted, edging past his partner as he walked into the kitchen. "It was just a playful scuffle. Hell, there were only ten of them, hardly enough to call it a fight. And none of them were brave enough to battle against Brooding Brody," he drawled, hitching his hip against the counter. He crossed his arms over his chest, a cynical smile twisting the hard curve of his devil's mouth, but Michaela couldn't tell if he was teasing or not.

"And Max was okay?" she asked, her attention focused on Brody while Torrance filled the sink with hot, lemon-scented dishwater and Mason finished off the sandwich he'd made while waiting.

Brody nodded in response to her question, but didn't move away from the archway. Instead, he crossed his own arms and propped his right shoulder against the wall, the recessed kitchen lighting glinting off the burnished stubble on his square chin, softening the stark lines of his scars. "Eric took him away before we left. He'll take good care of him, Doucet. No harm will come to your brother during his training."

Michaela worked to ignore the devastating effect of his deep voice—that husky, intoxicating baritone that slipped into her with a sweet, provocative slide and made her hot beneath the skin—but it didn't work worth a damn. The tight, black cashmere sweater that had kept her warm outside now sat too heavy over her damp skin, filling her face with heat. Lowering her gaze to the steam rising from her tea, the china cup fragile within the straining hold of her hands, she asked, "And after that? After the training?"

"If he doesn't pass, then we'd all stand together to ensure his safety, if it comes to that," Mason told her. She flicked her gaze up to see his easy grin as he added, "But if he's anything like you, that's not going to be a concern. If there's one thing I know about the Doucets, it's that they're tough as nails."

"Thanks," she murmured with a wry twist of her mouth. "I think."

"Don't worry," Torrance laughed, sending her husband a teasing look. "Mase's compliments are still a little rough around the edges, but he means well."

The Runner flashed his wife a wicked, hard-edged smile and playfully wagged his brows. "Face it, Tor. You *love* my rough side."

"Behave," Torrance admonished under her breath, but her green eyes glittered with excitement, her cheeks flushed a warm shade of rose. The love the two shared was so potent, so rich and heady and intense, that it seemed to fill the room, making Michaela painfully aware of how…alone she was. All she'd had was Max, and now even he had been taken from her.

"Max *will* pass his training," Brody rumbled, breaking the awkward silence. "And until all of this is over, I'll...*be with you.*" It almost sounded as if that last bit had stuck in his throat, and she wasn't the only one who'd noticed.

"If you're not up to the task," his partner drawled, reaching behind him to snatch up one of the cookies out of the perpetually stocked cookie jar, "I could always be a pal and step in for you, partner."

Brody didn't so much as twitch, but she could see the vein that began throbbing in his temple, pulsing beneath the dark sheen of his skin as he tilted his head and glared at the smirking Irishman. Energy, red-hot and raging, surged around him like a fiery glow, so real Michaela almost flinched from the burn. "Like hell you will."

"Why not me?" Cian laughed, sending her a teasing wink. The irreverent Runner obviously loved goading his partner and friend, but Michaela could sense something deeper than mere irritation in Brody's reaction, and she didn't need any of her so-called powers to see it.

"Why not you?" he softly snarled. "Because you'd be too busy bedding her instead of protecting her, that's why!"

Cian choked on another sharp bark of laughter, while Michaela made a soft sound of surprise, thoroughly insulted to think that he'd lumped her into the same class as all the other women who willingly fell into Hennessey's arms simply because of his looks. "I'm going to assume you're letting your irritation talk," she murmured, "and that you didn't mean that to sound as insulting as it did."

"Don't bet on it," Cian snickered, just before Mason elbowed him in the side on his way to the sink with his plate. The Irishman rubbed at his ribs, but couldn't stop his soft chuckling, and the frustration in Brody seemed to coil like a viper.

All it took was a woman's keen intuition to realize that he thought she'd rather have the pretty-faced Irishman watching over her than him. And while it was one thing for *other* women to prefer his dark-haired partner, something inside of Michaela compelled her to say, "As charming as you are, Hennessey, I'm…that is, I think the current arrangement will work just fine."

"Wow," Cian drawled, gifting her with a boyish smile as he rubbed one hand against the sharp angle of his shadowed jaw. "I don't think I've ever been turned down so nicely before." He looked toward his partner, arching one midnight-black brow. "Seems the lady is happy with *you* after all, boyo. Congratulations."

Brody's scowl deepened and a charged silence settled over the room, the only sound that of the running faucet as Torrance worked her way through the dishes. Too restless to sit still, Michaela shifted to her feet, pushing her chair back in at the table before taking her cup to the sink. "I'll finish up, Torry. I need something to keep me busy."

Torrance gave Michaela a quick hug, then slipped into a chair beside her husband. Together, they began talking with Cian about Jeremy and Jillian's wedding, which would take place later that week in the Alley. Michaela began to lose some of her tension as she listened to their easy, quiet chatter, when she suddenly became aware of Brody standing beside her. His left hip rested against the counter, long arms crossed back over his chest, and she felt that little catch in her breath again. She tried to act natural, but his strangely seductive presence speared through her system like the residual traces of a fine wine, making her senses hum.

From the corner of her vision, she watched his gaze settle on her mouth, before lifting to her eyes. "I know you're probably afraid of me," he stated in a quiet rasp.

"Afraid of you?" Michaela shook her head as she looked toward him, wondering where he'd gotten such an idea. "Why would I be afraid of you?"

He arched one auburn brow in an expression that reminded her of his partner, wearing a cynical look of disbelief, as if the answer should be obvious. But the truth was that she didn't fear him, at least not in a physical sense. No…her caution came from a different source—a basis more intimate than mere intimidation. It came from one that played his scarred, seductive image across the darkness of her mind when she closed her eyes at night; that made her pulse flutter whenever he was near. That reminded her time and again that men weren't to be trusted.

Not that she was going to explain any of that to him.

"I mean it, Brody," she told him in a soft voice, the armor around her heart breaking a little at the shadow of vulnerability she could see there in that dark gaze. "I'm *not* afraid of you."

For several moments, he looked as if he'd argue, those compelling green eyes narrowed on her profile as she turned her attention back to the dishes. Finally, he sighed and said, "This isn't going to work the same as it did with Pallaton and Reyes. I'm not going to waste time watching you from the outside looking in."

A shiver slipped down her spine, but she managed to keep her voice steady. "How do you mean?"

"From what Wyatt told me, they tried to keep a reasonable distance, but I'm going to be on the *inside* with you at all times.

If something happens, I need to be close enough to make a difference. Like it or not, I'm going to be like your shadow."

She slanted him a sideways look as she asked, "You didn't agree to watch over me just to keep me from causing trouble for the pack?"

He shook his head, and she watched, mesmerized, as the auburn tips of his thick hair shifted over the soft cotton of his black T-shirt, the material hugging the firm muscles beneath. "There's more going on here, Doucet, and you know it. I'm doing this for you, not them."

"My name is Michaela," she sighed, shifting her gaze back to his, irrationally irritated by the way he continually called her by her last name. It was so impersonal, which was exactly why she figured he did it—and it occurred to her that they were like two opponents circling one another, wary of the other's motives.

"I know your name," he muttered, his tone dry.

Michaela lifted one shoulder. "Couldn't prove it to me, since you never use it," she countered, noting the strange blend of exasperation and wariness in his sexy, almond-shaped eyes. "So you plan to protect me while keeping me in line, then?"

"I doubt anyone could keep you in line," he snorted, the corner of his mouth twitching in a reluctant grin. "What I *am* going to do is keep you safe."

"That's not what—"

The green of his eyes flashed with emotion. "Forgot what they said at the clearing, okay? As much as I don't care for Riggs, he knew that one of the Runners would accept responsibility for you so that we could keep you alive. There isn't a goddamn chance that Drake plans to let you live," he rasped, the softness of the words in no way lessening their impact. "Not when he knows he can use you to get to us, just like they did with Max. The only problem is that Max lived. Now I think they'll come after you even harder, or turn it into a game and play with us."

"By keeping me scared?"

"Yeah."

Grabbing at another plate, she ignored the shaking in her hands. "Drake really is the one behind all the trouble, then, isn't he? The one Anthony Simmons was working for, who's tempting Lycans to turn rogue, teaching them how to shift during the daytime?"

Michaela knew the past few weeks had been chaotic for the Runners. On top of learning that a traitor was working to expand the number of rogue wolves in the area, they'd discovered that those who had turned had been taught how to dayshift. That was the first clue that had pointed the Runners toward an Elder, once they'd learned that the ability to teach a wolf how to take his shape beneath the sun was a power possessed only by those who served on the League, meant to be used as a defensive weapon during times of war.

After the Runners had realized they were hunting a traitorous Elder, Stefan Drake had become their obvious suspect. Drake and his followers made no secret of their fanatical hatred for humans and Bloodrunners alike, but it wasn't until Jeremy had accepted his place within the Silvercrest pack and returned to Shadow Peak that they were truly able to investigate Drake.

Thanks to Pippa Stanton, the lone female Elder, Jeremy had learned about Drake's grudge against the League itself. According to Pippa, Drake had never forgiven his peers for forbidding the assassination of his wife after she left him for a human. They also knew Drake was responsible for the recent attack on Jillian's life. Using his own daughter as a weapon, Drake, along with the help of an unknown Elder, had performed a task believed impossible by most Lycans, pulling Elise's wolf from her body against her will. Once the change was complete, Elise's beast was controlled by Drake, and would have killed Jillian if it weren't for Jeremy and Mason's intervention. When Jeremy later confronted the Elder, accusing him of the crime, one of Drake's followers, a man named Cooper Sheffield, had tried to kill him, dying instead by the Bloodrunner's hand.

To make matters worse, Drake wasn't the Runners' only problem. Over the course of the past month, Michaela knew that Brody and Cian had been investigating a series of gruesome killings. Four human females had been found murdered, three in the mountains and one in the city. At each scene, there had been no trace of Lycan musk—only the acidic scent produced by a Lycan who had dayshifted, which was untraceable. Each of the victims had clearly been a rogue kill, their hearts eaten from their chests in some kind of psychotic, symbolic gesture. Only one of the victims had clearly been the work of Anthony Simmons, the rogue who had targeted Torrance's life, and who had been killed by Mason in a Challenge Fight shortly afterward. The other three crimes were still unsolved, and the Runners couldn't be sure that Drake himself was behind them, his accomplice on the League…or one of his twisted followers.

"Drake all but admitted his guilt to Jeremy after the attack on Jillian's life," Brody rumbled, his deep voice suddenly pulling her from her troubling thoughts and back to their conversation. "He already hated us before, but now he has a reason to risk taking us out. It's either get rid of the Runners, or accept that we're going to destroy him and whatever he has planned." He shrugged, and Michaela found herself momentarily fascinated by the way the casual gesture traveled across the broad width of his shoulders, his muscles flexing beneath the thin cotton of his shirt.

She tried to keep her focus, but damn, she couldn't get enough of those shoulders. Hoping she didn't sound dazed with lust, she managed to say, "So what happens now?"

"Would you like me to take you home tonight? We can stay in Covington for a day or two so that you can get your things together, close up your shop, then head back up."

"Close up my shop?" Her hands went still beneath the running water as she rinsed the suds away from a mug. She'd already made arrangements with one of her employees to run things at Michaela's Muse, her paranormal specialty shop, for a few days—but she hadn't considered that she might be away longer than that.

As if following her train of thought, Brody said, "I want you in the Alley, Doucet. In my cabin." The dark sound of his voice shivered across her senses, but his expression remained unreadable, as if they were discussing nothing more interesting than the weather. "I don't trust what's happening in the pack and we're too vulnerable in town."

She wanted to argue. She had a life, a business in the city. And yet, none of that would ever be the same again. Max wouldn't be coming back home with her. Working with her. Living with her. The pain crushed down on her again, but she battled against the tears. "Let's go down tonight," she said shakily, hoping he didn't hear the tremor in her words. "I can get what I need from home, then go by the shop and close things down. My customers will just…have to understand."

"You don't have to close. David would be more than happy to keep it open for you," Torrance suggested from the table, having obviously been listening in on their conversation. David Sharp was a loyal, longtime employee who had worked at Michaela's Muse while getting his degree in advertising and had recently returned home to Covington.

"I don't know," she murmured, picking up a coffee mug. "He's a sweetheart, but I couldn't ask him to—"

"Sure you could," Torrance said softly. "It shouldn't take you more than a day to go down and get the accounts all settled. You can even show David how to do the payroll, then leave everything in his hands until it's safe for you to go back."

Michaela gave a wary nod, knowing she had little choice if she wanted to remain in business, and turned back toward the sink, moving on to the last dish. "So what time do you want to leave?"

Brody didn't answer—just stood there watching her with a strange, intense expression hardening the grooves that bracketed his mouth. "What?" she whispered, wondering what was bothering him.

"Nothing," he muttered. Then he uncrossed his arms and started to shift away from the counter, only to stop. Shoving his hands deep into the front pockets of his jeans, he suddenly asked, "Can you use it on me?"

Michaela blinked at him in confusion. "Use it? Use what?"

He jerked his chin at her, his dark eyes narrowed and heavy-lidded. "That witchy thing that you do."

"Witchy thing?" she repeated, trying to stifle a laugh when she realized he was deadly serious. "I can assure you, Brody, that I'm not a witch."

"I want to know, Doucet."

"Know what?" she pressed, finding some perverse pleasure in pushing his buttons. And he was still calling her Doucet, which just made her feel ornery.

He stepped closer, invading her personal space, and the moonlight spilling in through the open kitchen window played across his face, revealing the stark angles and hollows. His nostrils flared, as if he were breathing in her scent, and she realized that from this close, she could see his scars in vivid detail as they cut over his face, slashing from his left eyebrow, across the bridge of his nose, down to his opposite jaw. Her fingers itched to reach out and stroke them, wishing she could wipe away the deep-seated pain that lingered in his eyes. He tried to hide so much behind his angry scowls, but she saw through them. The liquid depths of his bottle-green eyes were like a window into his soul, beautiful…and yet, so filled with hurt, as scarred within as he was without.

"Just ask me, Brody," she whispered softly, trying to tell him with her gaze that he could trust her. "I promise I'll be honest with you."

Something wild and hot and primitive flared in those mysterious green depths, lost as quickly as it appeared beneath the lowering of his lashes—and in a husky, silken slide of words, he said, "I want to know if you can you read me."

Chapter 4

They made the drive down to the city in relative silence, the radio delivering a quiet string of blues, the sensual tenor of an alto sax keeping rhythm with the steady beat of the tires upon the road. The second Brody had cranked the powerful V-8 engine, a quiet, exhausted lassitude had poured through her like warm, rich honey. Even now, it melted Michaela into the seat of the truck, while Brody's scent filled her head, surrounding her in the smooth, intimate darkness.

She took a deep breath, and savored it. God, he smelled good. Not pretty or flowery, but like a man. His scent was as crisp and rich as the outdoors, as the forest itself. Woodsy with traces of musk and salt. Completely delicious.

Sitting there beside him in the midnight dark, Michaela was uncomfortably aware that she'd never known a man whom she found more attractive, more compelling. The more time she spent with him, the more she felt inexplicably drawn to the quiet Runner, as if she wanted to wrap her arms around those broad shoulders and simply hold on to him. Comfort him, easing the hard tension she didn't need mystical powers to feel pouring off him in waves. And take comfort from him in return, drawing on his strength until she didn't feel so hollow inside, so broken and barren and wrecked. If he'd only show her a little warmth, she knew she'd be in serious danger of letting her emotions get the better of her. But he remained as cold and remote as ever.

And the fact you're upset about it proves that you're losing your mind.

She scowled at her know-it-all conscience and turned to stare back out her own window. Beyond the cozy confines of the truck, a light drizzle began to fall, adding to the strange feeling of intimacy. When his deep, whispery baritone intruded into the soft monotony of sound, she jumped, startled.

"Sorry. I didn't mean to spook you," he murmured, sliding her an uneasy look, as if he expected her to cringe away from him in terror, now that they were alone.

She gave him a small, self-conscious grin and tucked a curl behind her ear. "You didn't. I guess I'm just jumpy…still on edge after everything that's happened. I was so lost in my thoughts I didn't hear what you said."

He made a subtle gesture with his shoulders that did something wonderfully wicked to those hard muscles beneath the clinging cotton of his shirt. "I just wondered how you got that little gift of yours. The one you said doesn't work on me."

Her grin bled into a soft burst of laughter that she tried to hide under her breath, half watching her fingers play in the folds of her skirt while soaking up as much of him as she could from the corner of her eye. Sorting through her explanation in her head, she decided to start at the beginning. "My maternal grandmother, who lived in the bayou, was a gifted seer, and I guess I was lucky enough to have some of her powers make their way to me, though I'm nowhere near as strong as she was. I have a really good sixth sense about things, and sometimes I'm able to read people."

"Read them how?" he asked, sounding curious.

"I'm not quite sure how to explain." She shrugged, nervous under the force of his attention, even as he kept his hands and eyes on the road. But he was focused on her, every part of him. She knew it, felt it, and it was a heady, breathtaking sensation that made her want to scoot closer to him. He looked so strong and solid sitting beside her, so invincible and tough. It made her want to just crawl inside of him and pull him around her like a fortress, like the most amazing security blanket she could ever find.

Blinking in surprise, Michaela winced, startled by the discomfiting thought. She wasn't the kind of woman who went looking for a man to take care of her or to hide behind. She was a woman who prided herself on her independence and sensibility, but then, the last few weeks had been anything but normal.

Maybe you're due for a little comforting.

Another dangerous thought, that, and she shook it off, pulling her mind back to her explanation. "Sometimes, if a person is experiencing powerful emotions, I can sense them. It's like being able to see into their heart. I can't read their minds like my *grandmère* could, but I can...I can read their *will,* I guess."

"But not everyone's?" he asked, rubbing one hand against the scratchy surface of his jaw.

"No. Only some people. If a person wants to hide their feelings strongly enough, it's hard for me to pick up anything. And at times, the harder I want to see, the more difficult it is for me. Some are like a wall—others easier. Mason's feelings for Torrance are so strong, I had no problem picking up on them the first time I met him. But sometimes, the closer I am to a situation, the harder it is to see anything. It's almost as if my interest crowds the power."

He slanted her another quick, questioning look, then turned his attention back to the road. "You said you can't read me at all, but what about Cian?"

She rolled her eyes at his boyishly hopeful tone, snickering softly. "If I could, I wouldn't tell you. It wouldn't be fair, because you'd just use whatever I said to torment the poor guy."

A crooked grin played briefly at his mouth, making him look entirely too sexy. "Picked up on that, did you?"

"It's uh, kinda hard to miss. You two go at each other like brothers. It's ruthless."

"The bastard likes to push my buttons," he sighed with good-natured humor, the light sound warming her heart. It was surprising to see him like this, the corners of his eyes crinkled with laugh lines and a small smile playing at his beautiful mouth. Michaela didn't know what had brought it on, but she enjoyed the effect. An easygoing Brody was even more devastating than a brooding one, and she shivered with awareness, crossing her arms over the painful thudding of her heart.

Mistaking her reaction for cold, he reached out with his right hand to adjust the vents, making sure the warm air was blowing in her direction. A strange, electrified silence settled between them, and though she was staring at her lap, Michaela could feel the press of his eyes on her as he cast another look in her direction, this one lingering, briefly, on her profile, her mouth. Her lips tingled, and she rolled them inward as his left hand tightened on the steering wheel. The silence grew, thickening like a roux set over the simmering heat of a pan—and she watched the softened lines of his expression slowly slip away, replaced by his customary brooding darkness.

"So you own and run your own business," he finally said in a low, gravelly voice.

Whoa. As quickly as that shivering sense of awareness had come, it disappeared, like a rainbow bleeding back into the misty, rain-dappled beauty of the sky. And it wasn't the words themselves that chilled her. No, Michaela could tell from the sudden change in his tone that there was something behind the innocuous statement, and her stomach clenched with all-too-familiar disappointment. "And?" she murmured, silently berating herself for being such a nitwit, knowing her reaction was foolish. With everything going on in her life, she didn't have time to be sensitive over the moody Runner's opinions, but damn if she wasn't. For some stupid reason, she'd wanted him to be…different. To see her in a way that others didn't.

He shrugged his shoulders at her sharp tone. "Nothing."

Oh no. She wasn't letting him off the hook that easy. "Uh-huh. You brought it up, so you might as well go ahead and spit it out, Brody."

And she had a good idea of what it would be, aware of how most people pegged her as an eccentric basket case, walking around with her head in the clouds, once they learned that she owned a paranormal specialty shop. But the truth was that she had a good head for business and had simply chosen a market that she found fascinating as well as financially promising. She had her feet planted firmly on the ground, even if her mind was open to the world beyond what most humans considered normal.

"You just don't look like the business type." The look he cut her way said so much more than his words, and heat rose in her face that had nothing to do with the hot air gusting toward her. Oh yeah, she didn't need to read minds to know what "type" he thought she was. Her entire life, her looks had never given her anything but trouble, affecting how people treated her, judged her, thinking she was nothing but a pretty face with fluff for brains. Thinking she was good for some fun, but nothing serious. Her last boyfriend, Ross Holland, had enjoyed her body, but when it came to his blue-blooded public image and budding political aspirations, he hadn't wanted a woman whose sensuality was so blatant—so "in your face" as he'd put it. In Ross's eyes, her business had only been another strike against her.

She didn't want to admit it, but it hurt to realize that Brody apparently looked at her in the same, narrow-minded light. "Believe it or not, I don't sleep to dream, Brody. You shouldn't make assumptions about me based on physical appearances or what I do for a living."

"Sleep to dream?" he repeated, his brow furrowed over the deep green of his eyes. "What does that mean?"

Michaela struggled to keep her voice even. "It means that I don't have my head stuck in the clouds, worrying about when my next pedicure's gonna be and who'll buy me dinner on Friday night. When I sleep, I sleep hard because I work hard. I don't live in a fantasy world, playing dress up. My business takes up all of my time and I've worked my backside off to make it successful."

"I didn't mean to offend you," he grunted in a low rasp, surprising her. "And I imagine I'll get to see firsthand just how hard you work, since we'll be spending the next day or so at your shop."

"I guess you will," she muttered, looking down to realize her knuckles had gone white, she was fisting her hands together so tightly. She hadn't realized she was so touchy on the subject, but apparently she was. Or maybe she was just touchy about Brody's opinion. An unsettling thought, and another one she didn't want to look at too closely.

Without glancing in her direction, he went on to say, "And seeing as how we're going to be in the city for the next few days, are there any boyfriends I should know about? I don't want to have to deal with some jealous bastard who gets his nose bent out of shape because we're staying together."

"No," she sighed, squeezing her eyes shut, wondering how the hell this was going to work. The guy had her twisted up in knots and they'd only been together for a few hours. How was she going to endure days, if not weeks? She was too aware of him, too on edge.

"No what?"

Her mouth thinned and she opened her eyes, staring at the dark stretch of road through the front windshield. "No boyfriends."

A rude sound vibrated in the back of his throat. "Right."

Michaela shook her head in baffled amazement. She wasn't easily flustered, damn it, but something about Brody Carter made her feel stripped down to the raw, vulnerable, as if she were vibrating with energy, tension and anticipation. "I'm not sure what you mean by that."

He lifted one hand off the wheel, shoving his long, scarred fingers back through the auburn threads of his hair in an utterly male gesture of frustration. "If you want to lie about it, fine, but women like you always have a line of guys waiting in the wings, six or seven deep at least. I'd bet my life savings on the fact that you're involved with *someone,* Doucet."

"Then you're an idiot," she snorted, "and if you took that bet, you'd be a broke one at that."

He grunted in response, and she turned her head to glare back out her window. She kept quiet the remainder of the drive, not even giving him directions, since he already knew where she lived. But when they pulled to a slow stop behind the dark Mercedes parked in front of her house, she couldn't stop the low groan that fell from her lips, unable to believe her rotten, miserable luck. *"Merde,"* she cursed. "That's all this day needs."

"A friend of yours?" Brody asked with a smirk, eyeing the shadow of the man lurking on her front porch.

Michaela konked her forehead against the cool glass of her window once, then twice, and turned to send him her best glare. "I may be a lot of things, but I'm not a liar. There *is* no boyfriend."

He jerked his chin toward the waiting man. "Then who the hell is he?"

"Nobody. He's a big ol' nobody," she muttered, undoing her seat belt.

"I'm still waiting for a straight answer." His eyes narrowed as his face became etched with some unnamed emotion that was fierce and dark.

"He's my ex," she sighed, wondering how she could have ever been so stupid as to believe herself in love with a jerk like Ross Holland.

"Ex-what?" he grunted, his shock evident in his expression. "Husband?"

"Thank God, no," she supplied with a low, husky laugh. "Ex-*boyfriend*. But it's been over for…too long to count."

"Count it anyway."

The look she slanted him was equal parts surprise and exasperation. "Last year, okay?"

"And he's still coming around?" He shifted that dark stare back to Ross. "Hasn't he gotten the hint?"

"No," she replied dryly. "He doesn't seem to grasp the concept that he can't have his old girlfriend *and* his new wife at the same time."

He absorbed that for a moment, taking his eyes from Ross and watching her again with that deep green stare, making her feel as though he could see beneath her skin, beneath her guard, and take an intimate stroll through her mind. "He's married?"

It was obvious he wanted the story, and wasn't going to let it drop until he had it. "You're going to make me spill all the gory details, huh? Fine, here goes. It's not like this day could get any worse, so what do I have to lose? We'd been dating for about six months, when little Miss Sunshine Socialite made it clear she was available. His family loved her, and she had the pedigree and prestige they'd been looking for, while I was something he was ashamed of, like a secret from the carnival freak show. Ross is one of those whom I can't read, but once I saw him for what he really was, I told him never to come near me again. He married little Miss Sunshine, but won't give up on the fact that he can't have her *and* me."

After delivering the embarrassing account of her colossal stupidity, she reached to open the door, but Brody grabbed hold of her arm, his fingers fever warm against her skin, reminding her that he was so much more than human. As a Lycan, his core body temperature ran much higher than normal, even hotter when it was closer to a full moon. "Where do you think you're going?" he rasped, immediately releasing her arm, and as she held his stare, she noticed a warm glow beginning to seep through the deep, dark green of his eyes, as if backlit by the searing flames of a fire.

She wet her bottom lip, wishing she could get a read on him, but as always, whenever she threw out the soft, diaphanous net of her power, she met the hard resistance of his will, catching nothing. Taking a deep breath, she explained, "I'm just going to tell Mr. Nobody that he needs to get lost."

He shook his head, that oddly lit gaze cutting from her back to Ross's distant figure on her porch, and she was aware of his right hand clenching into a tight fist against his hard-muscled thigh. "I'll tell him," he said silkily. "You stay here."

Oh, no. Not in this lifetime. The last thing she was up to dealing with tonight was a fight between those two, and she knew from the hard cast of Brody's expression that he was looking forward to it. For a fleeting moment, Michaela actually wondered if he was jealous, before reminding herself that he couldn't care less about her personal life. No, he probably just needed to work off the frustration of getting stuck with her until Max's training was complete and her life could get back to some kind of semblance of normalcy. Brody didn't care anything about her personally. He was just a good guy who didn't want to see another innocent person get hurt.

But if that's the case, then why did he sound so possessive at the clearing?

To be honest, she didn't know, and wasn't even sure that she wanted to. After having her heart trampled, she didn't think she was up for another round, no matter how incredible her hormones thought he was. At worst, he just felt sorry for her. At best, he probably figured they could have some fun between the sheets while he was stuck with her. Michaela knew better than to think that anything more than that could come from something between them—just as she knew she couldn't risk it. No, something told her that the damage Brody could inflict on her would be devastating compared to the stupidity she felt at allowing herself to get used by Ross Holland.

She now viewed her involvement with Ross as an attempt to grasp at something she was worried she'd been missing, but Brody…God, this strange, unsettling interest searing through her system felt more like a necessity. Something that pulled on her, drawing her in, and that made him more dangerous to her sanity than her ex could ever be.

In the end, Ross had left her feeling used—but Brody Carter could leave her in pieces.

"Look, Brody, I appreciate what you did tonight. I know you only did it because you're friends with Torrance and Mason, and because you probably feel bad for me, after what happened to Max, and I appreciate it. Really, I do. But I don't need you to worry about Ross. A sleazy lowlife like him I can deal with. If anyone comes at me with claws and fangs, howling at the moon, then by all means, they're yours. I promise."

Despite the hot burn of frustration in his gut, Brody found himself biting the inside of his cheek as he fought the urge to grin at her words, thinking she was a lippy little package. She tried to hold his stare, until succumbing to an adorable yawn, ruining the "I can handle everything on my own" image she was going for. He admired her spunk, but there was no denying that he liked the fact she needed him.

What he didn't like was liking it.

You're not making any sense, you jackass. She's screwing with your head.

He wanted to deny it, but there was no point. Every part of him, every cell, every thought, had centered on her since he'd first seen her at the clearing earlier that night. And if he were honest, even before that.

"Come on," he murmured, reaching for the door handle. "You're all but dead on your feet. Let's get rid of pretty boy there so you can get some rest."

"This isn't what you signed up for," she argued, her gaze narrowed on her ex through the windshield. "Really, Brody, I can deal with this."

It was on the tip of his tongue to point out the obvious fact that if that was true, the prick wouldn't still be bothering her. But he kept quiet. She looked exhausted. So beautiful that it hurt a part of him deep inside to even look at her, but weary. Gray smudges darkened her big eyes, her mouth tight, skin pale. And the slow, melodic drawl of her accent had grown thicker, which, he'd noticed, happened when she was upset. She'd been to hell and back tonight, and he had no intention of letting some jackass give her a hard time. "My job is to keep you safe, so there's no point in arguing about it. Let's just get this over with," he muttered, opening his door.

Reaching across the cab, she latched on to his forearm, the touch of her hands on his body sending a tremor of shock through his system. "Damn it, Brody. What do you think you're doing?"

"Calm down, Doucet. I'm not doing anything. Just gonna walk you to your door. You can tell him to get lost all on your own," he told her, trying to sound relaxed while deep inside, in a part of him he'd thought he'd buried, he was burning with a cold, steady fury that he refused to look at too closely. But he couldn't forget it was there, just as he couldn't stop thinking of the many different ways he'd like to take Ross Holland apart, piece by piece.

And the hell of it was that he couldn't blame his anger simply on the fact that the creep wasn't getting the hint about Michaela wanting to be left alone. No, he knew better. He hated him because the bastard had had her. Didn't matter that Brody had no intention of letting himself fall victim to her considerable charms. He still hated every man who'd ever known the sweetness of her mouth, the softness of her skin. Who'd ever pressed his lips beneath the fragile edge of her jaw, drawing her delicate, milky-white flesh against his teeth, and marked her as he thrust himself into the slick, hot depths of her body.

Something ugly and vile and vicious ripped at his insides with the thought, and he realized with a silent snarl of frustration that hate was too light a word for his reaction. No, what he felt was deeper than hate, deeper than jealousy. It was something primal, visceral. Something base and primeval, bleeding both from the possessive nature of the beast and the man.

Irritated by the track of his thoughts, he ripped his gaze away from her soul-deep blue eyes and stared at the human. He stood just beyond the soft glow of the porch light, but Brody's keen vision allowed him to see clearly. His gut twisted as he took in the guy's appearance. He was tall and broad, on the lean side, not bulky. And he was…pretty, for God's sake. Cover model handsome, with thick brown hair and crystal blue eyes, features as even and perfect as a Hollywood sex symbol.

Brody wondered how a guy like that got down and dirty

in the sack. Ross Holland looked like the stiff-lipped type who probably folded his clothes and brushed his teeth, rolling his socks up neatly in his shoes before he slid beneath designer sheets, every hair in place as he flashed his signature smile. If that was the kind of man Michaela Doucet went for, Brody figured he'd probably scare her half to death with nothing more than a kiss. Because once he had her mouth, it wouldn't be sweet and easy and polished. It wouldn't be pretty or refined. His beast was too hungry for that—too focused on wanting this one wild, willful woman.

What it *would* be was raw. Consuming. Taking and drawing and demanding from her everything that he could take from the erotic slide of his tongue against hers, from the warm, lush sweetness of her inner mouth. And there was no damn way it would stop there. Brody couldn't imagine touching her and not losing himself to the animal craving lurking beneath his skin, the hunger of his beast letting loose in a vicious, violent taking. Which was why he needed to get the fact that it was never going to happen through his thick skull, there and then.

Never. Going. To. Happen.

"Please, Brody," she whispered, cutting into his private lecture. Her fingers grasped his arm tighter, and he could feel the tremor that moved through her, the slight vibration of emotion echoing against his bare skin. It was pathetic, how her simple touch unmanned him. "I…I can't handle any more fighting tonight. Wait here and I'll get rid of him, okay?"

He ground his jaw, furious with himself and her and the entire goddamn world, but finally nodded, jerking his chin toward her door. "Go on, then."

"Thanks," she whispered with a shivery smile, turning

quickly to climb out of the truck, while he leaned back in his seat, feeling like an idiot.

It went against every instinct he possessed to let her get out and walk toward another man. But as Brody watched her approach the porch, Holland moving into the light as they spoke, he reminded himself that no matter how he looked at it, it wasn't his right to dictate her personal life. No, that was a privilege that went beyond bodyguard, into emotional territory that was none of his business. It sucked, but he had to face the facts.

Despite how badly he wanted her, Michaela Doucet wasn't—and would never be—*his* woman.

Chapter 5

Rubbing at his gritty eyes as he leaned against the back wall of Michaela's Muse, Brody took another deep gulp of coffee, wondering if he'd ever had a worse night's sleep. It had been hell—no, worse than hell—being tortured with the slow burn of temptation.

After Michaela had climbed out of his truck last night, it hadn't taken her long to get rid of the ex. He'd hated letting her handle the jerk on her own, but he'd known it was for the best. The guy had met her on the steps, and they'd talked for no more than a minute, the human's pale eyes cutting from Michaela to his truck again and again, narrowed with suspicious jealousy. Just when he'd had enough and was reaching for his door handle, the bastard had turned and stalked away from her, heading to his car and screeching down the street in what he'd probably thought was a macho display of speed, which had just made him look ridiculous. Brody had grabbed the bag he always kept in his backseat then and met her on the porch.

Unwilling to let her out of his sight, he'd planned on taking the floor in her bedroom for the night, but she'd surprised him, once he'd made his intentions clear, with a spare bedroom that housed a pair of twin beds. Thinking about it now, he almost laughed, knowing they must have looked like something out of an episode of *I Love Lucy*. The corner of his mouth kicked up at the thought, and he shook his head.

With everything he had on his plate—the hunt for the rogues and the search for a way to bring Drake down, trying to find the psychotic maniac responsible for killing the blond humans, and his duty to keep Michaela safe—he didn't know why he kept having this bizarre urge to grin. It wasn't like him, damn it, and he didn't like it, same as he hadn't liked the way he'd relaxed around her during the drive into the city, before he'd realized what was happening.

And he definitely didn't care for the burn of desire in his gut—the one that kept growing tighter, harder, hotter the more time he spent with her.

What worried him even more than how much he wanted her, though, was how much he was beginning to actually *like* her. He'd been prepared to have to fight his hunger, but he hadn't expected to simply *enjoy* her so much. But with every passing moment, it became more and more evident that Michaela Doucet was unlike any other woman he'd ever known. There was so much more to her than what met the eye, layers upon layers that he wanted to uncover, peel away, until he could get to the juicy center of her heart, her very soul, that lay within.

Needing to keep himself occupied, he set his coffee aside and went back to work. While Michaela was busily getting things squared away for her absence, Brody had offered to make himself useful, even though he felt uncomfortable as hell around the fragile, delicate merchandise, like a bull in a china shop. Thankfully, she'd found the perfect job for him in the form of boxed bookshelves in the back corner, waiting to be assembled.

The units were needed to replace the ones destroyed by Anthony Simmons and his flunkies a few weeks ago, when the rogue had vandalized her shop as a way to strike out against Torrance and Mason. The mess had been cleaned up and the store reopened for business, but there were still odds and ends that needed to be finished. The shelves were one of them. While Michaela was buried in paperwork at the counter behind him, sorting out schedules and payroll, Brody kept himself busy assembling the units.

He'd just finished the first one, and was tearing into the tall cardboard box housing the second, when he heard her say, "Do you want something that will hold back your hair?" The soft, husky sound of her voice stroked his senses like a lover's touch, slipping across the surface of his skin, beneath it, trailing down the length of his spine with the damp heat of an openmouthed caress. He squeezed his eyes shut against the blistering need she so carelessly invoked. All she had to do was talk to him and he went hard, his body hot, muscles tight, every cell actually hurting with the need to touch her.

"No thanks," he murmured, pissed that he could feel the beginning warmth of a blush staining his cheeks as he looked over his shoulder to see her offering him a soft leather strip to tie around his hair. Jesus, he hadn't blushed since…hell, he couldn't even remember the last time.

Smiling, her head tilted slightly to the side, she said, "But isn't it hard to see with your hair hanging in your face?"

His eyes snagged on the sensual curve of her mouth, provocative and innocent all at once, and he blinked, unable to look away.

Son of a bitch. When she smiled at him like that, it made him start thinking impossible things that he had no business thinking about. Even if she was offering what that deliciously tempting smile suggested she was offering, he knew it wouldn't work— and the last thing in the world he wanted to see was that sweet smile melt into horror once she'd finished with him in bed.

"I don't want the goddamn tie," he suddenly growled, making her jump at the savageness of his tone.

"Okay," she whispered softly, still smiling at him, as if he hadn't just barked at her.

Damn it, why was she being so nice to him? What did he have to do to make her stop? And why did he feel like such a complete and utter ass? "Trust me," he grunted, turning back to the tall cardboard box he'd propped against the wall. "It's better this way. You don't want me scaring away your customers."

From the corner of his eye, he watched as she moved a little to his right. "Why would you scare away my customers?"

He snorted under his breath. "You need glasses?"

"Um, no."

"Then you've seen what I look like," he muttered, slanting her a hard glare, as if daring her to keep the little-Miss-Innocent act going.

But she didn't flinch. She just held his stare, her confusion evident in the soft crinkling of her nose. "Yes," she said simply. "I'm more than aware of what you look like, Brody, but what does that have to do with anything?"

"Christ," he hissed, wanting to grab hold of the feminine curve of her shoulders and shake some sense into her. "What the hell is it with you?"

The corners of her mouth slipped into a frown. "Am I missing something?"

Clenching his jaw, he jerked his gaze back to the sleek piece of shelving he'd grabbed from inside the open box, the honey-colored wood beneath his fingers beginning to give. Forcing himself to relax his hold, he ground his explanation out through gritted teeth. "My scars, Doucet. They tend to scare the hell out of people. The more I can cover them when around humans, the better. So just drop it."

"I'm sorry," she murmured in a quick rush, rolling her lips inward. "I didn't think…I just…" She shook her head, looking frustrated. "I didn't know you were sensitive about them."

"I'm not," he snapped, feeling like an idiot, aware of the heat slashing across his cheekbones burning hotter, completely humiliating him. "I just don't like drawing attention to myself," he added gruffly, pulling the next piece of shelving from the box.

"For what it's worth, I think…I think maybe you're wrong, Brody."

He turned his head, staring down into her big blue eyes, her lashes so thick they cast a shadow against the creamy paleness of her skin. "About what?"

"If people stare at you, it's probably not because of your scars," she admitted in a soft, tremulous voice that shivered with some unnamed emotion fluttering beyond his grasp, like the rapid flight of a butterfly. "It's because you're…well, you must know that you're…I mean, how…"

"Doucet," he growled, ready to tell her to spit it out.

At the same time she said, "How attractive you are."

The words landed between them with the explosive force of a nuclear weapon, thudding into the cloudy space of misconception, until all he could do was blink at her blushing face, wondering what kind of game she was playing. He searched for a flicker of amusement in her eyes, but could see nothing more than the slow, steady warmth of a desire that nearly made him combust then and there.

His muscles tightened, a trickle of sweat slipping down the searing heat of his temple, stinging the corner of his eye, while he clawed onto his self-control with every shred of sanity he could find. The hazy details of the store faded—the dim voices of a crowd in the next-door café, the dulcet notes of a Celtic CD playing on a stereo, the low burr of electricity coming from the cash register—until there was nothing but Michaela. Those big, beautiful eyes staring up at him with such wrenching emotion. Her intoxicating scent making his mouth water, his gums burning with the prickling sting of his fangs just waiting to slip free. She wet her lips—her tongue tiny, pink and delicate—and he wanted to take control of it. Wanted to grab hold of her and ravage the sweet, inner well of her mouth and that kittenish little tongue until she was sobbing and begging and pleading for more, for everything he could give her.

His fingers released the wood, flexing with impatience, his lungs heaving as he slowly turned toward her, the air between their bodies feeling thick, heavy, the tension building, growing, expanding, her luminous eyes shocked wide, as if she felt it, too. Brody took a step closer to the heat of her body, towering over her, both of them softly panting, his blood boiling with the hunger scorching its way through his veins.

He'd just started to lift his right hand toward the silken fall of hair spilling over her shoulder, one long, midnight curl sweeping provocatively across the voluptuous swell of her nipple—when a shrill sound echoed through the store, instantly fracturing the moment. They both flinched, jarred by the sharp, intrusive ringing, and he immediately turned away from her, giving her his back, wondering what in God's name he'd been thinking.

"Th-that's the phone," she stammered in a low, breathless voice, and he listened as she moved away, heading through a doorway and into her back office to answer the call. She'd already sent David home for the day, after going over everything he'd need to handle while she was gone, and now it was just the two of them.

The seconds ticked by, stretching out, until Brody completely lost count of how much time had passed. He just stood there, eyes squeezed tight, body aching as he struggled to force himself to relax, drawing the air in and out of his lungs in a concentrated rhythm that should have started calming him down, any damn second now. Shuddering, Brody finally cracked his eyes open and ran his upper arm over his forehead, his T-shirt clinging to the damp heat of his skin. He was on fire and he hadn't even touched her!

The churning, uncomfortable sense of awareness she incited seemed to have taken on a new skin, a new shape. The more time he spent with her, the more he wanted her. Before, when he'd first met her, he'd been afraid of getting too close to her. Now he didn't know how he would survive without the feel of Michaela Doucet under his hands, under his body.

It'd never been that way for him before. He'd needed sex, wanted it, and he'd slaked his hunger with women whose faces were forgotten the moment he left their beds, which was just the way they wanted it. The last time he'd allowed himself to get close to a woman, it had ended badly. He'd do well to remember the lesson, but damn, he didn't want to think about Jenny Riggs, the Elder's younger sister, right now. Still, it was with a small jolt of awareness that Brody realized the thought of her name no longer made him clench with frustration. That was…different, as if the Cajun's presence had wiped his mind clean of other women, replacing the tainted memories with a fresh, untarnished slate. But even if he couldn't recall what it felt like to have another woman under him, he remembered the bitter taste of rejection in his mouth, the shame of feeling like a used piece of meat when it was over.

The memory settled over him like a heavy, oppressive cloud, until like a breath of sunshine, Michaela walked back into the room. Brody groaned under his breath, the soft sound like that of a man being tormented, pushed to the edge of his sanity, the visceral craving evoked by her particular scent affecting him like an all-too-real pain within his body. He could feel his desire for her, lust-thick and heavy, lying in wait beneath the surface of his skin, keeping company with his prowling beast— and knew it was a hunger that would never be satisfied.

And never was a hell of a long time.

Drawing in a deep breath of impatience, he growled low in his throat as she drew nearer. Suddenly the room felt like a prison, the hunger in his veins a noose that he couldn't shake.

"Brody, you're trembling. What's wrong?" she asked in a soft voice, standing behind him again, her concern evident. He'd assumed she'd do the smart thing and avoid him when she returned, but he was quickly learning that Michaela Doucet was not an easy woman to predict.

"Nothing's wrong," he grunted, shifting away from her, toward the tall pieces of the bookshelf still lying within the open box propped against the wall.

"You're lying."

Whipping around, he towered over her, trying to ignore how the soft, dark blue wraparound cotton dress clung to the voluptuous, feminine lines of her body. "How the hell would you know?" he growled, feeling like a man pushed beyond endurance.

She blinked up at him, the pansy-soft curve of her lips, so luscious and pink, trembling with emotion, the look in her eyes liquid and tender. "I…I don't mean to pry, but there's a kind of pain in your eyes today. I think you're hurting inside."

Of all the things she could have said, he figured that was the one that could piss him off the most. Curling his lip, he snarled, "Let's make one thing perfectly clear, here, Doucet. I didn't ask for a goddamn reading."

With a soft hint of hesitation, she took a step closer to him, tilting her head back in order to hold his stare. "I told you that I can't read you, and I didn't mean to upset you."

"You didn't upset me," he growled under his breath, careful to keep his voice low so that they didn't draw attention from any of the people walking past the store. "And nothing's wrong. In fact, my only problem is a woman who won't keep her nose out of my damn business."

For a moment, she looked hurt, stricken, before taking a deep breath and shaking off that bleak expression. Damn it, what was wrong with him? She'd been through an emotional wringer in the past twenty-four hours, and here he was lashing out at her, biting her head off when she tried to be nice. It took everything he had not to reach out and touch her…comfort her.

He was on the verge of doing just that when the chimes attached to the front door sounded, and as Brody watched her pull herself together, then turn and walk away, all he could think was *saved by the bell.*

At the sound of the door, Michaela buried the hurt she'd felt at Brody's words and plastered on a bright smile that turned genuine the moment she spotted one of her favorite customers shuffling in, Meredith Shelby's pale gray hair wound in a tight knot on the top of her petite head. Rushing forward, she gave the local psychic a hug, kissing both her cool cheeks, before stepping aside to allow Meredith a clear view of Brody. She knew better than to try and shield him from the woman's view. Nothing and no one got past the eighty-year-old's eagle eye.

"Oh my. And who might this lovely be?" Meredith asked, her voice still holding a trace of her English heritage as she gave Brody a slow, thorough once-over.

Placing her hand on Meredith's arm, Michaela led the woman to Brody. "I'd like to introduce you to a friend of mine, Meredith. This is Mr. Brody Carter."

Giving him no chance to object, unless he wanted to get physical with her, Meredith reached out and snatched hold of Brody's right hand, clasping it within her fragile grasp. He flushed, his eyes wide as he stared down at the little gray-haired woman. Meredith bent over his palm, tsking and murmuring to herself, until she finally lifted her head.

"I'm very disappointed in you, Mr. Carter."

He opened his mouth, then promptly shut it, obviously having no idea what to say in response, and Michaela had to stifle a giggle.

As if there were nothing unusual about her scolding a

perfect stranger, Meredith held his hand and went on. "You're fighting your natural instincts, acting as stubborn-headed as a mule, and that just won't do. You're smarter than that, boy, but you're letting fear control you, holding you back from the thing you want most in this world."

He swallowed, the movement visible in his throat, and managed to say, "What's that?"

"Oh, sweetheart, I can't tell you," Meredith replied with a slow smile. "That would ruin the fun."

Brody's face hardened to the point that he looked as if he might crack, a low sound of restraint vibrating in his chest.

Undaunted, Meredith patted his chest in a comforting gesture. "There, there. It's all right. You're guarded now, but you're going to make a fine husband and father one day."

Shaking his head, he made a rude sound of disbelief in the back of his throat. "No disrespect, ma'am, but there's not a chance in hell of that happening."

The elderly woman arched one perfectly refined brow. "No?"

"I'm not the marrying kind," he stated, his mouth a hard, flat line.

Meredith winked at him, her eyes sparkling with mischief. "No man is, lovey, until he meets the woman who finally opens his eyes."

"I can assure you that my eyes are opened just fine."

"Oh, I do like you, Brody," she announced, her smile widening. Turning to Michaela, she said, "He's a wild one, this young buck you've landed. Do well and hold on to him, Mickey girl."

Blushing, Michaela knew the only way to deal with Meredith was to let her run right over you, and simply try to survive the experience. "Er, I'll, um, do my best, ma'am."

"I'm sure you will. Now show me that latest shipment of tea leaves you called me about." Patting her bun, she explained her hurry. "I have an appointment with the stylist in a half hour and want to be on time."

Helping Meredith make her choices, Michaela handled the transaction, aware of Brody keeping a cautious eye on them as he began fitting the bookshelves together.

At the door, Meredith turned back, pinning Brody with a pointed look of concern. "And call your grandmother, young man. She misses you something fierce."

The second the door slid closed behind the little gray-haired spitfire, Brody shook his head in wonder and exhaled a deep breath of relief. Waving to her friend one last time through the window, Michaela turned toward him, the corner of her mouth twitching with a grin. "So what did you think of our Meredith?"

"Charming," he muttered. "I feel like I've been run over by a tank."

A soft laugh fell from her lips. "She liked you."

"Yay for me," he drawled, rolling his eyes.

"Brody! Was that a joke?" she gasped with feigned surprise.

He grunted at her playfulness and turned back toward the shelves. When she moved closer, her mouthwatering fragrance blocking out the subtle blend of incense in the air, and voiced the question he'd seen in her eyes, he wasn't surprised. He'd known it was coming.

"What did Meredith mean, about your grandmother missing you?"

Aligning the side panel with the back of the shelving unit,

he slotted the screws into their grooves and picked up the screwdriver. "Nothing."

"Come on, Brody," she murmured. From the corner of his eye, he watched her perch one shapely hip against a display case full of intricate Celtic jewelry. "Why is it you get to know all my secrets, but won't tell me anything about yourself?"

Twisting the first screw into place, he tried to focus on anything but how good she smelled, how right it felt to be near her, calm and chaotic all at once. "Because I need to know about your life so that I can protect you."

"And I don't need to know anything about you in return?"

Finishing with the last screw, he moved to the other panel, muttering, "That's right."

He could feel the heat of her gaze as it slipped down his profile, over the bridge of his nose, lower, lingering on his mouth. "You really don't like me much, do you, Brody?"

"You're pretty enough," he muttered gruffly, rolling his shoulder as he focused on his task, "but I don't place much stock in beauty."

"Ouch." Her tone was contemplative, soft. "Can't ask for a more honest answer than that, now can I? I'd be offended, except I think you're being rude on purpose, trying to push me away so that you don't have to tell me about your grandmother."

"She lives up in Shadow Peak but we've avoided each other for years." He let out a deep breath, feeling like an ass, wondering why he couldn't just keep his mouth shut around her. "And the reason we don't talk isn't a pretty story, Doucet."

Quietly, she said, "I didn't imagine it was."

He didn't know why, but he found the words spilling out of his mouth in a low, emotionless rumble. "My father was a Silvercrest Lycan who fell in love with a beautiful human, and she repaid his love with an endless string of affairs. Even though he felt the call of a life mate for her, I guess she was either too coldhearted or too self-centered, or maybe just too dead inside to return his feelings. When she had an affair with another mated Lycan male whose wife demanded action by the pack, she and the guy were sentenced to punishment by the wife's family under one of the old laws that has since been rewritten."

"How old were you?" she asked, the words hushed, and he could tell she was trying to hide her own emotion, knowing he'd close up if she showed him so much as an ounce of pity.

"Young, just turned eight, but I understood what was happening. Like a little fool, I tried to rush to my mother's rescue, and ended up receiving a punishment of my own for daring to interfere. Each member of the wife's family was allowed to give me a single lash with their claws. All the blows were delivered to my back, until it was her father's turn." Snorting, he said, "I guess he was pissed at the others in his family for going easy on me, so he pulled me up by my hair and slashed my face. My father, who was already being restrained by members of the pack, was so furious that he challenged the Lycan later that night and they both died during the Challenge Fight."

There was a slight tremor in her voice that she couldn't disguise as she asked, "And what happened to your mother?"

He shrugged, careful to keep his eyes on the screws as he twisted them into place. "She lost too much blood from the punishment and the pack wouldn't allow Jillian's mother, who was Spirit Walker at the time, to do anything to help her. She died later the next day from her injuries, and the guy she'd been screwing around with abandoned his family and the pack. No one ever heard from him again."

"Wh-what happened to you?"

"My dad's mom took me in," he grunted. "But she was a right old bitch. Didn't want to be saddled with a kid any more than my mom had. She made sure I understood why she was stuck with me—because of my parents' recklessness and stupidity. And she made it her mission in life to teach me the control they'd both lacked, making damn sure I'd never forget it."

Control? What about love? Michaela thought, her heart breaking for the little boy who must have felt so alone, so unwanted. What about cuddles and bedtime stories and kisses on his skinned knees?

Deep, burning pain pierced her chest at the thought of all he'd missed as a child. Was that the lesson the women in his life had taught him, that he wasn't wanted? Wasn't worthy of their love and affection? Had the lessons from his past made it impossible for him to get close to any woman—to give them the chance to get close to him?

Rage for his mother and grandmother poured through her veins in a hard, rushing spill of anger and disbelief. How could any woman not cherish her child? Not do everything in her power to protect him from the world? Suddenly, despite her inability to read him, Michaela began to understand the complicated Runner, to see him in a clearer light. No wonder he was so wary of allowing others to get close to him.

"I'm sorry for what you went through," she said gently, noticing the way he flinched when she stroked her hand across the firm curve of his shoulder, wishing she could wrap him in her arms and hold on to him. Stupid wish, since she knew she would only end up being rejected. At worst, used. But wishes weren't always wise, or even healthy, blooming from that innocent part of our souls that held eternally to faith and hope.

He rolled his shoulder, shifting away from her touch. "No need to be sorry, Doucet," he muttered. "It's ancient history and I was stupid to interfere. I was impulsive and I paid for it."

"That's not true. You were very brave, and you loved her. What you did, it was incredibly heroic. You should be proud of what your scars represent. They're a symbol of your integrity."

Brody groaned under his breath at her huskily spoken words, wishing she'd just shut the hell up, feeling like an idiot for opening that vein and spilling his memories in a crimson wash of shame. He didn't know why he'd done it, except for the fact that he wasn't himself around her. All she had to do was smile at him, look at him, breathe for God's sake, and his hard-earned control and legendary restraint were shredded. He wanted to lash out at her, tell her to get lost, but the words were stuck in his throat, along with his heart, which was hammering like a freaking train.

A second later, the door chimes sounded again, and he silently swore, cringing at the thought of having to go through another inquisition. Wondering if he could sneak into the back office before she introduced him to another customer, he picked up a scent that was out of place, even in the strange parade of customers that had been coming and going throughout the day. The tiny hairs on the back of his neck stood up in alarm, and he sniffed the air, spinning the instant he caught the thick scent of Lycan musk.

"Oh my God," Michaela gasped, at the same time Brody grabbed hold of her, shoving her behind him as he turned to face the couple walking into the middle of the store.

Michaela's fingers grasped onto the back of his shirt, twisting the soft cotton into angry handfuls, and he knew she'd recognized Dustin Sheffield, the dark-haired, golden-eyed Lycan from her brother's *Novitiate's* ceremony. It was Dustin who had kicked Max when he'd fallen to the ground. His father, Cooper Sheffield, once one of Stefan Drake's key supporters, had been killed by Jeremy after the attack on Jillian's life. Now, with his father gone, it'd been rumored that Dustin had stepped into the role of Drake's right-hand man.

Taking a leisurely glance around the shop, Dustin whistled softly under his breath. "I heard Simmons had quite a field day with this place, but it looks so spiffy and clean. What a shame."

"What the hell do you want, Sheffield?"

Ignoring the question, the Lycan flashed a slow smile, then leaned down to whisper in the ear of the cute blonde clinging to his arm. Vapid and blank, her big eyes blinked slowly as she listened to him. No more than eighteen, the human girl giggled at whatever he said and turned to wander toward the far side of the shop, studying a display of crystals while blowing bubbles with an enormous wad of purple bubble gum. Dustin watched her ass in a low-slung pair of jeans that revealed the hot pink fabric of her thong underwear, then turned back toward them, one brow arched in a cynical lift as he tilted his head to the side, trying to see around Brody's body. "Is there a sexy little Cajun hiding behind you, Carter? I can't see her—" he took a slow, deep breath "—but I can sure smell her."

Michaela released Brody's shirt and moved to his side, her chin high, eyes narrowed with fury as she stared at the smirking Lycan who winked back at her. Brody wrapped a protective arm around her waist, hauling her even closer to him as he kept his attention focused on Dustin.

Stopping beside a display of pewter figurines and chalices, Sheffield's hard eyes traveled over Michaela's body, lingering on the lush swell of her chest. Obviously aware of his stare, she crossed her arms, shielding herself, and the corner of the bastard's mouth twitched with a grin.

Pitching his voice seductively low, he drawled, "Do you know who I am?"

She nodded with a jerky movement of her chin. "You're the sadistic asshole who kicked my brother."

"Aw, don't be a bad sport, angel. I was doing him a favor. If he's going to make it in our world, he needs to toughen up. Just ask Carter, here. Your Runner is known as one of the most brutal hunters there's ever been. They say he can kill a man without even batting an eye."

"Brody kills gutter scum who deserve to die," she murmured, surprising him by rising to his defense. "All you did was act like a bully."

A low, sinister laugh fell from the Lycan's lips. "Now you're just trying to hurt my feelings," he rasped, the golden hue of his gaze bleeding away, replaced by a deep, infinite black that revealed nothing, utterly devoid of emotion. "But guess what, sweetheart? It won't work."

Jeremy had told Brody and the other Runners that Dustin was close to turning, if not already, rogue. It was something you could just feel, after you'd been hunting as long as they had, the way an elderly arthritic man could predict rain. A sense...a feeling, not unlike the way Michaela had described her own abilities.

More than anything, it was in the eyes. Cold, emotionless, a rogue knew nothing beyond its hunger for death and satisfaction. There was no warmth, no soul. Just that hard, relentless push for a dark, violent rush of pleasure.

Brody wanted to take the bastard down, but his first priority was keeping Michaela safe. "For the last time, Sheffield, tell us what you want and then get out."

The grin curling Dustin's mouth shifted into something sly, suggestive, and he shook his head. "Something tells me that you'd put up a fight if I told you." Picking up one of the figurines, a lovely little sprite arching her back, arms flung high over her head in sensual abandon, Dustin ran his fingers over the feminine lines of its body, his gaze never leaving Michaela as he drawled, "But if you're really that interested, Drake sent me down to make sure you were doing your job, keeping her on a short leash."

"And he chose you for his messenger boy?" Brody snorted, aiming for his ego. "So with Simmons dead and your old man gone, I guess Drake is really having to scrape the bottom of the barrel for support these days, eh?"

Sheffield made a tsking sound under his breath. "Drake used Simmons's thirst for revenge to make a move against Dillinger, but the idiot turned out to be too weak to see it through. It was embarrassing, if you want to know the truth. As for my old man, he let himself get careless. But me, I'm smarter than both of them. I know how to keep myself alive. And I don't plan on going until I've gotten a taste of all that life can offer," he murmured, giving Michaela's body another slow, hungry look.

"Get your eyes off her right now," Brody demanded in a low, deadly rasp, "or I promise you're going to regret it."

"You can't touch me, Runner. None of you can. Drake's hatred has made him more powerful than anything you've ever known, than anything you can handle."

"See, that's where you're wrong, Sheffield. And if you're not careful, all you and Drake hold dear is going to come crashing down around you. Sooner or later, the humans are going to find out about the rogues. What do you think they'll do then?"

"You're so pathetic," the younger man snickered, shaking his head with mock pity. "The Silvercrest are embarrassed by you, and yet you still put their needs above your own, protecting them from discovery. Personally, I say let the humans find out the truth about us. They're no match for our strength. They're nothing but food."

A rich, husky rumble of laughter shook Brody's chest. "Food that would end up kicking your ass."

"Hmm, I wouldn't hold my breath about that if I were you," Dustin whispered, a gloating sheen of satisfaction coating his skin. "After all, her precious brother cried like a baby when I took a bite out of him."

For a moment, time stood still, suspended, and then Michaela exploded into action, a hoarse sob breaking from her chest as she lurched forward. Brody reacted instantly, throwing his arms around her, trapping her against the front of his body. She struggled in his hold, same as she had at the clearing the night before, but he didn't blame her. He wanted to tear Dustin apart, as well.

"You sick son of a bitch," he snarled, his own rage crashing against his control, battering it down. Only the need to protect the woman in his arms kept him in place, kept him from acting on the slow burn of fury rushing through his system. Tangling his hands in Michaela's hair, he cupped the back of her head and pushed her face into his chest as the first racking sobs shook her feminine frame, her anger and frustration escaping in a torrent of emotion. Cutting a cold, deadly look of menace at the Lycan, he said, "Get the hell out of here. Now."

Dustin made a soft, crooning noise under his breath. "Don't cry for Max, beautiful. I'll even be a sport and say hi to him for you."

Wrenching in his hold, she turned and shouted, "Stay away from my brother!"

"It's sweet that you're worried about him, but pointless. If anything," the Lycan murmured, his voice low and soothing, like a lover's, "you should be worried about your *own* skin. After all, if things don't go well for Max, your blood will be on Carter's hands."

She went still in Brody's arms, staring at Dustin in confusion. "What are you talking about?"

The Lycan's dark brows rose on the smooth expanse of his forehead. "Didn't he tell you?"

"Tell me what?" she demanded.

"If your brother fails, he's not the only one who'll die. All threats have to be neutralized, which means your watchdog would be expected to take your life. Wonder if he'll enjoy killing you as much as he's enjoyed all his other kills?" he mused, slanting her a laughing look as he set the sprite back in its place. "Who knows, maybe he'll even enjoy doing you while you're still warm, before finishing the deed. There's something wild about him that says he likes it a little rough."

Though he tried like hell to hold himself in check, Brody's restraint finally snapped and he pushed Michaela behind him as he surged forward, his fingertips burning as deadly claws pricked just beneath the surface of his skin. If it weren't for the human girl on the other side of the room, he'd have allowed them to slip free, but fought back the impulse. Instead, with one hand he grabbed a handful of the Lycan's shirt and drew his other arm back, preparing to smash the bastard's smirking face, while Dustin shoved at his shoulders.

"Come on, Runner. Give it your best shot," Sheffield taunted, just as the front door chimed and a group of eight young college students filtered in, laughing and chatting, oblivious to the tension at the far side of the shop. Releasing his hold, Brody shoved the Lycan away from him. His hands fisted at his sides, chest heaving as he struggled to claw onto some shred of his control.

"Better luck next time," Dustin drawled with a hoarse laugh, and with a crooked smile, he turned and walked past the oblivious students, out the front door, the wide-eyed blonde following faithfully behind him.

Chapter 6

That evening, they made the drive back to Michaela's house steeped in the same charged silence that had been hanging over their heads ever since Dustin Sheffield's visit. Brody had called Cian and brought him up to date on Sheffield's confession about Max's attack, and then he'd talked to Mason, who said he would notify the League. Not that they expected anything to come from it. Because of Dustin's close ties to Drake, until they had solid proof that Sheffield had gone rogue, and not just Brody's word, they knew the League would refuse to assign a Bloodrun on the Lycan.

And while he was sure Michaela had believed him when he'd awkwardly tried to assure her that he'd never cause her any harm, despite Dustin's taunting remark to the contrary, the tension between them had remained thick. Or maybe that was just the growing web of sexual awareness that he couldn't shake, its clinging, powerful strands ensnaring him tighter with each passing second, until he could barely breathe without panting for a deeper pull of her maddening, mouth-watering scent.

He parked in front of her house, and they both climbed out of the truck, the cool evening breeze wrapping around them, bringing hints of a coming storm, the air crisp and damp. As they made their way up the front walkway, he caught sight of a white swing hidden in the shadows at the far end of the porch. It creaked gently back and forth in the gusting wind, and his blood scorched its way through his veins as he studied it.

Too easily, Brody could imagine the beautiful human lounging there on the wheat-colored cushion, swinging lazily while a sultry summer breeze ushered in the twilight, a knowing smile curving her lush mouth as she beckoned him closer with the feminine crook of her finger. For a moment, the tender, seductive image was so powerful that he almost believed he could reach out and touch the warmth of her flesh, the heavy silk of her hair. Explore the heavenly textures of her body beneath his callused, work-roughened fingertips.

And daydreams are going to get you nowhere, you jackass… other than in a shitload of trouble.

Why was he having such a hard time grasping that concept? This—this bizarre sense of obsession, hunger and fascination—it wasn't him. The others, sure. Hell, Mason and Jeremy were so in love with their mates they were practically floating. And he could see some woman wrapping Cian around her finger someday, if she could find a way to put up with the smart-ass bastard. Even Pallaton would eventually be tamed.

But not him.

And yet, when he faced facts and owned up to exactly

what he'd have been willing to give up for the chance to touch Michaela Doucet, just once, it was staggering. Brody couldn't stop his mind from lingering across the visual details of her body as she led the way up the path toward the house, the barest hint of her profile visible as he followed behind her, her face as luminous as a pearl beneath the hazy glow of the streetlamp. Would her skin be that soft and pale everywhere, revealing the tracery of veins beneath her voluptuous breasts, her belly, the tender flesh of her inner thighs?

Muttering to himself, Brody wondered how he was going to survive another night under the same roof with her without touching her, battling against the visceral, sharp-edged hunger that wouldn't leave him in peace. He'd been insane to think he could watch over her, protect her, without losing his ever-loving mind.

Completely lost in the thick, unctuous tangle of his thoughts, he'd just set foot on the bottom porch step when he heard a vehicle behind them, its tires screeching to a stop in front of her small yard. Turning, Brody cursed hotly under his breath at the sight of Dustin Sheffield grinning at them from the passenger side window of a sleek, black Silverado.

Brody didn't recognize the driver, but Dustin sat with his arm braced in the open window of the door, the smoke from the cigarette perched between his lips, curling like a serpent above his head.

"What the hell does he think he's doing?" he muttered, aware of Michaela coming back down the porch steps to stand at his side.

"Pushing your buttons, no doubt," she whispered, grabbing his left arm, as if she could hold him back. "Please don't give him what he came here for, Brody."

Since, by this time, he was dragging Michaela along with him away from the porch, he stopped halfway down the stone path that bisected the front yard, unwilling to take her too close to the truck. "What are you doing here, Sheffield?"

Dustin exhaled a silvery stream of smoke and smiled. "Just being neighborly, making sure the little lady got home okay tonight. Didn't want her to be upset after what she learned today."

Brody curled his lip. "You're pushing your luck, and I don't give a crap about Drake and your pathetic threats. Only thing that concerns me is making sure you understand just how serious I am about you staying away from her. Do I make myself clear?"

"Crystal," the Lycan laughed, his smile widening as he flicked the cigarette butt into the street. Reaching behind him, he shifted as he pulled something out of the back pocket of his pants. Brody heard Michaela's gasp and knew she instantly recognized the pale lace bra Dustin brandished in the open window, rubbing the soft material between his fingertips, while his lips twisted in a taunting grin. "Hope you don't mind, Runner, but I borrowed a few pieces of the Cajun's lingerie for Kimmie today and wanted to return them. Dressed her up in it before I screwed her stupid little brains out, the scent of your woman filling my head. God, what a high," he sighed. "I was gonna return the panties…but, well, let's just say they were a little worse for wear." He snuffled a soft laugh, then lifted the bra to his nose, took a slow, deep breath and moaned deep in his throat. "Mmm, and no wonder you were so eager to volunteer to be her white knight, Carter. Little Cajun's sweet, like candy." His tongue flicked out, and he touched it to the delicate lace. "Good enough to eat, in fact."

A deep, snarling growl jerked out of Brody's throat and he lunged forward, while Michaela clung onto his arm. "You son of a bitch!"

Chuckling, Dustin tossed the bra in Michaela's direction and the truck immediately sped away, its tires screeching against the damp asphalt as it swerved and roared down the street.

"What do you think you're doing?" Michaela cried, breathless as she struggled to keep hold of Brody's arm while he tried to pull her off without hurting her.

"I'll tell you what I'm doing," he seethed, his voice so guttural, she could barely understand him. "I'm going to do what I should have done this afternoon and chase him down, then beat that little shit's face into the ground for daring to even look at you!"

"Stop it," she snapped, holding on to him with all her strength. "I'm not going to let you do this! It isn't going to change what's happened to Max, and it isn't going to help anything!"

"Do you know where he got that thing?" he shouted, pointing at the bit of lace lying in the grass.

She sucked in a sharp breath. "From my house, obviously."

"He could have gotten you," he snarled, his expression so livid, Michaela was sure he was going to slip from his human shape any second now, allowing the primal fury of his beast to break through. She could see the tips of his fangs gleaming wickedly in the moonlight, just beneath his upper lip—could feel the visceral, animal energy pouring through him while his eyes burned like twin golden-green embers. "He was *here,* Doucet! What if you'd come home alone last night? Or today? What if I wasn't with you? He could have done anything he wanted to you. There's no way you could have stopped him."

She went pale as his words sank in, but she didn't back down. "It doesn't matter," she said hoarsely, knowing that keeping Brody safe was more important to her than any kind of revenge against the rogue Lycan.

"Like hell it doesn't," he growled, not even sounding human. "I'll be damned before I let him terrorize you this way."

"He isn't terrorizing me, Brody. Upsetting me, yes. But I know what he's doing." She blinked up at him, releasing her hold on his arm so that she could press her palms against his broad chest, aware of his heartbeat thumping heavily beneath her touch. "He's using me to get to you, I mean to the Runners, just like you said they would. It's all just a game to him. Even what happened with Max. But with you watching me, he isn't stupid enough to actually try to hurt me, because he knows the lot of you would have his ass if he did."

"Jesus, when are you going to get it?" he demanded, his tone thick with anger and impatience. "He wants you, Doucet. Once his kind sets their sights on a target, they don't just let it go. Trust me, I know. This is the kind of filth I track down month after month. He isn't going to just up and forget about you."

"Well, he isn't going to get me, is he?"

Brushing her hands away from his chest, he took a deep, shuddering breath, his expression still etched with deep lines of fury, though she could tell he was trying to calm down. "We're packing up tonight. I want you in the Alley. It isn't safe for us down here."

"Okay," she murmured, glancing down the street as she snatched up the bra, hoping like hell that none of her neighbors had heard their raised voices. The last thing they needed was to deal with a concerned good Samaritan or the police.

"I finished up at the store today and everything's ready for David. If you'll just come inside with me, I'll pack up a suitcase and we can go ahead and leave."

She turned toward the house, and he stayed her with his hand on her shoulder, the heat of his fingers burning its way through the soft cotton of her dress. "We go in together, with you at my back. I need to make sure it's safe."

Michaela nodded, and together they moved up the narrow pathway. She unlocked the front door, and they walked into the silent house, turning on lights along the way. In the kitchen they found a window with a broken lock, obviously where Dustin had snuck in. Nothing was touched or out of place, however, until they reached her bedroom upstairs. The second Brody flicked on the light, she gasped, pushing past him as she rushed into the room, turning in a circle in the midst of mindless destruction, the bra falling to the floor, forgotten.

She'd already known Dustin had been through her things, but she hadn't expected this kind of devastation. Her furniture had been slashed, deep grooves from what looked like claws marring the smooth cherrywood finish. Her bed and mattress had been shredded, feathers from her pillows and comforter blankcting the ruined clothing that had been dumped from her drawers and closet. On her dresser, her antique perfume bottles had been smashed, the painting that hung above her bed, the one her *grandmère* had given her before her death, streaked with crimson letters, as if a message had been written in blood.

Blinking the tears from her eyes, she tried to read the words, but she couldn't focus. "What's it say?"

Brody made a harsh sound in the back of his throat. "It says *Your blood will be on Carter's hands.*"

"Oh God."

"Doucet, I'm…sorry."

"Why?" She sniffed, hating the tears. It was just stuff, after all. Not worth getting emotional over. But this was her private space, and knowing it'd been breached felt as if someone had spied on her with a hidden camera. Leaning down to pick up a shattered picture of her and Max and Torrance at last year's Christmas party, she said, "It wasn't your fault, Brody."

"I hate that this bastard got close to you."

There was something in his words, an underlying thread that made it sound as though he actually…cared, but before she could look at it too closely, the screeching sound of a car slamming on its brakes came from the front of her house. She flinched, and Brody moved toward the bedroom window facing the front yard. Looking through the white wooden slats of her blinds, he swore a foul string of words under his breath, while the soft spill of golden light from the bedside lamp played over the auburn silk of his hair, catching at the deeper, shimmering strands of ruby and crimson. "I don't believe it."

"Who is it?"

"Mr. Nobody."

"Oh God. Ross?" He nodded and she groaned, unable to believe her luck could be this horrendously awful. Pushing her hair back from her face and swiping her fingertips under her eyes, catching at any wayward tears, she said, "I'll go get rid of him. Just promise that you'll stay here."

"I'm not a goddamn dog," he countered in a low, guttural rasp, turning to face her, an incredulous look on his face. "And I'm not letting you talk to him alone."

"Brody, be reasonable. You…you can't…you're too…" Taking a deep breath, she tried again. "Look, I don't know how to say this any other way, but your wolf is too close to the surface tonight. Your eyes are glowing and the tips of your…of your fangs are showing. You *can't* go out there. It'll only take me a minute to get rid of him," she said quickly, turning away from him to head back toward the hallway.

"I don't give a shit what I look like." Brody grabbed her arm with controlled strength and spun her back around. "I don't want you going anywhere near him," he confessed in a rough voice, and she could see the shocking spill of an emotion that looked incredibly like jealousy burning in his deep green eyes. Of course, she knew she must be misreading what was simply his protective nature. The man could be reasoned with, but the wolf in him dealt in absolutes. He'd been assigned as her bodyguard, and he meant to keep her by his side.

Pulling out of his grip, she headed down the hall. "You can watch through the window. I give you my word I'll stay close to the house. You'll be able to see me the entire time. But I want him out of here. Can you imagine what would happen if Dustin comes back and Ross sticks his nose in the middle of another confrontation? It'd be a nightmare."

Stalking behind her, he muttered, "Open your eyes, Doucet. This is already a nightmare."

She stopped halfway down the stairs, gripping the banister so tightly that her fingers turned numb. "If you want to hand me off to someone else, Brody, I'll understand."

He grunted under his breath, his voice thick as he said, "You're not getting rid of me that easily."

Ruefully aware of the relief pouring through her system, she set back off down the stairs, mindful of the heat of his big, powerful body following close behind her. When she reached the living room, he moved to the side of the door. She glanced up at his face, marveling at how he could look so angry and beautiful at the same time, a perfect blend of violence and grace. "Don't you want to watch through the window?"

Slowly, he shook his head from side to side, the scarred corner of his mouth lifting the barest fraction. "The door stays open, Doucet."

She didn't bother arguing with him, not when he wore that dark, predatory look of intent. "Okay, fine. This will only take a second, anyway."

Standing in the open doorway, Brody hooked his thumbs in his front pockets, braced his shoulder against the doorjamb and watched Michaela meet the Armani-suited human in the middle of her front yard. The neighborhood remained silent, but then she'd told him it was an elderly community, most of its residents keeping early hours. And being at the far end of the street provided a certain degree of privacy.

He could tell from Ross Holland's body language that the prick was furious to have found him there. Wearing a ghost of a smile, Brody kept his stare targeted on the guy's handsome face, watching him closely, just waiting for the idiot to make a wrong move. If the bastard even looked at her the wrong way, Brody was going to take it personally.

The guy muttered something to Michaela, and her shoulders drew back, spine rigid as she hissed back at him, their words lost in the gusting breeze that played havoc with her long, midnight curls, until Holland raised his voice. "You're dumping me for a scarred-up freak like him?"

"How dare you!" she seethed, advancing on the ass like an enraged she-cat. "I'll have you know that he's better-looking than you could ever hope to be. And what's more, he's a man,

Ross. A *real* man. He doesn't need to hide behind designer suits and power ties, the way you do, trying to disguise what a worthless little prick you are. And for your information, I dumped you a long time ago!"

Stunned by her passionate defense of him, Brody swallowed the heavy lump of emotion in his throat. He had the strangest sensation of warmth in his chest, like something cracking open, spilling inside of him—but at the same time, an uneasy feeling curled around the backs of his ears, solidifying as he heard the asshole snarl, "You'll be sorry for this."

Taking a step onto the porch, he frowned as Michaela said, "I'm already sorry. I'm sorry for letting you use me, sorry for ever setting eyes on you. Now get off my property and know this, Ross. The next time you set foot on it, I'm calling the cops *and* the news crews. What do you think your wife and constituents would think of that, Councilman Holland?"

His face turning a mottled shade of pink, Holland spit out, "You snide little bitch. No one talks to me that way, Michaela. Not even a mouthy little whore like you." He grabbed her as the last words left his mouth, but Brody was already moving. With a savage growl of outrage erupting from his chest, Brody rushed forward, seeing red—the whole scene taking place within a mere span of seconds. He was almost on them when the bastard pulled back his arm and smacked her across the face, jerking her head sharply to the side as she slammed to the ground. Brody instantly sensed the warm scent of her blood, his rage burning hotter, more violently than ever before. In a flying leap that hurtled him high in the air, over her body, he took Holland to the ground, rolling once and pinning the human to the damp grass beneath him.

"What the hell are you?" Holland gasped, staring at him

in wide-eyed shock, his face pale with fear. Brody knew he should have been concerned about revealing the animalistic side of his nature, but he was too furious to worry about the inhuman leap he'd made to take the creep down.

"Trust me, asshole," he snarled, his voice so guttural, he sounded more animal than man, "you don't want to know what I am. And I'll tell you why. Because the thing I hate the most in this godforsaken world is spineless pricks who hit women." He leaned closer, aware that his eyes glowed with an unearthly light, his gums and fingertips burning as deadly fangs and claws fought to break free, held back by the last, crumbling vestiges of his control.

"Jesus Christ!" Holland croaked, his perfect features twisted into a mask of terror as he stared into Brody's changing eyes. "You're some kind of...of—"

"I'm your worst goddamn nightmare. And if you ever come near her again, I will take you apart, you cowardly son of a bitch."

Holland stared up at him in mute horror, and Brody felt his beast shift beneath his skin, prowling the confines of his body, desperate to break free of its human prison and go at the bastard with teeth and claws. He'd never been so livid before, his fury like a physical thing in his body that had substance and weight, pulsing like a toothache in his gut, pressing against his skin from the inside out. Panting, trapped between the fury of the man and the bloodthirsty hunger of his beast, he kept Holland pinned to the ground, struggling to maintain that final tenuous hold on his control, until he felt the cool, gentle brush of Michaela's fingers against the nape of his neck.

"It's okay, Brody. Let him go," she murmured, soothing

him with nothing more than the touch of her skin against his. "He isn't worth it."

"The bastard deserves to pay for striking you," he snarled, shaking, sweat slicking his skin despite the cool chill of the autumn breeze.

"Please, Brody," she whispered, her voice small, shaken. "Just let him go. I want to go inside now. I just want to get away from him and never set eyes on him again."

Heaving a deep, ragged breath, he released his hold on Holland, standing as he watched the human roll onto his hands and knees, crawling across the yard, until he finally lurched to his feet and stumbled his way to his car. Climbing behind the wheel, he sped away without ever looking back. Brody watched until the taillights of the Mercedes disappeared at the end of the street, Holland nearly taking the turn on two wheels in his haste. He'd wanted to give the bastard a final warning to never come near Michaela again, but figured he'd made his point.

Flexing his hands out at his sides, he took another deep, shuddering breath, struggling to regain control of his emotions, until he turned and saw Michaela standing at his side. From one heartbeat to the next, he felt that vicious burst of rage transform back into sexual craving the second he set eyes on her. The only thing that stopped him from grabbing her up and taking her to the ground, sinking into her then and there, was the knowledge that she needed his comfort at that moment, not his lust.

But God, he was dying, the need killing him.

"You're done calling the shots," he rasped. "I was an idiot to let you talk me into it, you coming out here alone. And that was the last time it's going to happen. From now on, I'm stuck on you like a shadow, no matter who you're dealing with. Understood?"

"Yes," she whispered, the soft glow of the streetlamp illuminating the fear in her eyes, as well as the angry welt of red slashing across her cheek from Holland's hand, the corner of her mouth bleeding. "I understand."

Steeling himself to hold it together, Brody moved forward and lifted her into his arms, locking his jaw against the jarring, heart-pounding knowledge of how perfect she felt against him. His pulse was roaring in his ears like the ocean surf, rhythmic and strong, blocking out everything else. The world could have come crashing down around them and he wouldn't have flinched, wouldn't have known, every part of him focused with blinding intensity on the warm feminine body snuggling against him, as if he were her shelter in a world gone mad.

She rested her face in the crook of his shoulder, slender arms wound around his neck, softly panting breaths warm and damp against his skin, and melted into him, so trusting that it damn near broke his heart. Her scent drifted up from the pulse point in the base of her throat, and he nearly walked into the side of the house, missing the open doorway, his fascinated gaze snagged on that fluttering patch of skin, so soft and smooth, begging for the touch of his tongue, the carnal scrape of his fangs.

Gritting his teeth, Brody ripped his gaze away and focused on the stairs as he climbed to the second story, heading down the softly lit hallway. "Which bathroom?" he asked, his voice a quiet rasp, betraying the slightest tremor.

"The one next to my room," she murmured, and his gut clenched as he felt her mouth move against the sensitive skin of his throat, like a lover rubbing sweetheart promises into his flesh. Not that he'd ever had a lover who promised him anything, much less love or affection.

Yeah, and let's pass on the pity party, he silently snarled, disgusted with himself.

He found the bathroom with the door open, and moved into the shadowy space, settling her on the counter between two sinks. A dimmer switch controlled the lighting, so he twisted it until nothing more than a soft wash of gold filled the warm, inviting space, needing to see what he was doing, but wanting as much shadow to hide behind as he could get. He knew it made him a coward, but between Sheffield and Holland and this gnawing need to get Michaela Doucet naked and under him as fast as humanly possible, he'd already been pushed to his limits.

A quick look around showed a stack of fluffy white wash-cloths sitting on a shelf beside the shower. Flicking on the hot water, Brody let it run in one of the sinks, while he grabbed a washcloth, watching her from the corner of his eye. She sat silent and still, returning his heavy gaze, her expression calm…but in no way serene. No, there was a flush on the delicate crest of her cheekbones, a heaviness in her eyes, a glittering fire burning within that deep cerulean blue that revealed her own emotional struggle.

She watched him hold the cloth under the hot water, steam rising in a slow, sensual swirl from the porcelain sink, adding to the breathless sense of intimacy wrapping around them. He wanted her to tell him to get lost, scram, that she could take care of herself, offering him the perfect avenue of escape. But when he wrung out the cloth and lifted it to the corner of her mouth where her lip had broken open, her fair skin smeared with blood, she grabbed his wrist, saying, "It's okay, Brody,

I can do it," he shook his head, wordlessly demanding her submission. Her breath hitched and she sighed, letting go, and
he dabbed at the crimson streaks of blood as gently as
possible, hating that she'd been hurt—that the bastard had
touched her.

"You're shaking again," she whispered huskily, staring at his
chest, and he realized it was true. His muscles were rigid with
tension, body tremoring with the effort of keeping himself
from taking the thing he wanted most, the only steady part of
his body the hand that held the cloth, afraid that he'd hurt her.

"Tell me to leave," he groaned, his voice nothing more than
a low, tortured snarl of emotion. "Tell me to leave you the hell
alone, Doucet."

She shook her head no and big blue eyes as rich and clear
as a summer sky flicked up to his face, captured by the blistering heat of his stare. Brody watched, the roaring in his ears
growing louder, thicker, as she pulled her lower lip through
her white teeth, that peaches-and-cream scent growing
stronger, heavier, richer, pulsing off her body in dizzying,
head spinning waves, until he felt drunk on the lust pouring
thickly through his system.

"I don't want you to leave." Reaching up, she cupped the
feverish heat of his cheek in her cool palm, stroking one of
the scarred ridges that slashed his face with the baby-soft pad
of her thumb. "Thank you, Brody."

"For what?" he grunted, undone by the touch of her hand
against his skin.

A shy smile played across her beautiful, battered mouth.
"For being here, for taking care of me."

The cloth slipped from his grasp, falling to the floor with
a wet slap of sound, and he curled his hands over her shoul-

ders, the soft cotton of her dress cool beneath the heat of his hands as he fought to keep his grip from crushing her. His chest heaved, but he couldn't calm his erratic breathing. In that moment, it became frighteningly clear that controlling the violent burn of carnal hunger in his gut was even harder than mastering the fury of his beast.

"Christ," he growled, the word nothing more than a graveled scrape of sound, ripped out of his throat. He was painfully aware that his muscles were shaking with the savage need to touch her, everywhere. To press his mouth to her skin, in the damp, intimate places where that heady scent would be the strongest. To get inside her, and claim her for his own. But he had to fight it, fight himself, terrified of admitting the truth his heart kept screaming at him. "Don't do this, Doucet."

"Don't do what?" she asked, her mouth trembling with emotion as she stared up at him through her lashes.

"Tell me to leave. Now. Trust me, you don't want to go where this is going to lead."

"Brody," she whispered, her hand slipping from his cheek, trailing down the column of his throat, until she placed her palm against the raging beat of his heart.

"Damn it, this *can't* happen," he groaned, even as his hands slipped down her arms, wrapping around her biceps; at the same time, he stepped closer. Her knees spread in supplication, welcoming him into her personal, private space, like a siren opening her body to her lover.

Staring into his eyes, she held him trapped with the sheer force of her will, the quiet intensity of her need. "It can," she said huskily, blinking as a luminous wash of tears clung to her long, thick lashes. "It can if we both want it to. Is that what you want, Brody? Don't you want to touch me?"

Chapter 7

Michaela was stunned by her own boldness, but she refused to take back the shocking words. Brody's eyes burned with anger, lust and something that was seething just beneath the surface. Something she couldn't see, could only feel, the way you could watch the surface of a calm sea and know that something violent lurked just beneath the serene, glasslike plane of water. But it didn't scare her. Instead, she wanted to reach out for it, grab it and rip it to the surface, take the wildness of it into her hands and hold it, throw her arms around it and cover herself with it.

She wanted him to lose control, to give her everything. All of him.

"Don't I want to touch you?" he snarled in a low, guttural rasp, so close that she could feel the heat of his breath, see the tiny flecks of gold that glittered in the deep green of his eyes. "If you had any idea of what I want from you, woman, you'd run screaming, while you were still able to, and get as far away from me as you could."

"I don't want to run away from you. I should," she admitted, the throaty words almost solemn. "You have the power to break me, Brody. A part of me that's more fragile than my body or my pride, and even though that terrifies me, I still want you. I want to get closer to you than I've ever been to anyone. I want to pull you inside of me. I want to wrap your body around me. Keep you. Feel you. Taste you."

"Christ, you evil little witch," he growled, his control snapping so sharply she could have sworn she could hear the sibilant hiss as it shattered, and then he was there, crowding into her, the touch of his warm mouth electric against the coolness of her own, and it took her breath, stealing it straight from her panting lungs. He kissed like something that was feral and wild—as if he could taste every part of her through her mouth, pulling every breathtaking sensation up from the depths of her soul until he could feast on them with his lips and tongue and teeth.

"Your mouth," he rasped. "Am I hurting your lip?"

"No. God no," she moaned, unable to get enough of him.

He growled low in his throat and kissed her harder then. And he was touching her, too, those big, beautiful, scarred hands clutching at the shivery sides of her throat, thumbs pressed just beneath her quivering chin, his mouth slanting across hers, taking instant possession, demanding her submission. She gave it freely, knowing that she'd goaded him into this. A part of her stood back in fascinated amazement at her boldness; it was so unlike her. So *not* her. But this hunger, this maddening craving for him, had driven her to this place, and she had no intention of balking now. No, she was going to enjoy every sweet, deliciously intense detail. She was going to wallow in them, steep herself in the erotic textures and flavors of him, so rugged and male and perfect. Salty and dark, his scent and taste overwhelmed her, everything inside going hot and soft, melting for him. She ached, from deep inside all the way to the surface of her skin, her desire making her crazed for his touch, his taste.

"Brody," she gasped, tunneling her fingers into the warm, silken strands of his auburn hair and clutching him to her. Lifting her legs, Michaela wrapped them around his hips, tilting her pelvis forward until she could feel the thick, heavy ridge inside his jeans pressing against that needy, empty part of her. "God, Brody, touch me more," she pleaded. "Everywhere. Please."

As if commanded by her breathless plea, his hands lowered, slipping across her collarbone, over her chest, until the lush weight of her breasts was filling his hands, her nipples like hardened berries beneath his thumbs as he stroked them. They both gasped, breaths soughing together, and Brody slid one hand under the neckline of her dress, wrenching until the fabric tore with a sharp slice of sound. His fingers ruthlessly burrowed beneath the delicate lace of her bra, and he cupped her naked breast in the rough heat of his palm, rubbing, molding, massaging her, while the other hand ran down her back, curving around that sweet ass. He jerked her forward, to the very edge of the counter, fitting his jeans-covered cock into that sweet, warm notch between her legs.

"Pull your dress out of the way," he growled, his voice savage and dark, full of predatory demand.

She clutched handfuls of the fabric and wrenched it to the side, her mouth moving under his while he pressed forward, only his jeans and the delicate lace of her panties separating him from that soft, wet flesh, its succulent scent filling his nose, his head, hunger like a stabbing pain inside him, raw and insistent.

Now that he had her in his arms, under his hands, Brody couldn't get enough. She tasted like something he needed to live, now that he'd found it. Tasted like warm sunshine, hot and honeyed and sweetly addictive. He could taste the blood from her lip, its sumptuous flavor only adding to the perfection of her mouth, providing a deeper, headier, intoxicating layer of spice. The details crashed down on him, through him, obliterating the reason of the man, until there was nothing but this burning need to consume her. The pansy softness of her inner lip, the sleek well of warmth within, her kittenish tongue that played with his, as if she were as greedy for the taste of his mouth as he was for hers. The berrylike tip of her nipple stabbing into his palm, so full and tempting, the warm heat of her sex melting against the fly of his jeans.

He'd never had a woman give him back so much. Normally, he could always sense a part of them that they held in reserve, in fear, ready to retreat should he lose control. But not Michaela. There was no hesitation, no questioning. She kissed him back with an avidity that stole his breath; slender, feminine hands clutching at him as if she could draw him into her body. Low, provocative little sounds broke from her mouth into his, making his blood roar, his wolf maddened with the need to mount and claim. Their mouths moved against one another, first from one angle, then another, deep, gasping breaths stolen before they came together in another clutching, groaning need for more. His hands roamed wildly, down the line of her spine, her shoulders, ribs, the lush side swells of her breasts, shaking from the need to rip her clothes from her body and bare her to his gaze, to his touch. He wanted nothing more than to sink to his knees and press his face into that moist, precious, intimate part of her, taking her with his tongue, lashing and thrusting until she gave him everything he wanted, tasting every part of her.

The only thing that held him back was fear. Terror, actually. Because he knew what would happen when he finally lost that last tenuous hold on his control.

But she wouldn't let him retreat, goddamn it. She just kept pushing him with the hungry kiss of her mouth, the provocative touch of her hands on his back, lower, stroking herself against the granite-hard ridge of his cock, until he could feel the slickness of her flesh sliding against the rough denim of his jeans.

"More," she moaned, breathless, biting at his lower lip with her small, white teeth, and he lost it. His restraint broke, and he knew he was going to have her. How could he fight it? The truth was blatantly clear, stunning him with the force of a blow, refusing to be denied. Chanting a low, coarse stream of swearwords into her mouth, he pressed his hand between her legs and ripped out the damp gusset of her panties, the tender, delicate feel of her sex beneath his fingertips so good that he wanted to howl. She was hot, wet, the softest, sweetest thing he'd ever felt, and he immediately buried two thick fingers deep inside of her, his thumb brushing against the swollen heat of her clit.

She cried out, and he pressed deeper, sinking all the way up to his knuckles. Her sex was small, delicate and tight, and his fingers were big. Brody knew the penetration had been too much, too soon, but she didn't push him away. Her hands clutched at him as eagerly as her body, those strong inner muscles pulsing around his fingers, bathing him in liquid fire. Her heartbeat surrounded him, and as he stroked her with his thumb, he curled his fingers forward, stroking her deep inside, as well. She stiffened in his arms for a tight, breathless moment, then melted against him, shivering…whimpering with pleasure against his mouth as the sensations inside her swelled. He swallowed every sound, their breaths tangled, gasping and rough, as if they were in pain. But it was a good kind of agony, the kind that held that breathtaking promise of a shattering, engulfing ecstasy at the end that would swallow them whole, leaving them different…changed…renewed when the crashing wave of sensation slowly receded back inside of them.

He wanted more. All of her. Everything he could take.

"Doucet," he groaned, rubbing her name into her lips, and she arched against him, pulsing hard and deep around his fingers, killing him with her passion. "I want you to come in my hand, baby. All hot and slick and wet. I want it right now."

"Brody," Michaela said thickly, crazed with the need to feel his body, hot and hard beneath her hands. Somehow, she managed to claw his shirt up over his head without breaking their kiss for more than a moment, and tossed it to the floor. Then she moaned deep in her throat, running her hands over the bounty of masculine power she'd uncovered. His broad, beautiful chest, with its ruggedly defined muscles and small brown nipples nestled within dark hair, fascinated her, as did the veins wrapping the muscles in his powerful arms. She ran her fingers over the fever-hot skin of his strong shoulders, trailing them down the sleek muscles running the length of his spine, her breath hitching as she felt the ridged scars she knew were from the punishment he'd received for trying to save his mother. They were deeper, thicker than the ones on his face, and her heart broke for all that he'd suffered when so little, while his hunger as a man blew her mind.

The touch of his hands on her skin, the taste of his mouth, were unlike anything she'd ever known before. Dark, intense, primitive and rough. He didn't touch her because he wanted to seduce her—he touched her, tasted her, as if he *had* to. As if he craved her. Was starved for her. Sensations built like the sensual strains of a symphony, growing layer upon layer, until they roared through her head, through her system. She was lost in them as her need rose higher, hotter, heavier, her senses screaming for more intimate contact. She was crazed, wanting to touch him, have him, everywhere at once. All of him. The velvety dark heat of his mouth, salty and sweet, flavored with hot coffee and hungry male. The silken skin stretched taut over mouthwatering muscles, so hard and lean and powerful, honed to battle perfection, like a weapon.

And those wicked, wonderful fingers that were quickly unraveling her into a shivering, sobbing mess as he gently pinched her nipple between his thumb and forefinger of one hand, the other buried possessively between her thighs. She could feel it building, the sensations inside of her too overwhelming to contain, to hold on to, even though she wanted to clutch at them and savor them, never wanting to let them go. But he was ruthless in his insistence, demanding her pleasure, knowing just where to touch her, how deep to stroke…to thrust, and how fast, devastating her with his knowledge of her body, as if he knew just how to make her burn. And he did. She felt blinded by the intensity and shocking rush of swelling ecstasy that he ripped up from the buried depths of her soul, hidden so deep she hadn't even known they were there. But she was eating her way into his mouth, clawing at his shoulders, anything to get closer, to have more of him, and then it slammed into her, knocking her breath from her lungs in a loud, keening cry. Michaela flung her head back, the dark, decadent waves of pleasure pumping through her, pulsing in her sex, her earlobes, her fingers and toes, eyelids and throat. She felt his mouth press against the rapid flutter of her jugular, felt the erotic slide of his fangs as he stroked them across her vulnerable flesh, and in that moment, she knew he was going to do it.

He was going to *bite* her.

The knowledge cranked up the stunning force of her orgasm, and she cried out, fisting her hands in his hair, pressing his face to her throat, wanting it, willing to beg for it if she could find enough air in her lungs for speech. Star-studded crystals of infinite night stuttered against her eyelids, her skin tingly and hot and damp…muscles shaking, strained, and then she went under.

She was distantly aware of Brody cursing, tensing against her body, ripping his hands from her flesh, his mouth from her throat, as he tried to pull away from her, but she held on, unable to release him. She was falling…into his mind, into him. Scared, she struggled against it, but she just kept sinking, her power flung wide, her body in a total weightless free fall, until she found a part of her landing in the midst of a midnight forest, while the other half remained trapped in the present, sitting on her bathroom counter.

In a foglike trance, she could see both scenes, the present and the past, as if watching two movie screens layered on top of one another. Michaela knew she should have been terrified, but her reserves of fear and terror were drained by the distant scene of horror playing out before her eyes.

In the present, her arms closed around him, hands trailing over the scars crisscrossing his strong back, while in her mind, she could see the blood spilling down his young body as she watched him on his hands and knees, surrounded by the savage sight of bloodthirsty werewolves, their deadly claws dripping with the blood they'd already drawn from his slim back. A full moon hung low in the sky, his choked sobs filling her head as he buried his face in his small arms, until a dark gray wolf reached down and jerked him to his feet by his hair. Her screams blended with the outraged shouts of a Lycan male she could only assume was Brody's father. Crying out in terror, Michaela watched the gray wolf deliver the final blow that came to the child's face, nearly taking out his eye. Then he'd been thrown onto the ground, unconscious, left there as the pack stalked into the surrounding forest, and it'd taken four of them to drag Brody's father away from his son. His memories whispered their secrets to her, and she knew that Brody had stayed there on the bloody forest floor until his grandmother had been allowed to come to collect him, but by then it had been morning. He'd been so cold through the night, so alone…so in pain.

Her heart broke into a thousand pieces, tears coursing down her cheeks as she cried for all the suffering he'd endured, both physical and emotional, until suddenly she was jerked back to awareness. Gasping, she found Brody gripping her upper arms, shaking her, his voice urgent and hard. "Goddamn it, Doucet. Snap out of it!"

"I'm here," she croaked, blinking against the salty wash of tears in her eyes. "I'm back."

"Back from where? What the hell was that?"

She shook her head, trying to get her thoughts in order, her tongue heavy in her mouth, throat dry. "I don't know. It…it just happened…"

"What?" he demanded. "What happened?"

"I saw you, when you were little," she whispered, struggling to explain, her words choked with tears. "That night… when they cut you. I saw it, all of it."

His brow lowered over the unearthly green of his eyes. "I thought you told me you couldn't read me," he growled in a soft, chilling rasp.

"I can't. This…this was different. I don't know why it happened. I'm sorry, I…I didn't mean to do it, Brody."

She reached for him, but he lurched away from her, until his back came up against the bathroom wall with a dull thud, and Michaela finally noticed the…*difference* in him. His eyes burned, glowing even brighter than before, as if lit with a blazing fire from within. Wolf's eyes. And through his parted lips she could see the glistening tips of fully elongated canines— fangs—shiny and white. Her breath caught, but amazingly not with fear. She remembered thinking he was going to bite her while her climax had roared through her, remembered wanting it, before he'd started trying to pull away from her. Clearly, a part of him had been fighting the urge to take that bite, fighting to get away, but she'd held on to him, unable to let go.

Chewing on her lower lip, Michaela tried to sort out what had happened. Why had he panicked? Had he been afraid of hurting her? Terrifying her? Or was it something else? She knew, from what Torrance had told her, that a bite between mates led to a powerful bond, but she had no reason to believe she was Brody's life mate. An upsetting thought, that, but one that she refused to dwell on. Was he afraid, then, of changing her? Somehow, the moment had felt too sensual for such a grave outcome—and yet, hadn't her brother been changed by a bite?

Then there was the strange vision of his past. Was it because of her powerful feelings for Brody that she'd been able to steal that little glimpse into his mind? The gift of sight had been her *grandmère's*, but never had Michaela experienced anything even close to what had happened. She'd had feelings, echoes of emotion—but this had been so sharp and clear. She'd been able to smell the blood and the sweat, to hear the low growls of the pack and Brody's broken whimpers.

She took a deep, shuddering breath, and noticed his gaze dropping to her chest, eyes darkening as he stared. Glancing down, her face flamed as she suddenly realized what had snagged his attention. With an embarrassed gasp, Michaela jerked her dress closed in front, covering her breast, and smoothed her skirt over her knees, horrified that she'd been sitting there so exposed while he was angry at her. "I really am sorry, Brody. Should I…do you want me to pack up now?"

His gaze lifted, and in an emotionless monotone, he rasped, "No. I'll be on watch downstairs. Get to bed and rest. We'll head out first thing in the morning."

He didn't wait for her response or bother to explain why he no longer wanted to leave that night. He just turned and headed off into the darkness of the hallway, leaving her alone to sort out the tangled mess of her thoughts. Sliding off the counter, Michaela decided to take a long, steamy shower while she struggled to make sense of everything, of her own feelings. Locking the bathroom door, she slipped out of her wrinkled dress, while admitting to herself that she was still wary of her emotional connection to the brooding Runner, terrified of getting used again, the way she'd been used by Ross—and yet, didn't his actions speak for themselves? If Brody had only wanted her for sex, like Ross had, he'd just given up the perfect opportunity. Why? What was holding him back?

Yet another question she didn't have the answer to, but one thing became strikingly clear to her, the harder she thought about it. Stepping beneath the stinging spray of hot water, her legs still shaking from the force of her orgasm, she accepted that there was more between them than breathtaking hunger, more than the feral burn of lust.

Michaela just had to decide if she was woman enough to go after it—or if she was going to allow fear of another broken heart control her, keeping her back from the thing she wanted most. Not just the man, as wonderful and breathtaking as he was.

No, if she found the courage to fling herself at his feet and open her soul, taking the risk of putting her faith and trust in him, she wasn't doing it for anything less than the ultimate prize. Because as badly as she wanted his hunger and passion, his laughter and his smiles, the thing that she wanted most from Brody Carter was the part of himself she knew he was going to fight the hardest to protect.

If she found the courage to go for it, she wasn't accepting anything less than his heart.

They made good time the following morning as they headed west, back to the mountains, back to the Runners' private sanctuary known as the Alley.

Resting her head against the comfortable seat of the Ford,

Michaela closed her eyes and thought back to the moment when she'd first awakened to the bright glare of morning sunlight sneaking through the slanted blinds in her spare bedroom. For a breathless moment, she'd stared at the sun-dappled shadows on the ceiling, the piercing, poignant sweetness of her dream still lingering like a warm wave of pleasure in her veins.

She'd closed her eyes then, as well, savoring the remnants of the dream, clutching at the details with greedy mental fingers. After her shower the night before, she'd crawled into one of the twin beds in the empty spare room, determined she wouldn't sleep while she worried over Max and waited for Brody to come to bed, only to find herself succumbing to a deep, heavy exhaustion.

And she'd dreamed. Dreamed of sitting on a quilt in a bright summer meadow, the fresh scents of the nearby forest and flowers dancing on the air, while fluffy, sun-kissed clouds rolled through the deep azure blue of the sky. A quiet rumble of laughter at her side drew her attention, and she'd turned to see Brody sitting beside her on the patchwork quilt, holding a dark-haired baby girl who had the Runner's beautiful bottle-green eyes. He chuckled as he played with the toddler, laughing and cuddling with her, his green eyes shining with happiness while the sun dazzled off the rich luster of his auburn hair pulled back in a short ponytail at his nape. He'd lifted his head, sending Michaela a heavy look of desire, his white teeth flashing in a bright, sexy smile within the golden beauty of his face. She'd smiled back at him, sharing a powerful connection that had all but skittered with sparks, heavy and potent and sizzling—and then the little girl had grabbed his face with her preciously chubby hands, demanding his attention. He'd laughed as he tickled the child, the joy of father and daughter so powerful and sweet it had made her chest ache.

Lying in the narrow bed, she'd pressed her hand against the sharp, burning glow of happiness in her heart, wanting to hold on to it, keep it—accepting, in that moment, that if it weren't for her fear of getting hurt, she'd be willing to do whatever it would take to make that breathtaking dream a reality.

Now, as she opened her eyes and watched the Runner from the corner of her vision, his profile so rugged and strong as he steered them down the highway, she wondered just how powerful a hold this man could have on her. She'd spent so long being wary, building her walls, her defenses, but with Brody, none of that seemed to matter. He was like a force of nature battering them down, smashing her resistance without even trying.

How could she resist him when she wanted nothing more than to be close to him, to break through his own defenses and breach his heart? To prove to him that if he could find a way to care for her, even a little, and be true to her, she'd do everything in her power to make him happy, to give him joy. To take him into her life, her heart and her very soul.

In the grand scheme of things, she hadn't known him long—just a flash of time over the minutes and seconds of her life—and yet, she knew him more deeply than she'd ever known any other man. Knew his fears, his demons, his strength and courage, his selflessness and temper. Knew he was fierce and loyal, savagely sexual, and yet, tenderly caring.

He tried to act so tough, but he couldn't fool her. As angry as he'd been with her last night, when she'd pulled herself from bed that morning and headed toward her bedroom to dress and pack what few things she'd hoped to find still in one piece, she'd been stunned to discover her room cleaned. It must have taken him all night, and yet, he'd picked up all of her clothes, her bedding, restoring the destroyed room as much as possible. Her bras and panties sat at the foot of her bed, and she'd blushed at the thought of him handling her lingerie, both touched and bemused that he would go to all that effort. Even her clothes had been awkwardly folded and placed on top of her dresser, the mental image of his big hands trying to handle the feminine articles bringing a smile to her lips.

When she'd come downstairs and told him thank you, he'd rolled his shoulder in embarrassment and asked if they could get on the road.

While they traveled down the highway, Michaela watched as he covered a yawn with his hand and wondered how much sleep he'd actually gotten, if any. He'd been quiet during the drive, but then she knew he usually was, never one for idle conversation. She couldn't help but wonder, though, if he was still upset with her for the scene in the bathroom.

Deciding she'd had enough of being timid, she cleared her throat and simply asked, "Are you still mad at me?"

He stiffened at the sound of her voice, then slowly relaxed, his long fingers flexing around the top of the steering wheel. "I'm not mad at you, Doucet."

"Then why am I getting the silent treatment?"

He flushed, slanting her a quick look. "Sorry. I've just been running over everything in my head."

"Oh. You mean the investigation?"

"Yeah," he rumbled, his worry and fatigue evident in that single word.

Michaela could understand why he was so preoccupied. She wasn't even a Runner, and it was never far from her mind, the worry over what Stefan Drake and his rogues were planning. "What do you think Drake hopes to accomplish?"

Sighing, he scratched the ginger bristle darkening the hard line of his jaw. "Hell if I know."

Pulling her hair over one shoulder, she shifted in her seat until she was facing him, bending one leg beneath her. "When Jeremy and Jillian told us what things were like up in Shadow Peak, I couldn't believe that so many of the Silvercrest could be following Drake, believing his racist propaganda and accusations that you guys are lying about the rogues. Why can't they see what he's doing, the way he's manipulating them? Why are they so afraid to believe the Runners?"

"Because it's easier to buy his lies than it is to think for themselves," he replied, his deep voice heavy with frustration. "That's the downside of living in a society entrenched in such steep traditions. They've forgotten how to question the authority of those who tell them what to do, what to think. They believe themselves so powerful, and yet, they've lost their backbone, their free will, following the League like cattle, while Drake seems to control more and more of the League."

"Considering the way they treat you guys," she murmured, "why do you risk your lives by Running for them?"

He pulled back his shoulders, the corner of his mouth twisting in a wry smile. "I wish I had some clever answer, but the truth is that we Bloodrun because it has to be done. I can't stand the backward-ass Lycans who'd rather spit on a human than shake one's hand, but their blood still flows in my veins. In all of our veins. As Bloodrunners, we're sworn to protect them. To see them destroyed is to see a part of ourselves destroyed—and with each rogue kill, not only does an innocent human die, but the risk of discovery and exposure of the entire Lycan community becomes extreme."

"It's very honorable, what you and the others do," Michaela told him in a soft voice, unsurprised that he ignored the praise, knowing he'd be uncomfortable. Taking pity on him, she went back to the subject of Drake. "I was there for the meeting you guys had the day after Jillian had been attacked by Elise. I heard Mason tell you and the others about the Legend of Azakiel. Do you believe it?"

"That Drake used one of the other Elders to pull his daughter's wolf from her body? I don't know," he admitted, shrugging his powerful shoulders. "It sounds crazy, but it happened. And not just to Elise, but to the other Lycans who were in front of Jillian's house that day. No one has any other explanation, so maybe it's true. I've known weirder things to happen."

According to the legend, there was once an ancient Elder named Azakiel who seized control of a European pack after mastering the dark art of ripping forth another's wolf against their will. Mason's father and Graham, the Lead Silvercrest Elder, found the reference in one of the League's archaic texts, which told of how two Elders could combine forces and together produce enough power to wrench the wolf from an unsuspecting Lycan, be it night or day. As if the violation wasn't bad enough, the wolf, once drawn, was feral, angry and violent, its actions completely controlled by the ones who'd pulled it. The entire idea was horrific, and Michaela had shivered with fear as she'd listened to Jeremy recount the attack on Jillian's life a little over a week ago. It was a miracle she'd survived, and though they still didn't know which Elder Drake had used as his accomplice, at least they'd been able to finally confirm their suspicions that Drake was the traitor they'd been after all along.

"But what's he hope to gain by using this 'dark art' as they called it? I know you believe he's still recruiting rogues who've been taught to dayshift. Why does he need to be able to pull the beasts from his own people if he already has a loyal following of rogue werewolves?"

"We have some ideas, but nothing solid. Once we had time to step back and think about it, we realized the attack on Jillian was probably a practice run," he explained in a low rumble, his dark eyes narrowed on the road. "We figure Drake wanted to see if it would really work. He got Jeremy out of town, then made sure Elise overheard his conversation with Cooper Sheffield that day, knowing she'd go straight to Jillian. That's why he needed Jeremy gone, so that no one could stop him when he put his plan into action. But Jillian's little sister, Sayre, spoiled his plans when she had some kind of... whatever the hell you call it."

"A premonition," she supplied.

"Is that what you have?" he asked, pushing a strand of auburn hair back from his face. "Premonitions?"

"Me? No," she told him with a smile. "Although my Gran had visions. Flashes of the future or of...the...past..."

As her words trailed off, silence settled for a moment, heavy and thick with unspoken thoughts. "I'm curious," he finally murmured. "Now that you've had time to think about it, do you know what happened last night?"

Here it is. Decision time, Doucet.

Michaela knew she could admit what she suspected to be true, or tell him nothing. Honesty could keep him from ever touching her again, but she couldn't lie to him, even by omission. Staring at her hands folded in her lap, she swallowed the heavy lump of emotion in her throat and struggled to put her thoughts into words. "I told you that sometimes my interest in a person can crowd my power," she said huskily. "I think that's why I can't read your feelings—but when you're touching me…I don't know. It was like a meltdown. No shields, no barriers. I still couldn't read your feelings in the present, but the image, the scene from the past, just blasted me. I couldn't stop it from happening, but I didn't mean to invade your privacy that way."

Warily, she lifted her eyes to gauge his expression. He looked as if he wanted to say something, but his cell phone suddenly started buzzing on his hip. Reaching down, he lifted up the silver phone and flicked a quick glance at the number displayed on the screen. "Cian," he murmured, and answered the call.

Michaela could tell from his expression that it wasn't good news. He listened to his partner, then grunted, "We're already on our way up, so we can meet you there."

"What's wrong?" she asked the instant he disconnected the call.

He slanted her a dark look, his fury and frustration evident in the rigid set of his features, the brackets lining his mouth deeper than before, the sensual curve of his lips compressed in a hard line. "I hate to do this to you, Doucet, but we've gotta take a little detour."

"Why? What's happened?"

"There's been another killing," he rasped. "Cian's with the body now."

Chapter 8

The knowledge that another kill had been made pounded through Brody's brain with the brutal force of a hammer, stabbing behind his eyes like a migraine. Squinting against the sharp flare of pain, he stared out at the road ahead of them through a red-tinged haze of fury. He was filled with anger and bitter frustration, as well as a gnawing sense of failure. Despite their efforts, they hadn't managed to stop the son of a bitch who had been ritualistically killing young blondes for weeks now, before another innocent human victim lost her life.

His head felt as though it'd been split in two—and as if that wasn't enough, he was tormented by the terrifying discovery he'd made last night: the fact that Michaela Doucet was his life mate.

Beyond the windows of the truck, the autumn forest

passed by in a golden splash of color as Brody took the next exit off the highway, that dark knowledge wiring its way through his brain again and again, set on a continual replay loop.

My mate. My mate. My mate.

He supposed it explained the unprecedented lack of control he experienced when around her, as well as the violent surge of emotion, as though he'd plugged his senses, his heart, into a nuclear reactor. The cool, calm nothingness that had encased him for so many years had been cracked the first time he'd met her, then slowly shattered, leaving him a little more raw, a little more exposed, each time they came into contact. He'd recognized it, on a subconscious level, and yet, he'd done everything he could to avoid what he knew was the truth. But knowing he'd been on the verge of sinking his fangs into her throat last night—well, he could hardly pretend ignorance any longer. That had never happened to him before. Never. Not once, in his entire thirty-four years.

He'd been furious at the time, but only because it'd scared him when he'd realized how close he was to making that bite. As his mate, the bite would have created a blood bond between them—one that could never be undone. And she'd have hated him for it, which was why he'd tried like hell to rip himself away from her—only to have her go into that strange, dreamlike trance on him. When she came back to awareness and admitted what had happened, his fear had bled into stark, raging terror that she'd now be able to read him, as well.

The possibility had made Brody's blood run cold, because it meant she'd have known. Known how badly he wanted her, and not just for sex—though there was no doubt that he wanted her under him. He'd been months without a woman, the visceral need of his body and beast like a raw, aching wound within his soul. It was a craving that only Michaela could satisfy, a pain that only she could ease.

There was no denying that it made him feel threatened, trapped, the thought that her powers might change, that his feelings and hungers could be revealed to her. That was the most terrifying part of all, the possibility of her discovery that she was his mate, destined by nature to be his and no other's—not that he planned to do anything about it. Hell, just because nature sometimes screwed up was no reason to run his heart through a sieve like his old man had done. He'd seen firsthand that, despite its awesome power, nature could only add so much to the equation. Without love to strengthen the bond between mates, the risks for potential heartbreak were devastating.

And what about Michaela? She was an amazing woman— and she deserved someone who could cherish her, love her. Someone she could cherish and love in return. She didn't merit a lover who was more monster than man—one who she'd wake up beside one morning and wonder what in the blazes she'd been thinking.

Not one for self-torture, Brody figured he'd save himself the heartache and pain and pass on the whole having-his-heart-ripped-out part of the scenario. The smart thing to do would be to simply stay away from her, but how could he? Her life was in danger, and his wolf was too possessive to allow another Runner near her. He was just going to have to suck it up and find some way to harden himself against her intoxicating allure.

Yeah, you just keep telling yourself that, jackass. 'Cause it's worked so well for you so far.

Shaking off the irritating thought, Brody made a series

of turns onto roads marked with Private Property signs, before following a narrow dirt road that wound its way up the side of the mountain, bordering the Silvercrest pack land. He spotted Cian's Land Rover parked on the shoulder, pulled to a slow stop behind it, then turned off the engine and looked at Michaela. "I wouldn't bring you here if there was another choice, but the case is mine and Hennessey's and I need to see it. You never know what a second set of eyes might pick up, and we can't risk missing anything at this point."

Her throat moved in a convulsive shiver, betraying her nerves, but her voice was steady as she said, "It's okay. Really. I understand."

Climbing out of the truck, he walked around to open her door for her. "Come on. The sooner we get this over with, the sooner I can get you up to the Alley."

Though there was no sign of his partner or the crime scene from where they stood, Brody could scent Cian, as well as the victim, the stale odor of blood thickening as the wind surged toward them. "This way," he grunted, wishing he could just leave Michaela in the Ford. But it was too dangerous. The bastard they were after made his kills while in his dayshifted werewolf form, leaving no traceable odor, only a sharp acidic scent that was impossible to track. They didn't even know how close he had to be before they could pick up that vinegar-like odor, which meant Michaela stayed within an arm's reach of him the entire time they were in the open.

They only had to travel a hundred yards into the woods to find Cian and the body. His partner leaned back against a nearby tree, his right leg bent, boot braced against the trunk, while he stared over the gruesome scene with a cold, gray gaze. Brody had seen that chilling look in his partner's eyes too many times to count, knowing precisely what it meant.

The Irishman was furious.

Exhaling a slow stream of smoke, Cian flicked the ashes from the smoldering tip of his cigarette and gave them a somber nod as they stepped into the small clearing. The body lay in the center of the open, moss-covered space, naked, her face turned away from them, blond hair matted with blood, her arms and legs sprawled as if she'd been staked to the ground. But death was the only restraint holding her in place. From the look of her wounds, it'd been as violent as the others, a great gaping hole in the center of her chest, the heart missing from within, literally eaten out of her.

"There's no purse or identification anywhere around here," Cian rasped, the wind blowing the stygian strands of his hair across his face as he took another slow pull on his cigarette. "Hell, I can't even find her clothes. But I doubt she's more than twenty. Twenty-one at the most. And as you can smell, there's not so much as a whiff of Lycan musk on the body. Nothing but blood and death and that damn acidic odor burning the hell out of my nose."

"How'd you find her?" Brody kept his voice soft, an eerie silence hanging over the scene that demanded deference.

Cian took a long drag, then slowly released an ethereal stream of smoke. "Silvercrest scouts were patrolling the pack land borders and came across the kill. They called it in not even an hour ago."

Bending his knees, Brody knelt beside the body. Digging into the rich soil beside the vic's head, he lifted a handful to his nose and sniffed, but was unable to pick up anything other than the sharp odor Cian had mentioned. "I was hoping something would stick out, catch our attention. Something that might set it apart from the other crime scenes. But it's all the same."

"What about trace evidence?" Michaela asked, standing just to his left, by the victim's pale hip.

Studying the body, Brody explained, "We investigated the use of trace years ago, hoping to use it like the crime scene department, but our genetic material decomposes too quickly. That's part of what's enabled us to remain a secret for so long. Plus, there's no discernible difference between Lycan DNA and human DNA. And even if we did leave blood behind that was instantly analyzed, it would look human in composition."

"That's why the lack of a traceable scent has made it impossible to name the killer," Cian added. "Without the scent, which is the only evidence a rogue leaves behind that doesn't fade, we're unable to identify him. In the past, it's only been a problem when a rogue's scent was washed away by rain before we found the body, but by making the kill while in his dayshifted form, this particular killer is like a ghost to us, a phantom. There's nothing left behind for us to follow, nothing to hunt."

"But if the authorities found a body like this, wouldn't they be able to tell that this kind of attack wasn't human, even without any trace evidence?" she asked. "Just from the wounds themselves?"

"That's always been the greatest threat to our secret—a body like this being found. Normally, a rogue Lycan hunts on the fringes of society," Brody went on to explain, "because the game is easier, and the kill made near the safety of his or her pack land. But this one, he's growing careless. The girl he killed in Covington, the one dealing drugs, could have been found by anyone. It was pure luck that Sophia Dawson showed up first and had the presence of mind to call us. If the cops had arrived on the scene, there would have been serious consequences. Not even Monroe would have been able to help us cover it up."

"Monroe? He's the FBI agent, right?" she asked, looking down at him as she wrapped her arms around herself, while the wind caught her hair, lifting it from her shoulders. "The one whose sister married a Lycan from the pack?"

"Yeah," he replied, fighting the urge to go to her and take her into his arms. Instead, Brody focused his mind on the scene. There was one thing left to check that might point them in the direction of the killer—something he'd put off, concerned about how Michaela might react. Shaking the dirt off his hand, he reached out, brushed the tangled, matted strands of the vic's hair back from her face, grasped her small, pointed chin and tilted her face toward them. A low breath jerked from his lungs; at the same time Michaela let out a shaky gasp of relief.

"*Mon dieu,*" she whispered, dark eyes glistening with tears as she stared into the girl's sightless blue gaze. "I thought…I was afraid that it might be Kimmie, the blonde from the shop. The one who was with Dustin."

"Yeah," he sighed, straightening his legs as he rose to his full height. "Me, too."

"It's still terrible…it's just that, I didn't want it to be someone I had met. I would have felt awful that I hadn't tried to warn her away from him."

Brody gave a slow nod of understanding.

"Sheffield had a blue-eyed blonde with him?" Cian asked, taking a long drag on his cigarette, his midnight brows pulled together in a deep scowl. "Do you think he could be the one?"

With his mouth set in a grim line, Brody shook his head. "Hell if I know. But the thought has crossed my mind more than once since yesterday."

"Well," Cian sighed, sounding as tired as Brody felt, "when I talked to Mason, he said Reyes and Pallaton were already on their way up to the Alley. Thinks it would be a good idea if we all met up at his place and talked things out for a while. Sounds like Dustin should be a topic of discussion."

"And I want to know what kind of reaction Mason got from Dylan about Dustin's confession."

Flicking his cigarette into the damp moss, Cian scowled with frustration. "Don't get your hopes up, man. You know the League won't move until their hand is forced."

He muttered a short curse under his breath, hating that his partner was right, while at his side, Michaela trembled, staring down at the body. "He hated hurting her," she suddenly said in a voice so eerily quiet, it was almost lost in the howling wind, "once it was over."

Narrowing his eyes, Brody watched as a shiver traveled the length of her body, her lips rolling inward as a tear tracked down the left side of her face. "What do you mean?"

Without looking at him, she shook her head, her brow furrowed with lines of concentration. "It's just a feeling. I sense…conflict."

"The killer's conflict?" Cian asked, pushing off from the tree to move closer.

She nodded, the shivering in her lips now, her skin so pale, she looked like a ghost, while her long curls blew wildly around the paleness of her face. "Have you ever felt anything like this before?" his partner asked, gray eyes fixed on her face.

"No," Michaela murmured, feeling so cold, as if her bones had been coated with ice, a sickening sensation of dread wrapping around her, keeping company with her heartbreak for the pretty young woman lying dead at her feet. "I've never felt anything like this, but then, this is the first time I've come into contact with a violent death, so I…I don't have any basis for comparison. Maybe it's a result of the situation."

She had another theory, as well—one that she kept to herself. Just a gut feeling, really, but she couldn't help but wonder if her psychic abilities were being affected by the red-headed Runner playing havoc with her hormones and her heart. Cutting a wondering look at him from beneath her lashes, she found Brody watching her with a fierce expression, brows drawn, mouth hard, his color high. Was his presence boosting her abilities, like a jolt of lightning surging through a power source?

If it was, she wasn't going to tell him. Not after what had happened last night. The last thing she needed was to give him any more of a reason to be on guard around her.

"What else can you pick up?" Cian asked her, his sharp, speculative gaze moving between her and Brody.

"That's it," she admitted, lifting her face to stare up at the graying sky. "I wish there was more, but it's as if there's a cloud hanging over this place, heavy and thick and evil. He…he stood here and stared at her in horror, after it was over. Almost as if he couldn't believe he'd done it."

"Can you pick up on him now?" Brody asked, moving closer to her side.

She shook her head no, and he looked at Cian, saying, "I don't like having her out in the open like this," when she could tell what he really meant was that she was spooking the hell out of him and he wanted her as far from the body as possible. "We'll see you back up at Mason's. How long until cleanup gets here?"

* * *

"Not long," his partner replied. "Another fifteen at the most. I'll let them deal with the body."

Brody watched as Michaela told Cian goodbye, before they began heading back through the woods, taking the same path as before. They moved in silence, absorbed in their thoughts—until they were about halfway to the truck. With a low gasp, she came to an abrupt stop, grabbing hold of his arm with her right hand.

"What is it?" he asked, voice low, eyes narrowed on her pale face.

Shivering, she looked over her shoulder, staring back into the dense woods behind them.

"Doucet," he quietly growled; at the same time, he was sniffing the air, searching for any signs of danger, but the acidic odor from the crime scene had temporarily diminished his sense of smell. "Answer me."

"Brody, I know it sounds crazy," she whispered, her eyes wide with fear, "but I think someone's watching us."

"Cian?"

"No…no, it isn't him. I can still feel him back with the body. This is…oh God," she gasped, looking up at him, "you don't think it could be Ross, do you? I can't read him. Maybe he followed us."

"Even with that sharp odor still in my nose, I'd be able to smell a human if he was close by," Brody assured her, taking her hand and pulling her along with him, anxious to get to the truck. His natural instinct was to turn and fight whatever the hell was out there, but he couldn't put her at risk that way. "I promise you that Holland isn't anywhere around here, Doucet."

"You're right," she told him, nearly jogging to keep up with his hurried pace. "I'm just nervous, I guess."

Taking out his cell, he called Cian, warning him to be on his guard, all the while keeping Michaela moving as quickly as possible. "Anything else?" he asked her as they broke out of the trees, near the truck. "Can you pick up anything?"

"No, there's just this strange static in my head, and it feels…I don't know, like someone's eyes are following me, pressing in on me." Her own eyes were huge within her face, shadowed by fear. "You know the feeling?"

"Yeah, I know it," he rasped. What worried him was what to do about it.

Hurrying her into the truck, Brody climbed behind the wheel, gunned the gas, and got the hell out of Dodge.

Twenty minutes later, they arrived back at the Alley, just as the first drops of rain from a coming storm began to fall. Serving as a place for the Runners to live separate from the pack, while still on Silvercrest land, Bloodrunner Alley housed ten cabins, only six of which were currently in use. Although set within a rural, majestic setting, surrounded by the natural beauty of the forest, the Alley boasted all the modern amenities, from plumbing to electricity to satellite TV, while its isolated location afforded the Runners the privacy they preferred.

Heading straight to the Dillingers, Brody took a quick look around as he stepped into the kitchen and asked, "Where are Reyes and Pallaton?"

"On their way back from Wesley. They had a lead come in on a possible hideout for Drake's rogues."

"They get anything?"

"Naw. It turned out to be another dead end," Mason told him, reaching into the fridge to pull out cold sodas for him and Michaela, who had moved to sit beside Torrance at the table. A platter of ham and cheese sandwiches sat in the center of the pine table, along with potato chips and pasta salad—the growling of his stomach reminding Brody that he was starving. They sat down to a late lunch, purposely keeping the conversation light by silent agreement, since Michaela was still far too pale, only picking at her food. They were just clearing the last of the plates when a screeching metallic noise sounded from the front of the cabin.

Brody whistled softly under his breath, at the same time Mason growled, "What was that?"

Together, the group headed into the living room, all eyes zeroed in on the front door as Wyatt Pallaton shoved it open, his rain-soaked partner following close on his heels. They were drenched with water, leaving a wet puddle forming in a haphazard circle at their feet, and Torrance and Michaela quickly hurried from the room to get towels.

"Let me guess," Brody drawled, arching one brow as he crossed his arms and propped his shoulder against the wall. "Wyatt forgot to pack the soft top for the Jeep again?"

Reyes pushed her sodden tangle of blond hair out of her eyes. "If I weren't such a *nice* person," she announced with a chilling dose of menace, "I'd kill him."

Her partner frowned as he sent the irritated woman a baleful glare, his dark eyes, which he'd inherited from his Native American grandmother, glowing like a midnight stretch of star-studded sky. "If I'd known the heavens were gonna unload today, I'd have put the damn roof on before we left," he said tightly, the words all but ground through his clenched teeth. "I said I was sorry, so what else do you want from me? Honest to God, woman, just tell me and I'll do it. God knows it'd be better than listening to you go on and on."

The female Runner bared her teeth in an evil smile. "If I were you, I'd save that question for some other time, Pall—preferably when I'm not feeling like a drowned rat. Right now, you might not like what I ask for."

Wyatt made a grunting sound of frustration, which he quickly choked off when Torrance and Michaela came back into the room, their arms loaded with thick towels. "Thanks," he murmured as Michaela handed him one, then offered two to Reyes. They ran the towels over their heads, then dried their clothes as best they could, while Torrance threw three more towels over the puddle on the floor.

"Let's take this into the kitchen, where it's warm," Mason drawled, once they were no longer waterlogged. "I'll put on some fresh coffee."

"I'll take mine with some whiskey," Reyes sighed, wrapping one of the towels around her head.

"I'll take mine with whiskey, too," Wyatt muttered. "But hold the coffee."

Everyone snickered, and together they all wandered back to the cozy kitchen, Jeremy and Jillian coming in a few minutes later. The group had been sitting and talking for nearly a quarter of an hour when Cian finally came through the archway. It occurred to Brody that the Irishman's "dark angel" looks were the perfect complement to Michaela's stunning beauty, the thought sending a sour feeling to the pit of his stomach that felt suspiciously like the hateful burn of jealousy.

"Any trouble?" he asked when his partner took a seat beside him, his handsome features etched with strain and fatigue.

"Nothing," Cian sighed, stretching out his long legs as he leaned back in his chair. "Whomever Michaela felt, he never showed his face and I never picked up anything to track."

Michaela gave a self-deprecating smile. "It was probably just my imagination."

"You said that you heard static in your head," Jillian remarked thoughtfully, her hands wrapped around a thick blue mug of coffee. "Have you ever experienced anything like that before?"

"Only at the clearing," she explained, "after Max's ceremony. It was just before I left."

Mason cut a dark look at Brody. "Maybe our killer is so screwed up, his psychic signals or whatever it is that Mic's able to pick up on are coming through warped."

"Hence the static," Cian murmured, locking his hands behind his dark head, the corners of his wide mouth turned down.

"He could even be trying to reach you, Mic." Torrance suddenly gasped, leaning forward in her chair. "That's it! What if he's trying to communicate with you, but you're just not picking up the signal clearly?"

"God, I hope not," she murmured, her expression revealing her horror. Studying her from beneath his lashes, Brody noticed the way her hands trembled, betraying her nerves and fear, though she tried not to show it, her scent growing stronger with the rise of her pulse. "I don't want some maniac talking in my head."

A slight shiver rushed through her, the skin on her arms covered with chill bumps even though it was warm in the kitchen. Brody wanted to reach out and take her hand, but knew he couldn't.

Jerking his attention away from her before he did something stupid, like follow through on his primitive instincts, he listened as she talked with the others, while struggling to get control of himself. With no conscious direction from his brain,

Brody found himself watching the subtle love play between the mated couples. The brush of a hand against an arm. A secret smile. A shared look. The closeness, the connection. He'd been around them many times before and never felt this illogical urge to get up and run from the room, escaping the proof of their love. Despite wearing a light T-shirt, he was sweating, feeling trapped, unable to relax.

He prayed for a distraction, on the verge of panic, nearly sighing with relief when Mason, his hard tone cut with disappointment, looked at him and said, "By the way, I talked to Dylan. He took the information about Dustin's attack on Max before the League."

"And?" he prompted, scratching his palm across the edge of his jaw.

The Runner sighed as he leaned back in his chair. "As expected, Drake argued against taking action, claiming conflict of interest."

"He accused Brody of lying?" Michaela demanded hotly, her voice shaking with anger as she tuned into their conversation.

"It's okay, Doucet," he assured her in a low voice, even though he was furious with the League. "We expected it."

"It isn't okay," she argued, turning toward him so quickly that her hair fanned out around her shoulders. "You risk your life for them, Brody. The least they could do is treat you with respect. And that monster attacked my brother. He deserves to pay!"

Frowning, Brody said, "If you feel that strongly about it, why didn't you let me go after him last night?"

"*Merde!* Because you could have been hurt," she said tightly, her frustration evident in the thickening drawl of her accent. "Not that you'd have actually left me there alone, so stop acting like you would have. And just because I didn't want you going after him on your own doesn't mean I don't want to see him pay for what he's done!"

"I didn't mean to insinuate that you did," he murmured, unable to take his eyes off her. She was always stunningly beautiful, but when she had her back up, you could see the energy coming off her like incandescent sparks, vivid and wild and breathtaking.

"Did I just hear that right?" Cian drawled, squinting his eyes as he stared at Brody with an incredulous look of surprise. "Because it almost sounded like you were actually apologizing."

"Can it, Hennessey," he muttered under his breath.

"Before you two start going at each other's throats," Mason sighed, "I just want to remind everyone to watch their backs." His golden-brown gaze traveled around the room. "Something's coming, and I think it's getting closer. When it blows, it's gonna be big."

"Just so long as it doesn't blow tomorrow night," Jeremy murmured, flashing a warm smile at his fiancée as he lifted her hand and pressed a kiss to the back of her fingers. Looking toward Cian, he asked, "Did you get the cedar for the fire pits?"

"Don't worry, boyo," Cian drawled with a slow smile. "It's all taken care of. You and your little lady love will be able to enjoy your wedded bliss in the great outdoors without everyone freezing their asses off."

Brody pushed back from the table. "I'm going to go ahead and take Doucet up to my cabin so she can get settled in."

"Before you head up to Brody's," Torrance said, reaching across the table to take hold of Michaela's hand, "I wanted to let you know that we heard from Eric this morning."

"Did you talk to Max?" she whispered, her voice husky

with emotion. "Why didn't you tell me earlier, *ma chère?* What did he say?"

"You were so pale when you got here, I wanted to give you a chance to relax before I brought it up. And I didn't get to talk to Max, because he was upstairs with Elliot," Torrance explained with a smile. "But Eric said he's doing great."

Oh thank God, Michaela silently cried, struggling to hold back a hot wave of tears. There was a storm of emotion roiling just beneath the surface of her composure that threatened to overflow every time she thought about her brother.

Blinking back a salty wash of tears, she heard Brody ask, "Elliot's there?"

Torrance nodded. "When Elliot heard about Max, he called Eric and asked if he could come over. I guess the two of them have really hit it off. They're close in age, and have both been through a lot. Eric asked Elliot if he'd come and stay while Max is in training. He thinks Elliot's going to be a lot of support for Max right now."

Elliot Connors was a Silvercrest teen who had landed in some serious trouble a few weeks ago with one of Drake's rogues. The kid was lucky that the Runners and Mason's parents had taken him under their wing, offering him their friendship and support, since his own parents had all but washed their hands of him. He had a long road ahead of him, but Michaela knew he would make it. The few times she'd been around Elliot, she'd sensed nothing but a good heart. His soul was shadowed by pain, but he was strong enough to overcome his mistakes.

"Eric says Elliot and Max are getting along like they've known each other for years," Torrance added, "bonding like a couple of kids."

A sad smile twisted the corner of Michaela's mouth, and she tried to shake the melancholy sensation, but Torrance noticed. "What's wrong, honey? I knew it would upset you to talk about Max, but I thought you'd be relieved he's doing okay."

"I am. I just…I feel bad, I guess. Max has worked so hard to pull his weight, even though I've told him time and again that there's enough money now for him to go to school without working. He's never had a break. I just think it's sad that it took something like this to make him step back and take a deep breath. He doesn't even really have many friends back home. I'm glad that Elliot's there with him." Turning toward Brody, she said, "Do you think I'll be able to see him soon?"

"You want to go to Shadow Peak?" The look he gave her showed his surprise. "Are you sure you're up for it?"

She gave a soft, shaky laugh. "It's going to take more than a town full of werewolves to keep me from seeing my baby brother. They won't scare me, so long as you're there with me. No one would dare mess with you."

"Max is under Eric's protection," he said in a low voice, and she could have sworn his cheekbones were flushed with color, as if her praise embarrassed him, "but I'll take you up so long as he gives the okay."

Michaela smiled at him as he stood, unable to believe what he'd said. "You mean it? You'll really take me?"

The corner of his mouth kicked up in a boyish grin at her obvious excitement, breaking her heart, since she doubted he'd had much reason to grin as a child. "If you're sure that's what you want, I'll go give Eric a call right now."

Chapter 9

Brody couldn't help the chord of anxiety that accompanied him as he entered Eric's house and spotted Max standing nervously on the far side of the room, the young man's knuckles white as he gripped the back of a pine chair. Part of a dining set, the chair sat in an arched alcove off to the right side of the living room, the kitchen just beyond.

For a split second, Brody worried about the reaction Michaela would have toward her brother, now that Max was one of them and no longer human. It didn't take long, however, for him to realize his concern was misplaced. With an ear-piercing cry of joy that spilled into the room like a colorful swarm of butterflies, Michaela rushed past him the second she set eyes on Max, running across the hardwood floor and hurtling herself into her brother's arms. Max crushed her against his lean body, his shoulders shaking while he buried his face in the thick waves of her hair, obviously as overcome with emotion as his sister.

Brody shook his head in wonder and relief, painfully aware that he shouldn't have underestimated her. There was no hesitation as she embraced her brother, carefully avoiding the bandages on his injured shoulder, and yet, holding him as though she had no intention of ever letting him go—as if she could take all the pain he'd suffered the past few days and make it her own. Untainted and unguarded, her love existed completely without prejudice.

As if acting by silent agreement, he and Eric remained by the door. The tall, broad-shouldered Lycan stood silently at his side, hands shoved in his jeans' pockets as he watched the Doucets with dark gray eyes and a pleased expression that revealed his own relief at the successful reunion. When Max and Michaela sat down at the table, put their dark heads together and began quietly talking, Eric slanted him a knowing look. "Man," he drawled, "I didn't think I'd ever see the day, but you've got it as bad as Burns does."

"Got what?" Brody asked in a low voice, not wanting to disturb the siblings.

"Like you don't know," the Lycan snorted. "You've been bitten by the lovebug, man."

Brody made a rude sound in the back of his throat, cutting the jackass with an "as if" look. "Get real," he muttered, trying to appear unconcerned, while inside, his heart rate kicked into overdrive, roaring through his head. Christ, was it really that obvious?

Eric's shoulders lifted in a laughing shrug. "Hey, don't blame me for the yearning state of your heart. I just call it like I see it."

"You don't see jack," he snarled under his breath, wanting

to wipe that knowing look off the bastard's handsome face. "If I'm watching her, it's only because it's my job to protect her."

Recalling their earlier conversation—and eager to steer the topic of discussion away from himself—he added, "You mentioned on the phone that there was something you wanted to talk about."

"There is." Holding Brody's dark stare, Eric's expression turned serious as he rubbed one hand across the rugged angle of his jaw, the sleeve of his T-shirt shifting to reveal the bottom edge of an intricate tattoo wrapping his thick bicep. "I want to help. I want to be a part of the investigation into the rogues and what happened with my sister."

"We're after your own family," Brody scoffed, wondering what the guy was up to. "Looking to bring down your old man. We appreciate you stepping up to help Max, but what makes you think we'd trust you to help in our investigation?"

"Because I saved your friend's life," Eric pointed out, wearing a ghost of a smile. "And while I may be a lot of things, a traitor isn't one of them. My loyalty is to the pack, not my father. Any sense of familial obligation I felt to the man, he managed to destroy a long time ago all on his own."

"And how do we know you're not just playing sides?" he countered for sheer argument's sake. It was obvious the Bloodrunners, including himself, had already decided to trust Eric Drake. If they hadn't, they never would have allowed Max to remain under the Lycan's supervision.

"Playing sides?" Eric snorted in response to his question, crossing his brawny arms over his blue T-shirt covered chest. "Do I look like the playful sort to you, Carter?"

"Yeah, you're about as giddy as a rattlesnake, and just as ornery."

Rolling his eyes, Eric muttered, "You're too good for my ego, man." The Lycan paused for a moment, once again watching the Doucets as he ran one hand over the short scrub of his dark hair, before blowing out a rough breath. "Look, I know it's going to take time to learn to work together, but I wanted to let you know that the Runners aren't alone in this any longer. You have support in the pack. There are others who feel like I do, they're just too afraid to come forward and risk my father's wrath. But we can keep an eye on things here, relay information that might be useful. There's been a communication breakdown between the town and the Runners for too long. It's time we put an end to it."

"I'll have to talk to the others," he grunted.

Giving a confident nod, Eric smiled as he said, "You do that." He knew damn well that the opportunity was too good for the Runners to pass up. "And speaking of how you need a better foothold in the information loop, I have some news."

"What kind of news?"

"The kind that not many people know about yet. Not even Jillian." His expression grim, Eric said, "The *Pippa Stanton has gone missing* kind."

Brody cursed under his breath, while dread settled heavily around his shoulders, weighing him down. "Do you know what happened?"

"Not a clue. There's a small group that was asked by the League to search the surrounding woods, but nothing's turned up so far."

"I have a bad feeling about this," Brody muttered, raking one hand through his hair before cutting a narrow look back at the Lycan. "And no doubt that your old man's behind it."

Eric's brows drew together in a questioning frown. "I'm

assuming he's behind it, too, but do you actually know of any reason my father might target Pippa specifically?"

"Maybe," Brody averred, rolling his shoulder. "Maybe not."

There was silence for the beat of several seconds, and then Eric quietly growled, "Shit. You *do* know something, don't you?"

Only something that had been passed on to him and the other Runners in confidence, that couldn't be repeated. It was Pippa who had revealed the secrets about Drake's past to Jeremy and Jillian the week before, telling them the story of how the Elder's wife left him for a human. When Drake demanded his wife be hunted down and executed for her treachery, the League had refused. According to Pippa, he'd never forgiven the League for "turning their back on him in his time of need." From that point on, his hatred and rage had consumed him, until he became the twisted, fanatical leader that he was today.

Instead of addressing Eric's question, Brody asked one of his own. "Do you know when she was last seen?"

For a moment, Eric looked as if he'd press the issue, before shaking off his irritation. "Yeah," he sighed. "It was last night, at a League meeting. Her sister called Graham when it started getting late and Pippa still hadn't made it home."

Damn, that wasn't good. Brody had already been uneasy about bringing Michaela into the lion's den, so to speak, risking the visit to Shadow Peak, but had felt a certain measure of confidence that Drake and his rogues wouldn't dare try anything in broad daylight, when all eyes were on them. But knowing that he'd had the balls to target Pippa, another Elder, was proof that Drake's madness had outweighed his reason. If he was willing to take out one of the most powerful members of the League, he'd be willing to risk *anything*.

Glancing out the front window, he saw that evening was fast approaching, and he didn't want to have Michaela out after dark. Things were dangerous enough during the day, but come night-time... No way in hell was he risking it. An ambush on the road home would be too easy. And though Brody was confident in his abilities, he didn't relish the idea of single-handedly battling a contingent of rogues in order to keep Michaela safe, the way Jeremy and Mason had done with Torrance just weeks before.

"Okay, I'll let the other Runners know what's happening as soon as we get back. And if anything new comes up, let me know. You've already got my number." Without waiting for Eric's response, he headed toward Michaela, stopping just inside the alcove. "I know we haven't been here long, but it's time for us to go, Doucet."

Clutching one of her brother's hands, she looked at him over her shoulder. "Already? But we only just got here."

"I'm afraid so. It's getting dark and I need to get you back to the Alley." Shifting his gaze to Max, who was trying to look tough despite the sheen of tears in his dark blue eyes, Brody said, "I promise we'll make it back up as soon as we can."

"Your brother's going to make it through this just fine, Michaela," Eric said as they headed to the door. "Whenever Carter can bring you up, you're welcome to come and visit. And if you want, I'll be happy to keep in touch with you, so you know how he's doing."

"That would be wonderful," she replied, her voice breath-less with relief. "If you have a piece of paper, I'll write my cell phone number down for you."

Brody crossed his arms over his chest and muttered, "Forget it, Drake. If you have information for her, you can damn well call my number and give it to me."

"Brody," she gasped, sounding appalled. She probably wanted to smack his hand with a ruler for being rude, but what did she expect? He wasn't going to stand by and watch her exchange phone numbers with another man. Not in this lifetime.

With her cheeks flushed, she sent an apologetic look toward Eric, who was clearly trying not to laugh, his gray eyes glittering. "I'm so sorry," she whispered.

"No need," Eric said smoothly, grinning like a jackass. "I think I understand *exactly* where Carter is coming from."

Grunting under his breath, Brody ushered her out the front door, wishing like hell he could figure out not only where he was coming from, but where he was headed. Because from where he stood, it looked like nothing but trouble.

"What's the matter with you?" Michaela hissed the second she slammed the door of the truck shut. Breathing hard, she ripped her seatbelt into place so violently, she damn near strangled herself. Brody knew she'd been dying to lay into him since the moment they'd left Eric's, but had held her tongue until they were alone.

"Hell if I know," he muttered, the words thick with disgust as he cranked the engine, setting the heat on low for her benefit. He was already hot beneath the skin, burning up in nothing more than a T-shirt and his jeans.

"I'm curious, Brody. Just what do you think is going to happen if Eric calls me?"

He cursed under his breath as he pulled away from the curb, navigating the Ford down the narrow street lined by beautiful oak trees. "I know what he'd *like* to happen."

"Honestly, Brody. You don't want me, but no one else can be interested, is that it?"

"You want him to be interested?" he grunted, while what felt like a ton of bricks landed in his gut.

"No," she snapped. "That's not the point. My point is that you can't have it both ways. You can't keep me at arm's length, then demand that no other man get close to me. And for your information, I find your entire attitude insulting." As she paused to take a quick breath, he wondered if she even realized her voice was steadily rising, growing louder with her anger. "Believe it or not, I'm not some femme fatale constantly on the make for a man. *Mon dieu.* My life is a mess, Brody. My brother has become a werewolf, I'm being threatened by rogues, and both my shop and my house have been broken into and vandalized. I'm warning you right now, if you don't cut me some slack, I'm going to have a freaking meltdown!"

He slanted her an uneasy look, aware that she was truly furious with him. More so than he'd thought. Calmly, he pointed out the obvious. "You're shouting."

She took a deep breath that vibrated with fury. "You think this is bad," she shot back, "just wait till you see what happens if you don't say you're sorry. I'm sick and tired of you and every other man I meet always thinking the worst of me. I am not some brainless bimbo looking to get treated like crap!"

He blinked, while a swarm of reactions skittered through his system. On the one hand, there was a part of him that wanted to smile at the way she'd so passionately declared she wasn't a "brainless bimbo," finding her ridiculously adorable, even in her anger. The other part wanted to pull her out of her seat, across his lap, and ravage her mouth with a breathtaking kiss until there was no doubt in her mind exactly who she belonged to.

It was the second scenario that scared the ever-loving hell

out of him, and Brody found himself prodding at her anger with a verbal stick. "What do you know about being treated like crap?" he muttered. "Your life's been a freaking fairy tale compared to what most people know."

She flinched in reaction to his low, guttural slide of words, anger and hurt flashing like sparks in her eyes. He expected her to lash out at him, but she just sat there, hands twisting in her lap, chest rising and falling beneath her sweater, appearing more vulnerable with each deep, shivering breath. She looked as if she would melt into a hot wash of tears at any moment, but when she finally spoke, her calm, soft voice betrayed only the slightest tremor. "Believe it or not, Brody, you don't have a monopoly on a painful past. I may not have suffered to the degree that you have, but I have my own emotional scars. Ever wonder why I don't mention my parents?"

"I'd assumed they'd passed away," he rasped, sliding her another uneasy look, aware of a suspicious heat rising up the back of his neck and ears that felt uncomfortably like shame.

Her mouth twisted with a wry smile, arms wrapped around her middle as she turned her head to stare out her window. "Oh no, I'm sure they're alive and well somewhere, enjoying their burden-free lifestyle."

"What does that mean?"

Sighing, she looked back at him. "It means they dropped Max and me off with our *grandmère* one day when he was little more than a toddler, then just got into their car and drove away. None of us ever heard from them again."

"Son of a bitch," he cursed hotly, brows drawn together in a deep scowl over the vivid green of his eyes, his scars accentuated by the fierceness of his expression. "That was heartless."

"It could have been worse," she remarked dryly, turning her attention back to the scenery beyond the window as they drove through the town, picturesque cottages and various buildings visible on both sides of the road. Amazingly, Shadow Peak looked like any other small mountain community. If you were just passing through, you'd have never suspected that something sinister lurked beneath the charming surface. Something with fangs and fur and claws, that would scare most humans into a catatonic state of terror.

"How could it have been worse?" he demanded, the words thick with outrage.

"They could have stayed around," she murmured. "In the long run, I think Max and I were better off without them. My *grandmère* truly loved us. She raised us until she passed away when Max was fourteen. After that, we moved here to live with her sister, my great-aunt. She willed her house to us when she died a few years ago, so we stayed in Covington. I opened my shop, and the rest is history."

"I still think it was heartless," he muttered, ripping the scarred fingers of his right hand through the auburn strands of his hair, while steering with his left. "Something must have been seriously wrong with them."

Michaela had no argument for him there, having never been able to understand how a mother could fail to love her child more than anything in the world. With a small shiver, she thought back to the dream she'd had last night, the one where Brody was playing with a beautiful raven-haired, green-eyed baby girl. The memory of that dream shot a pang of warmth through her middle, dissipating the last of her anger, and she pressed her hand against the center of her chest, as if she could control the hammering beat of her heart.

Needing a distraction before she lost her head in wishes that were never going to come true, she deliberately changed the subject. "Speaking of relatives," she murmured, "are you going to contact your grandmother?"

He arched one russet brow. "Why would I do that?"

"I know she doesn't deserve it, but…after what Meredith said, don't you think that maybe it's time to open up and give her another chance, Brody?"

"I don't give first chances," he grunted, "so what makes you think I'd give her a second one?"

Shaking her head, Michaela didn't know whether to feel sorry for him or knock some sense into him. "You're just a one-man island, is that it?"

Cutting her a frustrated look of exasperation, he took the next right, turning onto the private road they'd taken into Shadow Peak, though they were still in what looked like the center of town, the street congested with traffic. "Don't sound sorry for me, Doucet. I don't need your pity. I like my life the way it is," he rasped, his tone suddenly as belligerent as it was defensive. "I'm doing just fine."

She shifted in her seat, tucking her leg up under her so that she could stare at his rugged profile, the late-afternoon sunlight glinting through the windshield revealing the creases at the corners of those deep green eyes.

"Are you really happy with your life, Brody?" she asked softly. "Don't you get lonely?"

Narrowing his eyes on the road ahead, he looked as if he wondered just how much she knew about him, how much she understood. She realized, in that moment, that he still didn't completely trust her, and after what had happened the night before, she didn't blame him.

"I can tell from the look on your face that you still doubt me, Brody, but I didn't lie to you last night. I might have had that one vision when we were so…um, involved with each other, but you're still about as easy to read as a gator's expression in the middle of the bayou at midnight."

He snuffled a rough laugh under his breath at her colorful analogy, turning to stare at her after pulling to a stop at the town's last traffic light, the green of his eyes deep and dark, swirling with a myriad of thoughts and feelings she knew he'd never admit to. "Don't worry," he murmured, his tone dry, gaze shifting back to the road when the light turned green. There was a husky undertone to his words that made her shiver with sensual awareness as he said, "I believe you."

"You do?"

"Yeah. If you could read my mind, you wouldn't be…"

"What?" she demanded, her voice breathless.

He shifted his long body in his seat, pulling back his shoulders. "Nothing."

"Brody…"

"Drop it, Doucet," he muttered.

Unwilling to let the topic go that easily, she opened her mouth to press him further, when the sudden blaring of a horn made her jump. Peering through the window, she saw that the sidewalks were now packed with as much pedestrian traffic as the roads. "This is crazy. Are the streets always this crowded here?"

"Not like this. If I had to guess, I'd say everyone's heading to the Town Hall because Drake's holding another one of his rallies tonight. Jeremy told us he's using them to incite the pack, brainwashing them with lies, spouting a bunch of nonsense about how the Lycans are being oppressed by human society and the Runners are lying about the growing number of rogues."

"It's getting close, isn't it?" she whispered, his words sending a sliver of alarm down her spine. "Just like Mason said. You can feel the tension hanging over this place, just waiting to blow."

"Yeah," he agreed, his tone roughened by worry. "You can feel it in the air when you breathe, like a storm coming in. It won't be long now."

Brody glanced at her from the corner of his eye, seeing her own worry revealed in the strain around her eyes and mouth, her beauty taking on a haunted quality that tore at his heart. "And when it happens, your life is going to be in danger," she said softly, the unspoken meaning behind that tender, emotional tone taking another notch out of his hard-earned control; at the same time his automatic defense mechanisms kicked into gear, as natural to him as breathing.

"Our lives are in danger now, Doucet," he muttered in a low, coarse rasp. "Why else do you think I'm with you?"

The hateful words landed between them with an ominous thud, and she winced, unable to hide her reaction. Closing in on herself like an oyster, she turned away from him, staring silently out her window as he drove them home to the Alley. Neither of them said another word until Brody came to a stop in front of his cabin.

"Brody," she said in a small voice, breaking into the breath-filled silence. "I know we're not getting along that great right now, but it seems we have bigger problems than being at odds with each other."

"Yeah?" he rumbled, turning his head to see her peering out the passenger's side window. "Like what?"

She looked back at him, her eyes wide within the paleness of her face. "Look at your front door."

Peering around her shoulder, he cursed sharply the second he realized what he was staring at. "Son of a bitch," he hissed, grabbing hold of her arm. He opened his door and pulled her across the front seat, out the driver's side, sniffing at the evening air, searching for any imminent signs of danger. "Stay close to me," he ordered in a chilling tone of voice, keeping hold of her arm as they moved around the back of the truck, toward the porch. When the wind blew the scent of blood toward them, she made a sharp gagging sound, closing her eyes as she fought her nausea.

"Is that what I think it is?" she whispered, her voice little more than a whispery thread of sound.

"Yeah," he grunted, clutching the back of her head and pressing her face to his chest, finally giving in to the urge that had been riding him all day and wrapping his arms around her, holding her in a tight, possessive embrace.

A red haze of fury tinged the edges of his vision as Brody stared over her head at the atrocity nailed to his front door. A knife had been embedded deep within the dark wood, Pippa Stanton's long silver braid hanging from the bloody scalp that had been nailed there, along with a message written in blood. The writing was nearly illegible, the blood dripping down the wooden surface like crimson rivers of death, distorting the letters, but he could make out the bloodcurdling warning. He just couldn't believe Drake's rogues had dared to kill an Elder, trespass into the Alley and threaten the woman under his protection. And there was no doubt this was a direct threat against Michaela's life—the warning simple and straightforward, with no room for misinterpretation.

Scrawled across the door like a message from hell, it read *The Cajun is next.*

Chapter 10

Michaela lingered in a hot shower until the water threatened to run cool, her mind working over the chilling events of the last few hours. After the gruesome discovery of Pippa Stanton's scalp, as well as the terrifying, blood-written warning, Brody had taken her down to the Dillingers' cabin. Reyes had been ordered to stay with the women, while the men searched the Alley. They'd been unable to pick up any trace of Lycan musk, although there was a lingering vinegar-like odor on the scalp. Evidently, the rogue had delivered the macabre warning while in its dayshifted form, which explained why the Runners who were at home in their cabins hadn't scented the trespasser.

And even though the Runners knew the rogue had been confident that his disguised scent would allow him to slip in under their noses, they were still stunned by the arrogance of the move. Drake's rogues were getting cocky—a fact that only substantiated the Bloodrunners' belief that something would happen, sooner rather than later.

After stepping out of the granite-tiled shower, Michaela found a stack of fluffy white towels folded beneath the sink, and wrapped one around her body, overlapping the edges at the front in a tight knot. Opening the door that led into Brody's bedroom, she propped her shoulder against the doorjamb, taking a moment to study the room, enjoying the intimate look at his private sanctuary—aware that she was searching for ways to keep herself distracted so she wouldn't worry about Max, that horrific warning and the painful declaration that Brody had made in his truck.

The style of the room was just as she'd expected—strong, bold and ruggedly beautiful, exactly like the man himself. His bed sat low to the ground, a rich mahogany platform frame supported by thick posts and legs. A matching chest and armoire sat on opposing walls, the only other piece of furniture an oversize chair in espresso-colored leather with gently sloping arms that looked great for reading.

She'd have loved to have been worry free and relaxed, just cuddled up in that big chair with one of her favorite novels, without a care in the world. But even more than that, she'd have loved to have seen Brody sprawled across that beautiful bed. Closing her eyes, Michaela lost herself in the heady, breathtaking daydream. She could see herself coming out from a steam-filled bubble bath to find him propped up against the headboard, waiting for her. He'd have taken off his shirt and shoes, a low wash of golden lamplight at his bedside setting the beauty of his hard body alight, picking out the burgundy highlights in his hair. His broad chest would gleam like bunched satin, his muscles perfectly formed, his ridged abdomen drawing her eye as she followed the silky trail of dark auburn hair that tapered into the waistband of a faded pair of jeans. A significant bulge would be pressed against the straining hold of his button fly, her mouth watering as she watched his right thumb stroke along that swollen ridge, his fingers curled against the rigid muscle of his thigh.

Licking her upper lip, Michaela could practically feel the desire shifting restlessly within her body, as if she had a beast of her own that moved within her, struggling to break free. And she knew precisely what its prey would be.

Brody.

But he seemed determined to keep his distance from her, now more than ever. It made her heart twist, because she wanted so desperately for him to reach out to her. To walk to her with his mouth curled in a sexy grin, and when he reached her, to close his arms around her, pulling her into the hardness and heat of his body. Holding her as if he wanted to absorb life from her.

With a sad smile, she reminded herself that he'd held her for a moment on the porch when they'd first made the grisly discovery, but not out of passion. Her *grandmère* would have said something wise, no doubt, about how beggars couldn't be choosers—but damn it, was she really asking for so much?

Opening her eyes, she stared at the bed they were never going to share, and became painfully aware that she *was* asking for too much.

"Why else do you think I'm with you?"

Michaela knew he'd spoken the truth, but it still hurt, the knowledge that if it weren't for the fact she needed protection, he'd still be doing everything within his power to avoid her.

Stifling a low groan, she wondered how she would deal with him tonight. It was hard enough to hide her fierce attraction under the best of circumstances—not that there'd been many of those—but tonight she was too…needy. Too hungry for comfort. Worry and fear had worn her down like the weathered heel of a shoe, leaving her sensitive and raw. She didn't want to face the night alone. Though she still grappled with her own fear of being used, then discarded—she could too easily see herself seeking the warm security of Brody's muscled arms, begging for his protective embrace.

A wry smile curled her mouth, and she choked back a sound that fell somewhere between a sob and a giggle. God, she could just imagine his reaction if she tried to touch him. Knowing Brody, he'd probably blanch and push her away if she found the courage to even try it. No—no matter how tempting it would be to turn to him, she was going to have to find the will to resist.

She'd already unpacked her suitcase, using the empty drawers he'd brusquely pointed to in the beautiful armoire, his body language stiff as he'd shown her around his cabin, as if he couldn't wait to escape her company. He'd said something about needing to get some work done in his office when he'd left her in his room, and she assumed he would spend the rest of the evening hiding there. She'd eaten some soup while she'd waited with Torrance, Jillian and Reyes, and assumed Brody had already grabbed something for his dinner.

Growing chilly in the towel, she dressed in a comfortable pair of black leggings and a long, loose black shirt, the dark color matching her somber mood. Taking her cell phone from her purse, she checked her messages, in case David had called from the shop, but there was only one voice mail from Ross.

Wincing, she listened to his outraged message, shaking her head as he accused her of dating one of her "freak" customers, claiming that Brody wasn't normal. If it were anyone other than Ross, she supposed she might have been worried about what kind of trouble he could cause with his accusations. But Ross was too concerned with his public image. If he'd caught Santa in the act of coming down the chimney on Christmas Eve, he'd have kept the stunning news to himself, afraid of what people would think of him, of what they might whisper behind his back.

No, even if he'd seen Brody in all his beautiful, beastly glory, he'd never breathe a word of it to another soul. And even if he did, he'd probably find himself carted off to the nearest psychiatric ward for sedation. Still, she'd texted him back that she had no idea what he was talking about, and suggested his time would be better spent thinking about what a jerk he'd been.

Having dealt with that, she sat down on the edge of the bed, wondering what to do next. Rain had begun to fall again, its heavy rhythm soothing against the cabin's roof. Should she go to bed, listening to the storm? Find a book to read? She had seen a collection of current thrillers on a bookshelf in the living room. Or should she do what she really wanted, which was walk out of the bedroom, go down the hall and find the man she couldn't get out of her mind?

He would most likely be ugly and rude, if not insulting, in an attempt keep her away. But even knowing that, could she ignore the need to be close to him? The driving urge to keep chipping away at his resistance until he finally stopped fighting this powerful force pulling them together? Could she resist the temptation?

And more importantly, did she even want to?

* * *

The jarring cracks of thunder rumbling across the night-time sky marked the tedious passage of time, its movement drawn out and heavy, like the thick, sluggish spill of honey from a jar. Brody felt each second that passed by, moving painfully into the next, his tension twisting into tighter, straining knots of frustration with each individual tick…tick…tick.

Staring at the muted colors on his computer monitor, he rubbed his tired eyes with the heels of his palms when the contours of the map began to blur together in a swirling kaleidoscope of color. He'd been staring at the same image ever since Michaela had turned on the water in the bathroom, the gurgling in the pipes mesmerizing him as effortlessly as the pied piper's famous tune.

He still regretted the words he'd spoken in the truck, even though he knew they were for the best. For some unknown reason, the woman kept being nice to him, when it was the last damn thing he needed. *Nice* made his heart think there was a chance in hell things could work out between them, when he knew it wasn't true.

They were beauty and the beast, come to life from a storybook setting. But this was no fairy tale. Pippa Stanton's scalp hanging from his front door was proof of that, as was the infuriating threat against Michaela's life. It made him so violently angry, Brody knew he could have torn the one responsible into pieces.

The viciousness of that thought reminded him of another key point: the fact that he was more monster than man, the craving of his wolf growing stronger, edgier, every moment he spent with her.

He didn't want to be loverlike and caring. He wanted to

consume her sexually, claiming her so thoroughly it obliterated the memory of any other man, any other lover, she'd ever known.

And when he did, he knew she'd turn away from him. Knew he'd scare the hell out of her…or worse, hurt her. He couldn't risk it, no matter how painful it was to fight his beast's demand to claim her flesh with his body, her soul with his fangs.

The only thing he could think of that would be worse than bonding himself to a woman who didn't love him, was seeing the look in her eyes when it was over…when he'd lost his control and claimed her with all the raw, carnal sexuality of the wolf that lived within him, its power over him growing stronger the longer he went without sex.

He should have just swallowed the bitter pill of reality, gone into the city, hit the bars and found a woman to lie down with. Someone he could use as easily as she would use him, but he hadn't been able to stomach it.

And so here he was, so on edge he felt like one wrong move, one slip of the tongue, one dangerous touch, and he'd make the most destructive mistake of his life.

Enough already. Time to get your mind off the woman and back on the case, where it belongs.

"Okay, okay," he sighed, opening his eyes and studying the map once more. It covered the mountains in a forty-mile radius, with the Alley at its center. Red circles marked the location of the victims they'd found, small black stars plotting the locations that had been searched as possible rogue hideouts for Drake's teenage gang of killers. Though they suspected many of the teens in town who were part of Stefan Drake's "pureblood" movement were close to turning, they knew many already had, having been recruited, and at times even forced, by Drake and his cohorts. There was no doubt

Drake had nefarious plans for his little rogue army—the Runners just wished they knew what they were. An attack on the humans? God, his blood ran cold at the thought. Or an attack on the Alley, one meant to take the Runners out once and for all? Possibly.

Though they'd found several abandoned hideouts, they'd yet to come across the rogues themselves. The band had kept a low profile ever since the failed attack on Mason, Torrance and Jeremy a few weeks before, but the Runners knew they were out there, like a pack of predators hiding in the shadows, just waiting for the perfect moment to strike.

And though they hadn't found any bodies, they knew the Lycans they were hunting were killers, as well as rapists— they just didn't know how many victims had been claimed. Five? Ten? A dozen? Unlike the blond human girls who were being left out in the open for discovery, they'd yet to find the remains of the rogue gang's victims. Were they mass feeding, completely consuming the bodies? Were they taking them to their hideout, storing the remains there?

Though they hadn't found evidence of the kills, the Runners knew they were being made. After they'd rescued Elliot Connors, the teenager had admitted he'd been set up to kill a human girl, though her body had never been discovered. He'd even been able to send them to the place where the kill had happened, but by then the rogues had already abandoned the cave and moved on, an old animal carcass they'd left behind the only evidence of a feeding. The Runners suspected they were still splitting their time between the human city of Covington and the mountains, never staying in one place for long. And Elliot had only been allowed to interact with a small portion of the group, most of whom had been killed when they'd attacked

Jeremy and Mase, but he'd talked of them going out to hunt…
to feed.

At times, the entire nightmare seemed like madness, but
there was an organized chaos behind the fragmented pieces
that formed a larger picture. And yet, the Runners still had as
many questions as they did answers. With his small army of
rogues, why did Drake need this so-called Legend of Azakiel
that allowed him to pull out a Lycan's wolf against his will?
Who was Drake's accomplice? What was he after?

And how was the rogue killer of the blond humans connected?

Was the killer they were hunting, the one ritualistically
killing the human girls, part of the rogues? Was it Drake,
Dustin or someone else? An Elder? No matter who it was,
there was no doubt he was connected to Drake. The murders
had been made while the rogue was in his dayshifted form,
and they'd heard Simmons himself speak of the one who
would keep killing "the pretty blondes" before he'd died. If
it wasn't Drake, and Brody didn't think it was, then it was one
of his followers. But who? And why? The eaten heart was
symbolic, but again, in what way? All of the victims were
young and fair, with the exception of the redhead Simmons
had killed to screw with Mason's mind. All blond and blue-
eyed, similar in features and build, almost as if the same kill
was being made over and over again.

The only difference in the crime scenes that he and Cian
had investigated so far was the location, the first two near pack
land, then that third one found down in Covington. The fact
that the last body had been found near pack land again
probably indicated some sort of mistake, possibly a loss of
control, on the part of the rogue killer with the victim they'd

found in the city. Brody no longer thought that the city location had been an intentional move. No, if that'd been the case, this last kill would have presented an even greater threat of exposure—the body left out on a city street, instead of turning back up in the mountains again.

Feeling as though he was grasping at straws, Brody opened his e-mail and typed up a message for Monroe, asking the FBI agent for an updated missing persons report, narrowing the list down to young blond females with blue eyes who had gone missing within the state during the past several months. Maybe the search would turn up a lead, some sort of connection to someone within the pack.

Glancing at the pad of paper sitting on his desk, he reread the names he'd listed while waiting for his computer to boot up. He still had Dustin's name at the top of his list, reasonably so, since he'd already admitted to attacking Max—but the more Brody thought about it, the more it didn't fit. He couldn't see the Lycan losing control *or* making a mistake. Dustin might be his worst nightmare, but he wasn't sloppy.

Stefan Drake was next. Brody supposed the Elder could be playing out some twisted fantasy about a younger version of his wife, but when would he have had the time? Between recruiting rogues and masterminding whatever the hell he had planned, could he really be sneaking into the city for victims?

One of the rogues, then? But who? They didn't even know them all, suspecting the group to have grown from other nearby packs. And you couldn't go through the town and do a census. The Silvercrest weren't forbidden to leave Shadow Peak. Lycans could come and go as they pleased, and many of the young ones often spent time away from the mountains. And even the ones who'd "gone missing" were unlikely to be turned in by their relatives, who didn't trust the Runners any more than they would have trusted a human.

There were times when their work seemed like such a futile undertaking, because for every rogue they took down, it seemed that two more were just waiting to take his place. Something had to be done to stop the trend, and that had been before this current hell had started. Even after they caught Drake and managed to nail his ass, the Runners still had to hunt down the ones he'd tempted into turning.

It was enough to make a man contemplate a new line of work, that was for sure. Not that he was actually serious. No, as pathetic as it made him, Brody had meant every word that he'd said to Michaela when she'd asked why he Ran for the pack. He and the others took their positions and purpose seriously, and he knew none of them would ever walk away from it, no matter how frustrating it became.

Succumbing to his steadily growing headache with a foul curse, Brody swiveled away from the computer screen, fighting the urge to pick it up and hurl the equipment against the wall of his office.

Bracing his elbows on his spread knees, he cradled his head in his open palms, spearing his fingers back through his hair, and concentrated on taking deep, even breaths. In. Out. In. Out.

His next inhalation made his muscles clench in awareness, and he knew, without lifting his head, that Michaela stood in the doorway, even though she hadn't made a sound. Her warm, womanly scent wrapped around him, seducing his senses…seducing his heart. He could smell the warmth of the shower on her, the tang of her soap on her skin, shampoo in her hair. In his mind's eye, he tortured himself with the mental vision of her standing beneath the steamy spray of water, her body naked and wet and beautiful—knowing, instinctively, that she'd have welcomed him in there with her…if he'd had the balls to go after what he wanted.

"What are you working on?" she asked, the muted Louisiana drawl that softened her words melting into him, provocative and rich. He could listen to her talk for hours, turned on to the point of pain from nothing more than the sultry sound of that intoxicating voice.

Silently cursing his weakness, Brody lifted his head and jerked his chin toward the computer screen. "It's a map showing the locations where we've found bodies, along with places we've searched as possible hideouts."

She nodded, bracing one hand against the doorjamb. "Why do you think he came back to make this last kill on pack land, after risking discovery in the city when he killed the girl who was dealing drugs?"

"Who knows?" he sighed, leaning back in his office chair as he stared at her, her beauty taking his breath, same as it always did. "Maybe he lost control and didn't mean to make the kill in Covington. Could be that the close call scared him, made him more cautious."

As if echoing his earlier thoughts, she frowned, saying, "That doesn't sound like Dustin."

He rubbed at the tension knotted in the back of his neck, and asked, "What do you mean?"

"He's too arrogant, too cocky. And I was thinking about that feeling I had when we were with the victim. The conflict I felt in the killer. That doesn't sound like Dustin, either. From what I could read in Dustin when we saw him in Covington, he doesn't seem the type to mourn his actions. If he were the killer, I think he'd be gloating about his success. For that matter, I don't see Stefan Drake having that kind of reaction, either. Both have God complexes that would prevent them from feeling conflicted over their actions."

Scrubbing his hands down his face, Brody knew he had to agree. "You're right. We're still looking in the wrong direction."

Her head listed slightly to the side as she studied him, the damp curls of her hair falling like a midnight sheet of silk over her shoulder. She should have looked washed-out, with the black clothes and all that long black hair, but her skin shone with the luminous sheen of a pearl, cheeks and mouth flushed a blushing rose, eyes brilliant and bright and blue. "I know it's frustrating," she told him, "but you'll figure it out."

"I don't know. I feel like the answer's staring us right in the face, but we just can't see it."

"Has anything come up on any of the other Elders?"

"Naw. They all have their share of secrets and skeletons in their closets, but hell, who doesn't? We could make an argument for any of them as easily as we could make an argument against them." He sighed, leaning forward to brace his elbows on his knees once again. He turned his right hand over and stared at the lines on his palm, as if he could find the answers there as easily as Meredith had. "When we first started, we didn't know much about any of them, since we've been so isolated from the pack for so long, our interactions with the League as minimal as possible. But even now, we're still no closer to any answers, and Pippa was the only one willing to talk to us."

"And after what's happened to her, the others are going to be reluctant to stand against Drake, no matter how extreme he becomes," she murmured, stepping away from the door and walking into the room. Michaela didn't know what drove her forward. Loneliness? Need? Love? All of them? She only knew that she had to be near him. Stepping closer, she was no more than five feet away when he glanced up and jerked to his feet so quickly the chair crashed over behind him. Holding up his hand, he said, "Stop."

Michaela froze, standing in the middle of his office. She opened her mouth, but couldn't think of anything to say that wouldn't scare him away. And he was already wary enough. She could see it in his eyes, in the hard tension of those broad, beautiful shoulders and the tight stretch of the roped muscles and sinew in his arms.

"This isn't going to happen, Doucet. I can't touch you," he growled in a low, tortured voice, "because once I start, I'm not going to be able to stop."

She absorbed that, playing the words over in her mind. Pressing one hand against her stomach, she asked, "Is there someone else you go to, then?"

"There's no one else," he admitted, his tone gruff, as if the words were being ripped out of him. His strain revealed itself in the hard lines of his expression, the brackets around his mouth deeper, jaw tight, scars more prominent against the rise of color in his face. In a broken, guttural scrape of words, he said, "I haven't…, it's been…too long."

With a jolt of surprise, she understood what he was trying to tell her, but it stunned her. She'd assumed a man like Brody must have women lining up to be with him, and yet she was sure he was telling her that he'd been a long time without a woman.

Carefully, she asked, "Are you…are you afraid of hurting me?"

"Hurting you?" he repeated, a sharp, hoarse bark of laughter jerking from his chest. "Jesus, Doucet. It may not scare you that I'm as much wolf as I am man, but it should. I want…I need…" Struggling, he finally snarled, "Just trust me when I say that you wouldn't be tempting me if you knew what it would be like, getting under me."

"I think you're wrong," she said in a soft, quiet rush, daring to take a step closer to him. "And isn't that my choice to make, Brody?"

He gave a hard, sharp shake of his head. "No, I won't risk it."

Risk what? Hurting her? Losing control? Biting her?

"If you're not willing to take the risk, then I am," she whispered, taking that final step that brought her within mere inches of his body, so close his deliciously masculine scent filled her head, his heat warming her skin.

Lifting her right hand to his face, she trailed her fingertips over the slight ridges of his scars, wishing she could take his pain as her own. He carried his scars on the outside, while she carried hers within. Lessons learned from a lifetime of mistakes. And yet, it didn't feel like a mistake with Brody. It felt as if she'd finally got it right, as if she was right where she belonged.

The touch of her hand against his scars was Brody's undoing. One moment he was trapped, suspended in a state of agony, and then he was reaching for her, his hands curling around her biceps, pulling her to him. Instantly, he captured her mouth with his, and she was too goddamn sweet, her taste flooring him. The textures of her mouth assaulted his system, breaking him down, leaving nothing but this trembling, aching hunger, craving, in its wake. The pansy softness of her lips, that sweet slickness that lay just inside the lush swell. He could stroke that with his tongue forever and never get enough.

He kissed her harder, and she greedily accepted his aggression, matching it. No matter how desperately he kissed her, she responded with breathless urgency, as if he could draw the pleasure up out of her through nothing more than the touch of his mouth against hers.

The next thing Brody knew, he was trapping her against the wall of the office, surprised to realize they'd moved from the center of the room. Pushing her against the smooth surface of the wall, he curled his fingers around her right knee and lifted her leg, the spread position giving him room to press against that warm, liquid part of her, grinding the burgeoning ache of his erection against her. He buried his face in the sweet-scented crook between her shoulder and neck, scraping the tender length of her throat with his teeth. Her skin tasted dangerously perfect, and he repeated the primitive action that completely unraveled his control. Before he knew what was happening, the tips of his fangs slipped free, and she gasped, jerking against the heavy press of his body.

He lifted slightly away, and his eyes burned as he watched a thin rivulet of deep crimson slip across the pale perfection of her skin. His beast roared in triumph. He'd scratched her throat, drawn blood, the animal half of his nature longing to throw back its head and howl in victory. A low, thick snarl of possession broke from his mouth, and he leaned down, licking her throat, slowly lapping at the decadent taste of her, aware that his beast was drawing closer and closer to the surface.

Without any conscious direction from his brain, his claws began slipping the skin at the tips of his fingers, and he quickly embedded them in the wall on either side of her head, blood smearing against the white plaster as he gouged its surface.

At the same time, his head spun with the conflicting shouts of beast and man.

Grinding his jaw, he forced himself to take a step back, pressing his palms against her shoulders to hold her away from him—careful not to hurt her with the claws piercing through the tips of his fingers. She stared at him, and Brody knew she was going to fight him. That she wasn't going to accept defeat in whatever twisted game she was playing with his sanity.

And damn but did she play dirty.

Reaching between their bodies, she pressed her palm against the rigid, massive bulge of his cock trapped beneath the fly of his jeans.

"Doucet," he growled, grasping her wrist, careful not to squeeze too hard lest he crush her bone. Undeterred, she simply reached for him with her other hand. Gripping that wrist, as well, Brody squeezed his eyes shut, his voice a fractured whisper of sound as he snarled, "Goddamn it. What the hell do you think you're doing?"

Unwilling to give up without a fight, driven by the blistering need to be close to this man, Michaela leaned forward and pressed her lips against the damp side of his throat, his skin warm and delicious beneath her mouth, his scent the most wonderful thing in the world. "Please, Brody. I want to touch you, learn you. Hold you. Feel you pulse in my hand."

Releasing her wrists, he took hold of her shoulders again, shoving her away from him as he rasped, "What do you want from me?"

"I just—"

"What? You wanna have some fun?" he burst out, the

guttural words forced through his gritted teeth, eyes glowing an unearthly green within the burnished frame of his lashes. "Torture me? Is this to get me back for embarrassing you at Eric's? Are you playing with me? Or am I a charity case, Doucet? Maybe just something to pass the time with? A little walk on the wild side, getting your cut of the danger? It wouldn't be the first time a woman's used me that way, but none of them ever screwed with my head the way you do. *What. The. Hell. Do. You. Want. From. Me?*"

"You…just you," she gasped, her eyes stinging with a hot wash of tears, burning with anger and passion. So many words and explanations crowded against one another in her mind, crashing together like rocks caught in a violent, churning surf.

"I don't want to hurt you, Brody. I just wanted to make you feel good. To make you—"

"I don't need you to fix me," he seethed, the auburn strands of his hair falling around the rugged angles of his face as he stared down at her, looking every bit the part of a fallen angel, tortured and dark and angry.

"Damn it, I don't want to fix you! And I don't want to use you!" she shouted, thumping her fists against his broad chest. "I just want to be close to you! I'm different from those other women. Can't you see that?"

"Yeah, they wanted a piece of me for the danger. I'm betting you just want to try and make me into something that fits in your little picture-perfect world."

"That's not true," she argued, shaking her head, tears leaking from the corners of her eyes as her frustration grew, hot against the back of her throat.

"Like hell it isn't. But I've got news for you, sweetheart. It won't work," he snarled. "I'm not going to pretend to be something I'm not, just to make you feel better. And I'll keep on protecting you without expecting you to pay for it on your back."

"Why do you always have to be so ugly?"

"Might as well fit the personality to the face," he snorted, the corner of his mouth kicking up in a taunting smile, but there was more pain behind his words than sarcasm. And there was no doubt he'd be even angrier if he knew she could see it.

Her heart broke for the hurt she could see in his eyes, but it made her furious to hear the things he said to her—even more so when he kept putting himself down. Her own anger rising with stunning force, her voice shook as she said, "You're an idiot if that's what you really think, Brody. And blind, if you can't see how gorgeous you are. Being a wolf doesn't make you a monster or evil, and scars don't make you unattractive. They only have the power you give them. And as far as the women you've been involved with, I don't know what their problem was. Maybe you just have bad taste, because they sound like a bunch of bitches to me, and stupid ones at that if they weren't smart enough to hold on to you!"

He blinked slowly, as if shocked by her words, his expression closing in on itself, and she could see his shields thickening before her eyes. His face came closer to hers, nose to nose, the angry heat of his breath rushing against her mouth as he spoke. "I'm only going to say this once, so pay attention. Whatever it is you think you're doing, it won't work. You can't come into my life with your laughter and your smiles and make things right. I may be damaged, but it isn't your problem, and there's nothing you can do to change it or make things different."

He stepped back from her, gaze nothing more than a narrow slit, mouth a hard, flat line. "So stop with the damn seduction routine, because I meant what I said, Doucet. You don't have to whore for your safety."

All it took was an instant, and her hand cracked across the side of his face before she'd even realized she was going to do it. She was shocked by her action, but refused to back down as he lifted his hand, fingertips touching the red welt she'd left on his cheek. "What is it, Brody?" she whispered, swiping at the tears spilling down her cheeks, feeling lost in her own skin, as if she didn't even know herself anymore. "Do you always find a way to push away the people who care about you?"

"No one cares about me. Not for long, anyway. Don't you get it?

"You're wrong," she argued in a soft, nearly silent rasp. "You just won't give them a chance."

He turned his back to her then, and she lifted her hand, reaching toward his shoulder. Michaela had never slapped a person in her entire life, not even Ross. And though Brody had been intentionally cruel with his words, she wanted to apologize. But something inside of her choked on the words…her own defenses rising to protect her, and she pulled her hand away. "No one asked you to take this job," she said unsteadily. "When you want me gone, just say the word and I'll be gone."

She turned then and walked out of the room, back down the hall, toward his bedroom. Just before she shut the door behind her, Michaela heard a loud, crunching sound come from inside the office, making her flinch.

With a heartbreaking sense of certainty, she knew that Brody's frustration had finally gotten the better of him.

Chapter 11

Michaela opened her eyes to the misty spill of early-morning sunlight drifting through the bedroom window, her head aching the way it always did when she cried herself to sleep. And yet, it wasn't with a sense of defeat that she faced the new day. Though she'd gone to bed still questioning whether she had the courage to follow her heart, she no longer felt mired in indecision and fear. Oh no. With the refreshing glow of morning sunlight came the knowledge that she was willing to do whatever it took to get what she wanted...what she needed.

No price was too great—not even her pride. Though heartache and bitter disappointment had smothered her as she'd lain down between the crisp, cool sheets of Brody's bed, her dreams had freed her, filled with beauty and tenderness. With visions of Brody and the beautiful green-eyed baby girl, their laughter and smiles stealing her heart. As she rolled over to her back, staring at the sun-dappled ceiling, a sweet, refreshing wash of tears warmed her cheeks against the cool morning air. She knew, using nothing more than the yearning of her heart, that that powerful dream was worth fighting for. That it was meant to be hers. That Brody and the baby girl were *meant* to be hers.

No matter how hard he fought her, she was determined to do whatever it took to become a part of Brody's life—because Michaela wanted that dream to become a reality more than anything in the world. She wanted to hold her and Brody's child in her arms, nuzzle the velvety softness of her cheek and kiss the smooth perfection of her forehead. And in the sweetness of the evening, when their daughter lay down to bed, she wanted to take her man into her arms and hold him, love him, cherish him.

Her man. In all her life, she'd never thought of anyone as hers and hers alone—but he was. She felt it in her bones and her blood, in the very fabric of her soul.

Brody Carter belonged with her.

Drawing in a deep breath that filled her head with his rich, mouthwatering scent, she vowed then and there to see it through. It wasn't a decision she made lightly. If she wanted him, she had to be willing to work for him, to fight and claw and battle, because there was no way he'd make it easy.

Throwing on some jeans and a sweater, Michaela brushed out her long hair and used concealer to hide the dark circles under her eyes which seemed to keep getting darker by the day. As she stepped out of the bedroom, the cabin was silent and still, making her wonder if Brody was still sleeping. She tiptoed down the hallway and peeked into his study through the door that had been left ajar. Her breath caught at the vision he made, his long body sprawled out across the chocolate-colored sofa, his auburn hair gleaming against the rich luster of the soft leather. The only clothing he wore was a faded pair of jeans that molded his hard thighs, the top two buttons undone. He had his face turned away from her, one hand low on his bare abdomen, lying across the drool-worthy cut of his abs. The knuckles of that hand were swollen and bruised—evidence of the fact that he'd lost his temper the night before after she'd run out on him. Sure enough, there was a fist-sized hole in the drywall on the far side of the room.

Pulling her hot gaze back to Brody, Michaela stared for a breathless eternity, it seemed, wanting so badly to walk into the room, kneel down beside him and press her lips to that shadowy vee in the open fly of his jeans. Feel the heat of his skin against her lips, the musk of his sex, salty and warm, filling her head with each breath. She'd lap at his skin with her tongue, his low grumble of pleasure telling her he was waking up, the hard, blatant ridge of his cock pressing against the denim proof of his hunger, his desire, his need.

Then she'd release those last remaining buttons, and take that hard, massive part of him deep into her mouth, showing him how much she wanted him, how badly she wanted to make him writhe and moan. Make him feel good, wanted… even loved.

For a moment, her fingers tightened on the soft white finish of the door, but then she slowly released her grip and stepped away, shaking her head as she stared down at her sneakers. She couldn't do it. Not yet. She knew he still wasn't ready. Knew, without a shadow of a doubt, that he'd only reject her again.

To get what she wanted, she was going to have to tread carefully, with as much caution as determination. And she needed answers, needed insight into the enigma that was Brody Carter.

Luckily, she knew just where to get them.

Sitting at the Dillingers' breakfast table, Michaela took another comforting sip of tea and thought over what she'd learned from her best friend. While Mason worked with the others outside, setting up chairs for the wedding that was to take place later that evening, Torrance had told her what she knew about Brody's past relationships. In short, there hadn't been many. One-night stands with nameless, meaningless women—except for one. And the story behind that relationship finally explained why Brody was the only Runner who didn't get along with Dylan Riggs.

According to what Torrance had learned from Mason, Brody had been involved with Dylan's younger sister, Jenny Riggs, the year before. Though Jenny rarely spent time in Shadow Peak, preferring to live with her mother's birth pack in upstate Virginia, she had come down to stay the summer with her brother while she worked on her painting. She'd dated Brody in secret, finally breaking up with him when her brother had found out about the relationship. It seemed that while Brody was good enough for her to fool around with, Jenny had been embarrassed by the idea of the town finding out about her involvement with a Bloodrunner. She'd dumped him, left Maryland and never looked back.

Though it made her own jealous streak burn hot, Brody's experience with Jenny Riggs explained a lot about his resistance to a relationship with her. Michaela could have pressed Torry for information about Jenny all day long, wondering what she was like—but they were short on time and Brody's past relationships had been only one of the questions she had for her best friend. Speaking softly to keep from being over-heard, Michaela had then asked Torrance to tell her about a Lycan bite. While there was still a lot Torrance had to learn about the Lycan way of life, she was able to explain that a bite between mates created a powerful type of metaphysical link called a blood bond. The bond formed a deeper connection between the couple, to the point that it could even be used to help pinpoint the location of a mate. However, when a Lycan bit a human who wasn't his mate, it would result in his or her turning, as it had with Max, whether the Lycan was in his wolf or human form at the time.

Since Michaela had no intention of turning Lycan, she was going to need to be clear about whether or not she was Brody's mate before she begged him to bite her again. And she had been ready to beg. For some reason, whenever he touched her, the thought of his fangs sinking into her throat became incredibly arousing, adding a deeper layer to the hunger that coursed through her veins.

Of course, she also couldn't help but wonder about the fact that he'd obviously wanted to bite her. Did that mean that Brody's urge was born from a deeper need to bond her to him, because she was his mate?

Oh God. The thought made her pulse ramp up to breath-taking speed, her head feeling light as she sat at the table, waiting for Torrance to return. Her best friend had gone to answer the knocking at the cabin's front door, thinking it would be Jillian with some last-minute tasks. However, when Torrance walked back into the kitchen, she didn't have the pack's beautiful, golden-haired Spirit Walker with her. Instead, the visitor was an older Lycan, most likely in her early seventies, her auburn hair pulled back in an elegant French twist.

Torrance shot her an anxious *what-the-hell-is-going-on* kind of look as she stepped into the room, the guest coming in just behind her. Staring straight at Michaela with penetrating green eyes, the woman asked, "Do you know who I am?"

"Yes," Michaela rasped, keeping a careful grip on her teacup, making sure it didn't rattle as she set it down and came to her feet. "You're Brody's grandmother."

"That's right," the Lycan murmured, taking a seat across from her at the table. "I'm Abigail Carter."

"Your grandson is still sleeping, Ms. Carter," Michaela murmured, beginning to step away from the table, "but if you don't mind waiting, I can get him for you."

"No, no, that's all right. Take a seat, child." She waited for Michaela to sit down once again, making no secret of studying her with a critical eye, declining Torrance's offer of coffee or tea. After flashing her an encouraging smile, Torrance moved to the sink, where a mass of flowers had been left, and began trimming the stems. At the same time, Abigail Carter folded her hands on the gleaming surface of the table, saying, "There's no need to fetch my grandson. I'm sure he'd only refuse to talk with me anyway. No, it's you I came to see. I'd hoped to catch you like this, without Brody near, so that we could talk for a moment."

Warily, Michaela asked, "Why would you want to talk with me?"

The woman's expression remained as closed as her grandson's, giving nothing away, but there was a tightness around her eyes that suggested she wasn't quite as relaxed as she was trying to appear. Michaela threw out the soft net of her power, but caught nothing, a surge of frustration flaring as she realized she couldn't read this woman any more than she could read Brody.

Answering her question, Abigail said, "I've heard the rumors of what transpired at your brother's *Novitiate's* ceremony. Dreadful stuff, really. I don't know why the pack is so stubborn in its desire to support Stefan Drake, but then we often hold on to the idea that we find most comforting. It's easier for them to believe that the Runners' accusations are false, saving them the humiliation of admitting that they've allowed themselves to be led by a racist fanatic. But I'm afraid they won't open their eyes to the truth until it's too late. In that regard, I'm not so different."

"But from what you've just said," Michaela murmured, "you're clearly not one of Drake's followers."

"I'm not speaking about Drake, Ms. Doucct. But my grandson."

Frowning, Michaela shook her head. "I'm afraid I don't understand."

Abigail sent her a meaningful look, while a low vein of laughter vibrated her slight frame. "You're a beautiful girl, Michaela, but you couldn't tell a lic to save your life. You know exactly what I'm talking about. Let's not be coy. I'm too old and the topic is too important."

"Very well," she said, her temper flaring as she thought of all the heartache this woman had caused in Brody's young life, at a time when he'd needed her love and comfort. "If you want honesty, here it is. I'm wondering what possible interest you could have in your grandson, Ms. Carter. Brody has spoken of the upbringing he received at your hands."

"And?" Abigail asked, her voice slightly softer than before.

"And it was so cold," she explained, anger causing her own voice to shiver, "I'm surprised to see you're a flesh-and-blood woman, and not made of ice."

At the sink, Torrance made a sharp, choking sound of surprise, and Michaela knew she'd shocked her with her bluntness. She had been raised to always show respect to her elders, but the protective streak she felt where Brody was concerned made her so angry, it was all she could do not to stand up and demand to know why the woman had been such a coldhearted bitch. She thought she might have, too—if it weren't for the memory of Meredith's words to Brody, reminding her that there was a good chance Abigail had finally come to her senses and had a change of heart.

"I suppose I deserve that," the Lycan murmured, the corner of her mouth twisting with a self-deprecating smile. "God knows I've made my share of mistakes. And you've got fire, girl, which is just what he needs. He had that fire as a child, brimming with heat and emotion, and I chilled that in him. Taught him how to bury it all inside, until he learned the lesson even better than I'd hoped."

"So you don't deny that you were cold to him? That you withheld the love and comfort he so desperately needed?"

"I'm too old to waste time denying my mistakes. I was tough on him, I know. But after what happened to my son, I wanted to make Brody strong. Make him hard enough to stand on his own."

"And did you also set out to teach him that he wasn't worthy of a woman's love?"

Abigail shook her head wearily, the early-morning sunlight glinting off dark red hair so similar to Brody's. "An unfortunate consequence that I hadn't planned on, but then we rarely see things clearly while we're living them. It's only hindsight that gives us such a clear, painful picture of our errors. I thought I was protecting him from making the same mistakes as his father. He learned the lesson too well, though, and I've feared he'd always be alone," she confessed softly, before a small smile curled the corner of her mouth. "And yet, from what I've heard, it seems that you've managed to break through his armor."

Michaela lifted her chin. "Only because I refuse to let him scare me away."

"Like I said, you've got fire, girl. And I'm glad. It's what Brody needs, someone who'll shake that infernal reserve of his. Unlike his father, Brody has chosen well. And hopefully he'll learn to follow his heart before it's too late."

Her anger softening, Michaela said, "It's not too late for you, either, Ms. Carter."

"Perhaps, perhaps," Abigail murmured with a wistful expression as she rose to her feet. "But now I must be on my way. Enjoy the wedding, ladies. If my grandson is half the man I believe him to be, I have a strong feeling it won't be long before the Alley hosts another wedding. And this time, I expect to be invited."

With those softly spoken words, Abigail walked out of the kitchen, leaving both Michaela and Torrance staring quietly at the archway, their expressions mirroring their surprise.

"Are you going to tell Brody she was here?" Torrance finally asked.

"I…I don't think so, *chère*. Not yet. I want to see what Abigail does. If she's serious about wanting a relationship with Brody, then she can make the next move. Telling me what she wants and actually doing it are two different things."

Picking up her teacup, she carried it to the counter, adding, "It may sound heartless, but I'm more worried about Brody than her. He doesn't deserve to be played with."

Sighing, Torrance placed a comforting hand on Michaela's shoulder. "I agree. And I'll go ask Mase to tell the others to stay quiet about her visit."

After waking up in his office, Brody had swung his legs over the side of the chocolate leather sofa, hung his head between his shoulders and braced his elbows on his knees. For endless moments, he'd struggled to get his breathing back under control, the strangest dream he'd ever had still screwing with his mind. A disturbingly tender, heartwarming dream of him and Michaela sitting on a blanket in the middle of a field, playing with a baby girl who had looked just like her mother, but for the bottle-green eyes that had stared up at him with such joyful delight, it made his chest hurt.

He didn't know where in God's name the images had originated from, the thought of his own child as alien to him as the idea of walking on the surface of the moon. He'd just accepted as fact that it would never happen in his lifetime, so what was the point in wishing for it? But the dream had been so crisp, so clear, the little girl's laughter filling his ears, making him smile, while Michaela had sat beside them, staring at them with the most powerful look of love; he'd felt like the luckiest bastard alive.

Where had it come from? He ground his jaw, wondering if the damn woman had bewitched him…put a spell on him.

His mood, already slipping into foul, hadn't improved when he'd failed to find Michaela in his cabin, unable to believe he'd been so angry the night before he'd forgotten to set the security system. Panic had ripped at him with deep, gouging force as he ran out of his front door, not even bothering with his shirt and shoes. He'd run into Cian first thing, who was setting up the tables and chairs for Jeremy and Jillian's wedding. His partner had arched his brow when he saw him, then silently pointed at the Dillingers' cabin, a slow, knowing grin curving one corner of his mouth, a cigarette perched in the other. Snarling under his breath, Brody had set off for the cabin, finding Michaela laughing in the kitchen with Torrance, Jillian and her younger sister, Sayre, the women busy as they arranged the centerpieces for the wedding tables.

Riding the hard edge of fear and fury, he'd ripped into her for leaving the cabin without waking him. After the threat they'd received along with Pippa's scalp, he'd told her he expected her to be smart enough to know that she stayed by his side at all times. He'd expected her to snarl back, giving as good as she got, but instead she'd only smiled at him and apologized for making him worry, her mood as calm and poised as his was fractured and raw. And it didn't improve from there.

Now, with the wedding over and the celebration well under way, Brody sat at the head table, his jacket draped over the back of his chair, watching Michaela talk with Torrance while they stood beside one of the elegant fire pots that had been placed among the tables to provide warmth for the guests. Reluctantly, he admitted to no one but himself that fear for her safety accounted for only part of his foul mood. The other came from the fact that he wanted her all to himself, jealous of everyone she talked to, smiled at, danced with. Of the wineglass that touched her lips, the soft, navy-blue silk of the dress that draped so sensually over her body. He wanted to be the only thing covering her skin, warming her with his heat, with the hard press of his flesh against hers.

Frustrated with himself, he wondered if it was the romantic setting making him so on edge…so restless. Brody had only been to a handful of weddings in his lifetime, but he knew enough to understand that, like Torrance and Mason's two weeks before, Jeremy and Jillian's ceremony had been special. He was hardly the sentimental type, but he'd sensed the wave of emotion overcoming the guests as the bride and groom had exchanged their vows. Jeremy's deep voice had been husky, the reverent look in his eyes as he stared at his stunning bride enough to make the single men shift uncomfortably, while the women had swiped at their tears. It was obvious the couple loved each other to distraction, and after a decade of bitter heartache and separation, even Brody had to admit that it was wonderful to finally see them so happy.

Pushing one hand back through his hair, he tried to pull his gaze away from Michaela—but he couldn't do it.

As if she could feel the press of his eyes on her, she turned her head, a slow, siren smile curving across that beautiful, fantasy-inspiring mouth. She'd been smiling at him like that all day and night, driving him wild, making him so hungry he was amazed he'd been able to hold it together for as long as he had. He wanted so badly to take what she was offering, no longer caring if she was using him or not.

But what about the bite? Would he be able to resist? Christ, he didn't know. The only thing he knew with any sense of certainty was that the night had worn him down to his last nerve—and watching her share a dance with Dylan a few minutes earlier hadn't helped.

Monroe, who had been having a blast playing DJ, put on a slow jazz piece with a deep, heavy rhythm of alto saxophone. Taking the empty seat at Brody's side, Mason stretched out his long legs under the table, a lazy smile on his face as he looked out over the dancing couples. Mason's father, Robert, had asked Torrance to dance and was now playfully twirling her around and around, her long red hair streaming behind her as her laughter filled the air. And on the other side of the makeshift dance floor, the bride and groom danced so close together their noses were nearly touching as they gazed dreamily into each other's eyes. Everywhere he looked, guests were enjoying themselves. All but Pullaton, who was taking his turn patrolling the woods, ensuring no one came near the Alley with the intention of causing trouble.

Sighing, Mason took a long sip of his champagne, then said, "How are you holding up?"

Brody grunted under his breath as he watched Cian approach Michaela and ask for a dance. They moved together onto the parquet dance floor, the evening wind blowing her long curls until they wrapped around Cian's shoulder, and the tall Runner took her into his arms, both of them dark-haired and gorgeous, like something off the cover of a goddamn magazine.

In all the years that they'd been friends, since Cian had come to live with the Silvercrest, Brody had never been jealous of him—until this moment. For the first time, he now coveted his partner's effortless charm, his perfect good looks. It was as if nature were playing a bad joke on them all, singling Michaela out as his mate, instead of the handsome Irishman's. And yet, he knew there was no way he would ever let Cian have her.

"Michaela looks like she's having a good time," Mason murmured.

Softly, he snarled, "I'm going to take Cian apart if he doesn't get his hand off her ass."

"That's her back, not her ass," Mason snorted, before saying, "We need to talk."

Brody scowled. If he got a lecture on being more sociable, he was going to take his drink and dump it over Mason's head. "What about?"

Leaning forward to set his empty champagne glass on the table, Mason quietly said, "I talked to Dylan before the ceremony. He didn't want to say anything in front of everyone and ruin things for Jeremy and Jillian, but he had news, and none of it was good. The first thing he told me was that Drake is pressing for a vote to rescind Jillian's position, just as we'd expected. He thinks the League could call the meeting any day now."

"Nice wedding present," Brody sneered, his contempt for the League hardening the edges of his speech. "We'll have to stand with her and Jeremy when it happens. Offer our support."

"I agree," Mason sighed. "And believe it or not, his second bit of news was even worse. They found Pippa's body just before he got here."

He scrubbed his hands down his face, cursing under his breath. "Where was she?"

"Out by the old mill. She'd been staked to a tree, the word *traitor* carved into her stomach with a set of claws."

"Shit," he muttered, rubbing at the knots of tension in the back of his neck.

"Yeah, it was pretty bad," Mason grated, slanting him a dark look from the corner of his eye. "From what Dylan was told, sounds like she was covered with bite marks. I think they killed her as slowly and painfully as possible."

Leaning forward in his chair, Brody braced his elbows on his spread knees, his gaze finding Michaela as she danced through another song with his partner. "They obviously killed her because she talked to Jeremy," he said grimly.

"That's what I explained to Dylan, since we hadn't told him yet that it was Pippa who talked."

"Speaking of Dylan," Brody rumbled, "he looks rough as hell tonight."

"Yeah, I'm worried about him," Mason admitted. "It's not like him to show up to something like this without a woman on his arm, but who knows. I've already warned him twice tonight to let up on the liquor, which isn't like him, either. Maybe it's just the stress getting to him. I think he's been burning the candle at both ends."

"Maybe," he grunted, but as he cut his gaze to the haggard-looking Elder slouched against the side of Jeremy's cabin, silently watching the couples dance, Brody found himself wondering if it wasn't something more.

Chapter 12

The towering flames of the nearby fires warmed the night, while zigzagged strings of overhead lights glinted above their heads like shimmering stars as Michaela danced with Cian, the Irishman's tall, muscled body moving in perfect rhythm with hers. She enjoyed dancing with him, as much as she could enjoy dancing with any man who wasn't Brody—and Brody hadn't asked her. Cian was sinfully dark and beautiful, but he didn't make her heart race. Instead, she felt comfortable with Brody's partner, as if he were someone she could become great friends with.

Smiling up at the grinning Irishman, Michaela kept her voice soft as she said, "Thanks for asking me to dance. When Torrance partnered up with Robert, I was afraid Dylan was going to come over and ask me again."

"Don't you like Dylan?" he rasped, gazing down at her

with pale gray eyes that looked almost silver beneath the thick black fringe of his lashes.

Lifting her shoulder, she tried to explain. "I have no reason *not* to like him. It's just…there's something about him that puts me on edge."

He was silent for a moment, then said, "Is it something you're picking up from him, using your power?"

"No," she admitted, feeling foolish for even saying anything. "Dylan's one of those that I've never been able to get a read on."

"Hmm," he murmured, the corner of his mouth curling with a slow, contemplative smile. "Then it's probably just Brody's dislike for him rubbing off on you."

"I knew there was no love lost between them," she told him, lowering her gaze to his chin, lest her eyes reveal more of her feelings than she intended, "but it wasn't until this morning that I learned the reason."

"The Jenny story isn't a pretty one." Cian sighed, taking her into another slow spin as the sultry notes of a jazz song filled the nighttime air. "I was afraid he was going to let it screw up his life forever, but then you came along, and at just the right time, I think. I've never seen Brody so focused on a woman, not even when he was dating Jenny. With her, he always had his standard cool, calm control. And, lass, that's something that he's sure as hell never had around you. It's about time a woman came along who could shake him up."

Michaela rolled her eyes. "You make me sound like an earthquake."

A low, husky chuckle rumbled deep in his chest. "I think you're just what he needs. Whatever you do, sweetheart, don't give up on him. I know it won't be easy, but just listen to your heart, as my mother would always say. It will lead you where you need to go."

Michaela started to smile, when suddenly there was a touch on her bare shoulder, and she flinched, a clammy sensation of dread spreading over her skin. She knew, without turning, whose hand touched her, just as she knew it was going to lead to a scene. Casting an uneasy look up at Cian, she saw that his sharp gaze was focused on the man standing behind her.

"I'm cutting in," Dylan Riggs slurred, his slow speech betraying the fact that he'd hit the open bar one too many times that night.

"Not now, Dylan," the Irishman murmured in a low voice, obviously sharing her same opinion.

"You've had your turn, Irish," the Elder countered.

"And you've already had yours." Despite the casual tone of his voice, the Runner's words were cut with steel. "Let it go."

"You know, I'm getting damn tired of being told what to do tonight," Dylan growled, stepping closer, until Michaela could feel his heat against her back, the cut of her dress leaving too much of her skin exposed to his touch. With a sickly sensation in the pit of her stomach, she felt one of the fingers of his other hand trail lightly down the line of her spine as he rasped, "So be careful what you say."

"If you don't like being lectured," Cian warned him, the lilting burr of his accent thickening, "then maybe you should stop acting like a bloody child."

The hand on her shoulder tightened, fingers digging into her skin with bruising force. Determined to avoid a confrontation in the middle of the wedding reception, Michaela ignored the sting of Dylan's grip and bit her tongue to keep from crying out, but it was already too late. From her left came a deep, furious rumble as Brody snarled, "What the hell do you think you're doing, Riggs?"

"Just planning on enjoying the pleasure of the Cajun's company tonight," Dylan drawled. "You got a problem with that, Carter?"

What happened after that was nothing but a frenzied, chaotic jumble of images and sounds as Michaela found herself forced against Cian's hard chest at the same time Brody crashed into Dylan, slamming him onto a nearby table stocked with plates and glasses of champagne.

"Son of a bitch," Cian hissed, moving her to his side with a protective arm as Dylan swung at Brody, clipping him on the side of his mouth, just before Brody countered with a driving right that slammed into the Elder's nose. Blood spurted, covering the snowy-white shirt beneath Dylan's tuxedo jacket, while more blood poured from his left hand, drenching his sleeve. Broken shards from the shattered champagne glasses glittered against the table's surface, accounting for the cut on Dylan's hand.

"Stay back," Cian ordered her, stepping forward as more punches were exchanged. Michaela assumed the Irishman would break up the fight, but it was Mason who suddenly took action, hauling Brody off of Dylan. The Runner trapped Brody against the front of his body, pinning his arms behind his back.

"What the hell is your problem?" Mason snarled in Brody's ear, while around them everyone drew closer, trying to hear what was being said.

His chest heaving as he glared at Dylan, who was slowly pulling himself off the table, Brody grunted, "Get off me, Mase. The bastard was asking for it."

"Jesus, Brody, get a grip," Mason snapped. "It isn't like you to go around acting like a jealous ass."

"He was hurting her," Brody growled, jerking out of Mason's hold, his angry gaze cutting to Michaela's shoulder.

Turning toward Michaela, Mason's eyes narrowed with concern, as well as a thread of confusion when he saw the dark finger marks against her pale skin. "Are you okay?"

"It's…nothing," she whispered.

"Dylan?" Mason said carefully, looking back toward his friend, his brows pulled together in a deep vee over the shadow of worry in his eyes.

But the Elder averted his gaze to the white dinner napkin he'd wrapped around his cut hand, the linen drenched with blood from the seeping wound. Stepping to his side, Jillian reached for his hand. "You had better let me look at that."

"Forget it," he grunted, jerking his arm away from her, while a strange expression shadowed the lean angles of his face. "I'm fine."

Frowning, Jillian said, "I don't mind, Dylan. Really."

"I said forget it!" He took a deep, shuddering breath, then more calmly said, "You've got better things to do on your wedding night than worry about this. I'll be fine."

"You should let her heal it," Jeremy offered quietly, eyeing Dylan with a quizzical gaze, as if he wasn't quite sure what or who he was looking at.

"I don't need you to be my goddamn mother," Dylan snapped, releasing another quaking breath. Cutting his gaze back to Jillian, he muttered, "Sorry for the scene." Then he turned and walked away.

Almost at once, the entire group of onlookers seemed to release a collective sigh of relief.

"I'm sorry, Michaela," Mason murmured, rubbing the back of his neck as he turned her way, his ruggedly handsome face etched with deep lines of strain. "He's a good man. I think the stress of the past few weeks is just getting to him."

"It's more than that," Brody argued, pulling his ruined shirt off, balling it up, and wiping his face with it, the corner of his mouth bleeding from one of Dylan's punches. "Open your eyes. The guy's coming apart at the seams."

"What are you suggesting?" Mason demanded, narrowing his eyes.

"I don't know. I just…I don't think we can avoid facing the facts. If Drake's accomplice *is* another Elder, then Dylan could be the one."

"Just because you can't stand Dylan doesn't mean anyone else shares your opinion. He's our friend, Brody. Not a killer." Slanting a meaningful look at Michaela, Mason growled, "And all things considered, I would have thought you were getting past old issues and grudges."

"I may not like him," Brody ground out in a voice like gravel, "but that doesn't mean I'd point the finger at him for no reason. You guys are blind if you can't see he's been acting strange as hell."

"He's under a lot of pressure," Mason grimaced. "Like we all are."

"Just don't let friendship cloud your perspective," Brody rasped, his auburn hair brushing against the golden sheen of his powerful shoulders as the wind picked up, surging around them.

"And don't let hatred cloud yours," Mason countered.

"He wouldn't let Jillian heal him," Brody pointed out, and Michaela knew he was thinking of the fact that the pack's

Spirit Walker could see into the minds of those she used her power to heal.

"And Michaela can't read him," Cian added, rubbing his palm against the hard set of his jaw as he entered the argument.

"From what I've heard, she can't read Brody, either," Mason quietly snarled. "Does that mean we should lock him up in the woodshed and accuse him of being a traitor?"

"Enough!" Reyes finally shouted, obviously deciding to be the voice of reason as she glared at all three men. "In case it escaped your notice, we're in the middle of a celebration. So why don't we save it all for tomorrow, before the three of you start bashing each other's brains in?"

"Carla's right," Torrance whispered, sending an apologetic look toward the wedding couple, who stood a few feet away, Jeremy's strong arms wrapped around his wife's shoulders as she cuddled into his side.

"Christ, I'm sorry," Brody murmured as he sent the newlyweds a flushed look of contrition.

"No worries," Jeremy replied with a wry grin, repeating one of Michaela's favorite sayings. "At least no one will be able to say that the party wasn't exciting."

Some of the guests smothered sharp barks of laughter under their breaths, while others shared worried smiles as they turned back to whatever they'd been doing before the commotion. Monroe put on a new song, and Jeremy pulled Jillian back onto the dance floor for another dance, then Torrance did the same to Mason.

Eyeing his partner's tense posture, Cian murmured, "Why don't you be a doll and take Brody home early, Michaela. See if you can't help calm him down."

"Come on," she whispered, reaching out and taking his

warm hand, surprised that he let her, instead of pulling away. But he looked a million miles away, completely lost in thought as she said, "Let's go, Brody."

She'd just started to lead him toward his cabin, when Pallaton suddenly ran out of the woods, and everyone stiffened in alarm. Panting, the Runner stopped at the edge of the dance floor, jerking his chin toward the thick expanse of forest behind him, and in a low, guttural rasp, he said, "We've got company."

The night was cool, the moon bright within the blue-black stretch of autumn sky, thin clouds stretched across its dark canvas like pulled threads of cotton. Brody and his partner moved with stealthy purpose through the trees, careful to stay downwind, closing in on their prey, while Mason and Pallaton headed in from the other side.

Their differences momentarily put aside, the foursome had immediately moved to investigate, while Jeremy remained behind with his bride, Reyes taking Michaela and those guests who chose to stay to the Dillingers' cabin. While patrolling the perimeter of the Alley, Pall had picked up the scent of a group of ten or more Lycans in their human forms. Considering the threat that had been scrawled across his door the day before, Brody wasn't taking any chances with Michaela's safety. Fully prepared for battle, he and the others had already shifted the top halves of their bodies into wolf form, fangs and claws at the ready.

Unfortunately, the wind shifted as they drew nearer to their prey, allowing the Lycans to pick up the Runners' scents. Mason bellowed a short, sharp howl just to their north, telling them that he and Pallaton were trailing a smaller group that had branched off from the first, most likely retreating in fear.

The rest held steady, about twenty yards in front of them, either too cocky to run, or too stupid.

Personally, with the growing tensions between the pack and the Runners, Brody thought anyone foolish enough to venture near the Alley uninvited must be missing some valuable brain cells. The wind blew stronger, and he finally caught what he'd been looking for. *Dustin.* The flames of a fire could be seen flickering through the trees just ahead, and he and Cian moved in perfect synchronicity as they burst into the small, open patch of land surrounded by the thickness of the forest.

Sitting on a rock on the far side of the small campfire in a T-shirt and jeans, Dustin Sheffield shot them a slick smile, a longneck bottle of beer in one hand, smoldering cigarette in the other. Three of his friends stood behind him, their expressions indolent, though Brody could scent their fear on the air. Unlike Dustin, they were wary of facing off against him and Cian, now that the time had come.

"Well, well, well, if it isn't the legends themselves," Dustin drawled snidely, slowly clapping his hands. "Carter and Hennessey, two of the most bloodthirsty Bloodrunners who've ever existed. Tell me, boys. Exactly how many of your own kind have you murdered in the hopes of one day buying back a place among us?"

His voice roughened by the muzzled shape of his ebony snout, Cian barked a low, gruff burst of laughter. "I get the feeling you don't like us much, Sheffield."

"That's because I don't," the golden-eyed Lycan replied, causing his friends to snicker nervously behind him.

"Good," Cian rasped, his long, sinister fangs glinting white in the flickering firelight. "Because we think you're a sniveling little shit."

Standing, Dustin took a hostile step forward, the flames of the fire casting his young face in a demonic light, as if he were standing at the gates of hell itself. Brody thought it was a fitting analogy, considering he didn't think it would be long before the rogue actually found himself waiting on Lucifer's doorstep. "You can't talk to me like that," Dustin snarled.

"Yeah?" Brody rumbled, just waiting for Dustin to make a move so that he could rip into him. The only thing that kept him from dealing out the punishment Sheffield deserved for attacking Max was the knowledge that if he struck first, the League would deem it an illegal kill and sentence him to death. Not that he was afraid of dying, but he couldn't leave Michaela when it was his job to keep her safe. And just roughing Dustin up a bit wasn't an option, no matter how tempting. No, Brody knew that once he got his claws on the little bastard, he wouldn't stop till he was dead. "Who's gonna stop him, Dusty? Your daddy? Your pals? Sorry, but your daddy's dead, and your buddies are all pissing themselves in fear right now."

"You're forgetting Drake," Dustin murmured, the corner of his mouth kicking up in a taunting smile as he took a slow drag on his cigarette, the gusting breeze whipping his brown hair around the sharp angles of his face.

"You think he really gives a shit about you?" Brody laughed, shaking his head. "Hell, Drake'll probably kill you himself when he's done with you. That is, if I don't get you first."

"Aw, are you still sore about the pretty little Cajun and her brother?" Dustin smirked, exhaling a long stream of smoke. "Look around, Runner. No little lady to worry about protecting now. What'd you do? Leave her back at the Alley all alone?"

Brody took a step forward, and Cian stayed him with one

long, claw-tipped arm across his fur-covered chest. "Don't let him bait you, man. He's just getting worried. Isn't that right, Sheffield? You know, if Drake doesn't kill you, he'll probably just set you up to take the fall for the blondes."

Dustin threw back his dark head, a low, rusty laugh spilling from his lips. "Aw, nice try, Runner. But it won't work. Still, I'll let you in on a secret. I'm not the one you want for the blond little bitches. I'll take the blame for a lot of things, but not those pathetic whores. Too dramatic for my tastes. If I'm going to put myself to the trouble of a good meal," he drawled, his slow smile baring the tips of his fangs, "I expect to enjoy more than just her heart."

"And just whose whores are we talking about?" Cian asked.

The Lycan's mouth curled in a cocky grin. "Wouldn't you like to know, Runner."

"I bet I could make you tell me," Brody rasped, stepping closer, the heat of the fire searing against his fur.

Holding up his hands in a mocking gesture of surrender, the golden-eyed Lycan smirked as he backtracked into the woods. "I'd love to hang around to see what you have in mind, but there's no rest for the wicked. Another time, Runner?"

"You can bet on it," Brody rumbled.

Dustin winked at them, then turned and disappeared with his cohorts into the trees.

Michaela was standing beside the front window of the Dillingers' cabin when the Runners finally returned. She watched as the half wolves came back into the Alley, their sheer size staggering, enough to make fear thicken in your veins. And yet, she wasn't afraid, knowing they used their skill and strength to protect the innocent.

She picked out Brody immediately, his deep ginger fur glinting like blood-red rubies beneath the ethereal glow of the moon, green eyes burning vividly bright as he looked toward the window. He was terrifyingly beautiful, savage and powerful and deadly, and yet, all she wanted was to run to him. She wanted to throw herself against him and sink her fingers into that rich, thick fur, holding him as the shape of his wolf bled away, back into the equally powerful body of the man.

And then she wanted to take him to the ground and rock his world, blow his mind, enslaving him with her feminine wiles.

Snorting under her breath, she shook her head at her foolishness, thinking it was a nice fantasy—but one that didn't have a chance of happening. Despite how people tended to perceive her, she was actually kind of shy when it came to sex, always feeling a bit awkward and nervous, instead of a confident seductress. Still, if she had to learn to seduce Brody, then that's what she'd do. She wasn't going to let him keep fighting her forever.

Who knew? Maybe it wouldn't be so hard after all, considering how wild she went in his strong arms, her natural reserve destroyed beneath the force of her desire.

Moving away from the window, she stepped out onto the front porch, coming down the stairs. As she watched, the Runners allowed the shapes of their wolves to melt away, thick fur giving way to the sun-darkened flesh of man, though their eyes still glowed with preternatural fire. Cian gave her a sly wink, then turned and headed toward his home that sat higher up the glade. Pallaton joined him, the two talking quietly as they walked, while Mason nodded as he passed her on his way to his front door.

Suddenly, Michaela found herself alone with Brody. He

stood fifteen feet away, his broad, muscled chest expanding with his breaths, and she had the strangest feeling that he was drawing in slow, deep pulls of her scent, the sensation as evocative as an explicit touch against her skin. He was so beautiful, it was a physical ache within her body not to rush to him, running her hands over that smooth, bare chest and powerful arms, his skin slick and hot and manly beneath her palms. But she held her ground, aware that she needed to bide her time…tread carefully.

"Don't worry," she whispered when she moved toward him and the rugged lines of his face tightened with apprehension, making his scars more prominent, his eyes narrowed to piercing, cautious green slits. "I won't bother you tonight, Brody. I just want to make sure you're okay."

"Not bother me?" he snorted, shaking his head as she stepped closer to him, the hazy streams of moonlight and slowly dying flames in the fire pits setting the deep auburn silk of his hair afire, as if it were hot to the touch, like his skin. And he was hot. Shifting even closer, she could feel the erotic shock of his heat as it poured off him in waves. "Christ, woman, you bother me just by breathing."

Wanting to make him smile, if only for a moment, she playfully took in a deep breath, holding it with her cheeks dramatically puffed out. He narrowed his eyes on her, looking as if he thought she was crazy, before the sensual curve of his mouth twisted in a crooked smile and he let out a low rumble of laughter. "Come on," he murmured, jerking his chin toward his cabin. "Let's get out of here."

Releasing her held breath, she moved into step beside him. "What did you find?" she asked.

"Just Dustin and some of his gang."

Tension twisted in her stomach like a thousand piercing knives at the thought of Brody in danger. "Did you fight them?"

"Naw," he rumbled, shoving his hands deep in his pockets. "Though I would have liked to take that little shit apart. But he was too chicken to make a move against us. Ended up slinking away with his buddies."

The forest-scented wind blew harder, surging as a thunderstorm crackled far in the distance, and she shivered, suddenly hit by an unsettling sensation, not unlike being touched by a stranger. The rustling of the trees filled the air, but there was a strange current of static buzzing in her head, just for a split second, and then it was gone. Had it been the same as she'd experienced before, or was she simply psyching herself out?

"What's wrong?" Brody asked, and she realized that although he was trying to give the impression of cool nonchalance, he was actually as focused on her as she was on him. So much so that he'd picked up on her telling shiver.

She gave a small, self-conscious laugh. "Nothing. I just…I had the strangest feeling that someone was watching me just now."

"Not surprising. Guys have been watching you all damn night."

"You know that's not what I meant," she sighed, shaking her head.

He stopped for a moment, tilting back his head, nostrils flaring as he breathed deeply. She waited beside him, silent but for the pounding of her heart roaring in her ears, until he lowered his head and resumed walking toward his cabin. "I can't pick up anything. It's probably just Cian peeking out his friggin' front window." Slanting her a dark look, he grunted, "It's not like you weren't all over the guy tonight."

"What?" She breathed out on a soft burst of air, unable to believe what he'd just said. "I hope you're joking, Brody, because that's the most ridiculous thing I've ever heard. I've given you no reason to think I'm interested in any man other than you."

His shoulders stiffened, the bunched muscles in his chest and arms hard with tension. "And facts are facts, Doucet."

"What the hell is that supposed to mean?" she snapped, following him up his porch steps, careful not to twist her ankle in her heels.

"You don't sleep to dream?" he snorted, rolling his shoulder as he hid the side of his face beneath the auburn fall of his hair. "Well, neither do I. I saw how good you and Hennessey looked together tonight, and I'm not the only one."

"God, Brody, he's your friend." Her words were sharp with frustration, the blistering emotion searing through her veins until she wanted to pound her fists against his chest. "And for your information, we were talking about you the entire time we were dancing! You don't need to be jealous!"

"No?" he snarled, turning away from the front door he'd just opened to face her down. The interior of the cabin was shadowed behind him, the only light a muted glow from the kitchen light that had been left on. "God knows you deserve him. You're both too goddamn beau—"

"He's not the one," she gasped, cutting him off, her voice nothing more than a breathless, fleeting wisp of sound.

"The one what?" he grunted, his scent coming stronger… filling her head…making her dizzy with lust and love and this urgent, desperate craving that scorched the inside of her body, her surface so hypersensitive she trembled from nothing more than the sensual warmth of his breath against her skin.

Her face went hot, mouth quivering with emotion. "He's not the one I want. The one I lo—"

Lunging forward, he grabbed her by her upper arms and jerked her off the ground, bringing her face-to-face, eye-to-eye with him. "Do. Not. Say. It," he growled, the guttural words vicious and hoarse, his expression etched with tormented fury, as if he'd been pushed beyond endurance.

"Not. Another. God. Damn. Word."

Chapter 13

"Please," Michaela whispered, unable to give him the silence he'd so desperately demanded. *"I need you."*

He closed his eyes, body tremoring, the roped muscles and lean sinew straining beneath the burnished surface of his skin. She held her breath as she watched his eyes slowly open, the green shining golden and bright, glittering with predatory awareness. He pulled her fully against him, then, and she hovered over the ground, her breasts crushed against the solid heat of his chest, her dress a silken caress between their bodies. When he spoke, his words were guttural and raw, his breath sweet as it pelted her mouth, salty and warm, like his scent. "You win, goddamn it," he seethed, his lips pulling back over his teeth. "You want me at the edge, Doucet? Want to break me down? I'm there, sweetheart. *You. Win.*"

"I don't want to win," she whispered, trying to tell him everything that she felt with her eyes, knowing the words would scare him away. "I just...I just want to be alone with you."

He was all action and quick, violent bursts of movement then, rushing them through the open doorway, inside the cabin. The heavy wooden door slammed behind them, and the shadowed room spun as he took her to the floor right there in the middle of the living room, trapping her beneath his body as he caged her in on his hands and knees. With his auburn hair hanging around the rugged angles of his face, he stared down at her as if she were some rare, breathtaking discovery made in the midst of an Amazonian rain forest, something coveted for aeons, until finally unearthed. He looked as if he were afraid to believe she was real, afraid to believe that the moment was actually happening. "Why are you here, Doucet?" he whispered.

"Because I want you." She reached up to cup the hot side of his face, desperately needing to touch him, but he stopped her. Just before her fingertips made contact, he shifted his weight to one arm and snatched her wrist with his left hand, suddenly trapping it in his hold.

"Please, Brody. Let me touch you," she said huskily, needing to put her hands on him. She wanted to cradle his jaw and stroke her thumb across the ridge of his scars. Wanted to press her palm against his throat and feel the sensual movement as he swallowed, the pulse of his heartbeat, the ragged intake of his breath. Wanted to run her hands over his gorgeous body and experience the shift of all of that hard, mouthwatering muscle rippling with power beneath the sleek heat of his skin.

His eyes narrowed with anger and doubt and something deeper...darker. "Why, Doucet? Out of pity? Charity? Am I so pathetic that you think you can make my life better by lying down for me?"

Her temper flared as he threw the ugly accusation in her face, and a violent surge of frustration had her freeing her wrist and rolling over beneath him, her hands scrambling for purchase on the gleaming hardwood floor as she struggled to crawl away, her legs tangled in the skirts of her dress. Flipping her onto her back again, Brody took hold of both wrists this time, pinning them to the floor as he leaned close, growling, "Where do you think you're going?"

"I'm so tired of you being ugly to me," she shouted up at him, her words broken with emotion. "Every time I'm honest with you, you throw it back in my face. I'm tired of getting slammed for wanting you!"

Brody's pulse roared through his brain, as heavy and violent as the surf in the height of a savage storm, while her angry words echoed through the room, before settling silently into the shadowed corners. "Why?" he groaned, feeling as though the question was being torn out of him. He knew the smart thing to do was get up and run, as far and fast as he could—and yet, he couldn't do it. "Why can't I stay the hell away from you?"

"Because you're watching me," she answered in a soft, husky rasp. He didn't know what she saw in his expression as she stared up at him, but he watched her anger bleed back into desire, the thick weight of her lashes darkening her gaze. Her chest lifted with each of her shallow breaths, the shadowy swell of her cleavage drawing his gaze, begging for the touch of his mouth, the primitive scrape of his teeth.

I'll be the last wolf watching you, Doucet. Brody growled

the possessive words within the safety of his mind, painfully aware that he'd never be able to say them out loud. That he'd grow old with them, replaying them in his mind as he lived off this memory, clutching at it year after year, while his life slowly passed him by.

But he was going to have her. At least for tonight, damn it. He was going to offer her one last out…and if she didn't run, he was going to slake himself on her, feasting on the rich, sensual bounty that was Michaela, layer upon layer of intoxicating, womanly perfection. It required a painstaking physical effort, but Brody managed to release his hold on her, placing his hands on either side of her head, his knees bracketing her thighs. "If you don't want this, you need to run. Right now. Because once it starts, I don't trust myself to be able to stop. I have no control with you."

She blinked up at him, the color in her face burning darker, lips moist and parted and soft. "I don't need you in control. I just need *you,* Brody. I'm not afraid of you."

Ironically, before she'd even finished her hushed confession, the tips of his fingers began bleeding, the razor-sharp claws of his wolf slicing through the callused flesh. His breath hissed through his teeth from the keen sensation, his body feeling everything more intensely with her so close to him…under him, her mouthwatering scent filling his head.

She turned her face, staring at the lethal claws that could so easily hurt her, and he waited, breath held, for the look of horror to fall over her face…for the cry of fear to break from that beautiful, passion-red mouth. But as always with this woman, she took what he knew as reality and turned it on its head. "You're beautiful," she whispered, her gaze shifting back to his face, her eyes liquid and soft as she visually traced the slashing lines of the scars. "Every part of you. You don't scare me, Brody."

His fingers flexed in reaction, claws digging deeply into the wooden floor, creating a sharp, screeching hiss of sound that cut across the sensual canvas of their breaths like nails down a chalkboard. "I *should* scare you," he growled. "You stay, you're going to be under me all night, and it isn't going to be easy or sweet or nice."

I don't want easy, Michaela thought, so turned on, she felt as if she were going to melt into a puddle of boneless, lust-thick need beneath him. "I wouldn't expect it to be any of those things," she murmured, while the corner of her mouth curled with a slow, sensual smile. "All I want is for it to be real, Brody. For you to let go and take me in whatever way that you want."

"You don't know what you're asking for," he warned in a gritty rasp, but she could see his excitement, the hope that he was so afraid to feel. The vulnerable look in his eyes tore at her, making her want to wrap him up in tenderness as much as she wanted to hear him cry out in passion.

"I know what you are, what you're capable of," she whispered. "I may not be able to read you, but I know you wouldn't hurt me."

"You don't know jack, Doucet," he muttered, shaking his head. "But this is your last chance. Are you running? Or staying?"

Reaching up to curl her hand around the side of his strong, tanned throat, she said, "I'm not running, Brody. I'd like to see you just try and get rid of me."

A ghost of a smile twisted the corner of his mouth at her

words, and she could feel his pulse hammering against her palm, the heat of his skin so intense, she should have felt blistered from the contact. He leaned closer, his breath warm against her mouth. Just before their lips touched, she heard herself ask, "You're not worried about my power?"

His eyes burned, the green brilliant and bright within the heavy fringe of his dark lashes, his auburn hair falling around his face like a blood-red veil of silk, beautiful and thick. "No, I'm not worried about your power," he told her in a deep, velvet-rough voice graveled by need. "This time, when you break, Doucet, you'll be feeling too much—coming too hard—to have time to go messing around in my head."

"Mon dieu," she whispered in response, pulse beating wildly in the pale base of her throat, mesmerizing him.

She was flushed with desire, her eyes heavy, bluer than he'd ever seen them. Wanting her with a primitive violence that shook him, Brody finally touched his mouth to hers, tasting the sweetness of her lower lip with the tip of his tongue. She arched beneath him, her low moan vibrating through him, and with a hard growl, he opened his mouth over hers. Then he took, he possessed, he claimed. There was no other word for it. It was too carnal to be kissing, too urgent to be passion. It was need in its most primitive form, hungry and violent and consuming.

Desperate to touch her, he retracted his claws and curled his fingers over the bodice of her dress, then wrenched, ripping the fabric until the top half split down the middle. The creamy perfection of her breasts spilled out, skin as smooth and pale as a pearl, topped with berry-red nipples that beckoned for his touch. Her back arched violently at the first stroke of his tongue against one tight, hardened tip, the sensual flavor of her skin too good to resist, until he had to take her deeper into his mouth. And with every hungry, desperate pull, every slow, tasting lick, he pulled the ecstasy up from deep inside her, following the cues of her body, soaking up her responses, feeling as if he'd been made for this—for the heady, breathtaking purpose of giving her pleasure.

With his wolf seething in hunger, prowling beneath his skin, Brody moved from breast to breast, nuzzling and suckling and lapping with a hungry avidity that he couldn't control, couldn't temper, until her nails were embedded in his biceps, body writhing against the floor, long midnight curls spread out around the flushed perfection of her face. She was all luminous silk and rosy softness, the provocative, intoxicating scent of need growing hotter on her skin, stronger, until he couldn't hold back.

He wanted to savor her, to saturate his starved senses for hours on end, but his need, his craving, for this one beautiful, fiery woman was too great.

Ripping his mouth from the sensual bounty of her breasts, Brody shifted back on his knees and clutched slippery handfuls of her gown, wrenching it up and out of his way. Staring down at her, there was a heart-stopping moment where her beauty actually frightened him—her body so pale and radiant in the soft light, lush breasts bared to his smoldering gaze, nothing more than a tiny midnight-blue patch of silk covering her mound, legs deliciously long, tipped by sexy heels that strapped around her delicate ankles. The vision was so devastatingly erotic, he felt as if something important were going to snap inside his brain from the sexual overload, like a circuit breaking.

Shaking with hunger and the most sharp-edged excitement he'd ever known, he pressed his knees between her legs, forcing her to open for him. Unable to wait a moment longer, he took hold of the thin strips of silk that held the panties on her hips, and ripped, tossing the ruined lingerie to the side. Then he curled his hands behind her knees and pushed them high and wide, completely exposing that most exquisite, intimate part of her, the tender folds wet with desire, glistening and candy pink, so beautiful he wanted to throw back his head and howl. The only thing that kept him from doing just that was the fact he wanted to taste her even more. Wanted to bury his face against her sweet, delectable flesh and make love to her with his mouth. With his lips and tongue and the gentle edge of his teeth.

Before she could shy away from him or tell him no, he settled his broad shoulders between her thighs, shoving them deliciously wide, and touched his tongue to her. She was unbelievably sweet, warm…wet. Good enough to eat, which was exactly what he'd planned for.

"You're beautiful, Doucet," he whispered, the low words lust-thick and gritty. Then he lapped his way through the tender, silken folds, curling around the thrumming heat of her swollen little clit, feeling her heartbeat pulse against his tongue. She cried out, and he did it again…and again… learning her, taking as much pleasure from the explicitly carnal act as he gave. Cursing hotly under his breath, he growled, "Tastes too damn good," and then he closed his mouth over her, slipping his tongue deep inside, and hungrily thrust it into the lush, clutching depths of her body, unable to get enough. He turned his face one way, then another, thumbs holding her wide, so that he could get to all of her. Like water rushing up from a well, he could feel it building, the growing climax pulling her body tighter…and tighter, until she finally crashed into that star-studded, infinite stretch of keening, thrashing pleasure, her husky, choppy cries filling the air while her body arched, the heels of her shoes gouging into the floor as she grabbed his hair and pushed herself against him.

His wolf silently snarled in primal, visceral victory, and while she broke against his mouth, the sweetest, most perfect thing he'd ever tasted, Brody worked furiously at his pants with his right hand. Buttons ripped, scattered across the floor, the aching weight of his cock surging thickly into the damp heat of his palm. It had always been difficult for a woman to take his full length, seldom actually happening—and despite how wet she was, Michaela was tiny and tight. Deliciously so. He told himself he had to go easy, but as he moved over her, jaw locked, body hot and painfully hard, every muscle from his neck to his calves tensed in savage anticipation, and fit the heavy head of his cock against her—he lost it.

Her breath caught as he surged heavily into her, stretching her, her body closing around him like an endlessly soft, silken fist, and an animal sound broke from his chest, low and deep and scary as hell. He blinked the sweat from his eyes, panicked, knowing she was going to tell him to get off her.

Only…she didn't. Instead, she raised her knees, hugging his hips, and sobbed, *"Brody! Please…more."*

Shaking with amazement and relief, a low, wicked rumble of laughter surged past his lips, and he pressed deeper, loving the way her eyes went wide as he gave her another thick inch. Loving the way her mouth parted, teeth stunningly white against the dark stain of color in her lips. Loving everything about her.

And then he started to move…and it broke him down.

That perfect feeling of burying more and more of himself inside her, until she'd taken all of him, every inch of his cock buried up into her warm, clutching depths. Christ, there was no way to hold himself together. With a primitive snarl, he opened his mouth over hers, swallowing her sharp cry of surprise when he pulled back, then slammed at her harder, putting all his strength, all his hunger behind it, driving into her the way he'd fantasized about doing since the moment he'd first met her, each heavy thrust sweeter than the last.

And in the midst of the maddening pleasure, Brody felt his beast raise its head, sniffing at the ripe, sweet scent of her…and demand its satisfaction. His fangs slipped his gums, piercing and hot, tongue heavy within his mouth, his body readying itself to make the bite that would claim her as his own.

Growling, he screwed his eyes closed and stiffened his arms, levering himself away from her. He turned his face to the side, grinding his jaw, anything to keep from giving in to that blistering, blinding urge, knowing it was wrong. All wrong—for him and for her. She'd be terrified…angry. And he'd spend the rest of his life in misery, drowning in guilt.

Keep it together, jackass.

Brody concentrated on his heartbeat, on the roar of his pulse—and held still, buried hot and thick inside of her, while her muscles fluttered around him in an endless, breathtaking caress that felt better than anything he'd ever imagined. And through the hazy fog of urgent, animalistic hunger, he heard her calling his name. At first it came soft and fleeting, as if she were far away, but then it gradually grew louder, until she was shouting up at him, demanding his attention.

"Brody, look at me!" she pleaded, arching beneath him, her

cool hands stroking his chest, the tight tendons in his throat, the tensed muscles in his arms.

"Can't," he growled, his deep voice a guttural slash of sound, more wolf than man.

"I won't turn away from you, Brody. I know what you are, and I'm not afraid. You can be yourself with me," Michaela struggled to explain, the intensity of his possession making it difficult to put her thoughts into words. "You...don't have to be afraid."

And yet, he was. She could sense his fear as his wolf struggled to break free. Could see it in the glittering, oddly glowing light in his eyes as his lashes lifted and he warily turned to stare down at her, the sharp tips of white fangs just visible beneath the sensual curve of his upper lip. Clutching his face in her hands, she held him with her gaze, unwilling to let him look away—knowing that no matter how badly he wanted it, he wouldn't bite her. Not yet. Not tonight. "Stay with me, Brody. It's okay. Please don't turn away from me. I trust you."

Then she pulled his face close to hers and she kissed him, slipping her tongue between the dangerous points of his canines, and he growled into her mouth, the predatory sound tasting as sexy as it sounded. She couldn't get enough of him. He was addictive, hot and musky and so wonderfully male. He made her feel fragile and feminine, and she loved it. Loved knowing that she'd brought him to this sharp precipice of control. It was a dark, forbidden kind of knowledge, like Eve reaching for the sin-cursed apple—and she knew she wouldn't have had him any other way.

Michaela ran her palms down the muscled length of his back, reveling in the feel of him, the power of his muscles tensing and flexing beneath her hands as he started to move again, thrusting his body into hers, his rhythm deep and powerful and strong. She loved that he held nothing back. That he gave her all of him, everything that he had, taking her with all the power and intensity of the man *and* his wolf. Fever hot to the touch, she should have felt scorched by the heat of his skin, and yet, the sensation of being covered by his warmth, driven against the cool wooden planks of the floor beneath her back, made her writhe, aching for more.

"You deserve a man who's more than an animal, Doucet," she heard him snarl, voicing his demons, and she couldn't help the grin that played at the corner of her mouth.

"No," she moaned, the provocative friction of his hard body moving inside hers making her sob with pleasure. "I deserve everything you've got. All of it. Don't you dare hold back on me."

She pulled him closer then, pressing her lips to his scars, the pansy-soft kisses tender and reverent, demanding his surrender. Brody marveled at the proof of her acceptance, unable to believe that even with his eyes turned the deep, glowing green of his wolf, his claws once again digging into the floor beside her, and his fangs slipping free, she accepted him, telling him that she wasn't afraid. That she trusted him. And amazingly, because of that trust, he felt himself able to hold on to that small shred of control that kept his beast from becoming too savage and hurting her. From sinking its fangs into her throat and taking the warm, rich spill of her blood into his body.

Grasping her wrists and stretching them over her head, he buried his face in the feminine curve of her shoulder, and drove himself into her, as hard as he possibly could; thanking

God and anyone else he could think of, when a husky cry of pleasure filled his ears, instead of pain. He couldn't get deep enough inside her, inside of the tender, clutching grasp of her body as she came, so perfect and swollen and small. Hot. Slick. Breathtaking. The stuff of fantasies, white-hot and spellbinding. She devastated him, and as he followed her over into that vicious, raging storm of pleasure, spilling himself inside of her in searing, pumping surges that had him shouting against the tender curve of her shoulder, Brody realized that he was never going to be the same again.

In the aftermath of the most incredible experience of her life, Michaela lay in a sprawl across the muscled beauty of Brody's chest. They'd shed their clothes and shoes, his breathing slowly returning to normal, but she could still feel the tension in him, the hunger that lurked just beneath his calm surface. One of his hands rested possessively in the small of her back, his thumb stroking her skin in a lazy, sensual pattern that made her want to purr with pleasure, while his other hand smoothed over the long, tangled length of her curls.

She murmured a soft, incoherent sound of satisfaction as the hand on her back slid lower, over her bottom, then lower still, the callused tips of his fingers touching between her legs, caressing screamingly sensitive, slippery flesh. Her breath caught, and her body responded with a renewed wave of warm, wet heat. He growled low in his throat, the wickedly sexy sound vibrating deep within his chest, right beneath her ear.

And then, without a word, he rolled her over, one thigh holding her legs spread wide, his upper body resting on his bent arm, gaze vividly intense, glowing and green. He stared into her eyes, before running that smoldering stare down her body, while his fingers pressed possessively between her thighs, playing havoc with her senses. His thumb stroked baby-soft caresses against the thrumming heat of her clit, while two thick digits thrust up into her body, penetrating her, curling until they rubbed against that one deep sweet spot that made her scream, the sensations came so sharp and bright. Then he slid over her, covering her, moving with a speed and masculine grace that should have been impossible for a man his size. And yet he was all predatory strength and power, like something escaped from a primeval jungle.

"I'm sorry," he groaned raggedly against her lips, pressing kisses to the corner of her mouth, before raking the inside with his tongue, the kiss as bold and hungry as it was breathtakingly possessive. "I know you'll be tender...but I can't...can't be gentle, Doucet."

"I don't want gentle," she murmured, rubbing her mouth over the burnished skin of his throat, his shoulders, the muscles steel-like beneath the firm flesh. He pushed into her, working himself back inside, and she said, "I just want *you*."

"You've got me," he murmured, laughing a low, wicked sound deep in his chest. Then he hooked one arm under her bottom, the other around her back, and shifted to his feet, carrying her through the shadowed rooms of the cabin, his cock thrusting deeper inside of her with each step, the pleasure as sharp as it was intense. Hazy streams of moonlight lit the bedroom, and as he pressed her into the cool, crisp sheets, she gasped, the heat of his body on top of her making the sensation of cold beneath her back even sharper.

He held her gaze as he started moving again, withdrawing, then driving deep...thick...hard, back inside of her, stretching her to the point that it would have hurt if she hadn't been so desperate for him, her body soft and wet and slick. They rolled across the bed, the passion between them explosive, with her head hanging over the edge at one point, while he thrust into her again and again, giving her everything that he had. Giving her all of him.

Levering his upper body away from her, she watched him as he stared at the place where their bodies joined, and ran the rough tip of his forefinger along the strained edge of her swollen sex, the look in his eyes one of wild, primal possession. She could barely take him—and he liked it, loved it. Reveled in that dark, primitive knowledge. She could see it in his eyes, hear it in the fractured cadence of his breathing. Her back arched as the pleasure mounted, building stronger, and Michaela closed her eyes, trying to prepare for it, to hold it together when it crashed over her, not wanting to fall apart on him.

"No," he rasped, fisting his hand in her hair, his words gritty and thick with emotion as he growled, "Open your eyes, Doucet. I want to see it when it happens. I want to see the look in your eyes when you go over."

She lifted her lashes, and he went into her thick and hot, then just held there, packed tight within her, the look in his eyes so impossibly sexy, she couldn't take it. With her next breath, she broke around him, the pleasure rushing through her with the furious energy of a storm, and she screamed, head thrown back, held in his hand, body completely overtaken by the intensity of the sensations, white-hot and blinding. Lowering his head, he growled against the tender stretch of her throat, his fangs scraping against her skin in an erotic slide of temptation, and his body convulsed deep inside of her, the wracking spasms of his orgasm spearing her own into a deeper, spiraling darkness that consumed her.

And just as he'd predicted, she didn't fall into his mind with this orgasm, either. On the one hand, Michaela was relieved, since she didn't want anything to mar the stunning perfection of the moment. And yet, there was a tiny part of her that had wanted to see into him again...if only to learn more about him.

He held hard and tight inside of her for long, breathless moments, his body rigid, then finally collapsed over her, trying to move to the side, but she stopped him with the clutching hold of her arms, wanting the delicious press of his weight. "I'll crush you," he grated in a passion-rough voice, the deep rasp sending erotic sensations racing across her flesh like a brush fire.

"I don't care," she whispered. "Don't leave me."

Brody moved just enough to the side so that she could breathe, pulling her farther onto the bed, then buried his face in the fragrant silk of her hair spread out across his sheets. As exhaustion overwhelmed him, he meant to leave before falling asleep, telling himself he could lie beside her for just a moment longer—taking a few more stolen moments of heaven. And then suddenly the screeching call of a hawk hunting for a late-night snack sliced across the sky, and Brody awoke with a husky grunt, jerking to consciousness. He stared at the moonlit shadows shifting across the bedroom ceiling, wondering how long he'd slept, while his chest labored to pull in deep, gulping bursts of air.

Blinking his eyes, he glanced at the digital clock on the far side of the bed that read 2:00 a.m., then looked down to see Michaela's dark head buried in his shoulder, her mouth parted the barest fraction, breath warm and sweet against his skin. They'd obviously moved together in sleep, their bodies naturally finding more comfortable positions. She had one fist curled in the middle of his chest, her graceful hand looking as small and delicate as a child's, and it made his heart hurt, how trustingly she'd lain in his arms and slept with him.

It was, without a doubt, one of the most wonderful moments of Brody's life—as well as the most wrenching. Wonderful, because this woman was everything to him, a part of his very soul—and yet, heartbreaking, since he knew there wasn't a chance he could keep her.

Doing his best to slip away from her as slowly as possible, Brody eased his legs over the side of the mattress, bracing his elbows on his knees as he hung his head in his palms. He concentrated on taking deep, even breaths, struggling to ignore the tearing pain ripping across his heart at the thought of getting up and walking away from her.

"What happens now?" she suddenly asked into the quiet, moonlit darkness, the sound of her voice wrapping around the hard, drumming beat of his heart as it pounded painfully within his chest.

He wanted so badly to confess to her, to tell her everything that he felt inside—but held back. He didn't know why. Fear? Caution? Cowardice? A combination of them all? Even after she'd given him everything—her passion so loving and sweet, and yet, scorching and wild, leaving him wrecked with pleasure that was unlike anything he'd ever known—even after all that, he still didn't have the guts to be honest with her.

To tell her the truth.

"Brody?" she whispered, and he could hear the tears in her voice, his hands fisting as he resisted the need to turn around and take her into his arms, under his body.

"I'm sorry, Doucet. But this…this was all I could give you."

"All you *could* give me…or all you *want* to give me?"

"What I want doesn't matter," he stated, his tone flat, devoid of emotion. He'd taken it and buried it deep inside of himself, hoping like hell he was able to keep it there.

"It *does* matter, Brody. Do you think this doesn't terrify me, the idea of opening up to you, of letting you into my heart, of giving you that kind of power over me? I'm scared to death, but I can't seem to stop myself from needing to be with you. I know you could hurt me emotionally. Hurt me more than any other man has ever done, but it doesn't seem to matter."

"This thing between us, it just isn't going to work out," he grunted, moving to his feet, doing his best to ignore her wrenching confession. "It shouldn't have happened in the first place, because I knew better. I should have stayed the hell away from you."

"Is it because of Dylan's sister?" he heard her ask as he reached for the pair of jeans he'd left draped over the arm of the chair when he'd dressed for the wedding earlier that day. "Was she…was Jenny Riggs your mate?"

A low, harsh laugh jerked out of his chest. "God no."

She absorbed that for a moment, then quietly said, "Do… do you sense anything when you're near me?"

"Like what?" he grunted, ripping one hand through the damp, tangled strands of his hair so hard that his scalp stung.

"Like the…others? Mason and Torrance. Jeremy and Jillian. I thought maybe—"

"Even if I did," he grated, not really giving her an answer as he cut her off, "it wouldn't make a difference."

"Oh…" she said softly, and in that moment, Brody hated himself more than he'd ever hated anyone or anything in his entire life.

Clearing his throat, he turned around to face her, knowing his words were pathetically inadequate. "You're an amazing woman, Doucet."

"Yeah, thanks," she hiccuped with a small, watery laugh, staring at her lap, hiding her face from him behind the fall of her hair.

"If I could be different…" He winced as the words trailed off, painfully aware that he sounded like a total jackass.

She shook her head, pulling the sheet up over her body, hiding herself from his gaze. "You never lied to me, Brody."

He opened his mouth, but nothing came out, as if his ability for speech had just dried up. He just stared at her, the time stretching out into a long, seamless expanse of anger and hunger, frustration and hopelessness. Eventually, he turned and walked out of the room, shutting the door behind him.

The early-morning sun struggled to burn its way through the thick cover of storm clouds that had blown in during the night, the promise of rain thick in the air as thunder rumbled in the distance. Brody stared out the window over the kitchen sink, his nerves jacked up from the two cups of coffee he'd already downed, while his brain kept replaying that final scene from last night over and over in his mind. The details were gut wrenching and stark—no fuzzy perception to blot the depth of pain, to make him feel like less of a bastard. But even more than that, he felt like a coward. In his head, he could hear his ego making mocking noises at him, taunting him for being such a chicken shit.

You know what you want, you're just too terrified to take a chance on her. Too afraid to believe she could be for real— that she could want you for forever.

True, but what the hell was he supposed to do about it?

The sound of footsteps down the hallway had him breaking out in a cold sweat, that lush, mouthwatering peaches-and-cream scent wrapping around him like some biologically altered, fast-growing vine, imprisoning him, squeezing the air from his lungs. It released on a low, shaky breath when she stopped at the entrance to the kitchen, and he searched for the balls to turn around.

He hadn't slept after walking out on her in the middle of the night, and from the dark circles he spotted under her eyes as he faced her, neither had she.

And yet, she was painfully beautiful. She licked her bottom lip, and his muscles clenched, that tangled knot of hunger in his gut roiling, damaging him inside, like an emotional wrecking ball. What the hell was he doing? He wanted so badly to go to her, shoving her against the kitchen wall, imprinting his body against her own, until he could feel every inch of her. Wanted to rip those hip-hugging jeans to shreds and sink to his knees, pressing his face into the lush, breathtaking sweetness of her sex, his tongue and lips and mouth taking everything she had. All of it. Demanding it.

The memory of her taste sat on the tip of his tongue like a treasure, taunting him, and he fisted his hands at his sides, his claws breaking through until he could feel the piercing tips cutting into his own flesh, the warm wash of his blood filling his palms. Turning back to the sink, Brody flicked on the water and put his hands under the warm flow, washing away the evidence of his weakness. Christ, he had no control with this woman. None. Hadn't last night proven that?

Bile rose in his throat, and he choked back a low string of

curses that burned across the landscape of his mind, leaving scorched earth in their wake.

"Are you okay?" she asked, her voice closer, and he knew from her scent that she'd come into the room, standing maybe five feet behind him. He closed his eyes, struggling for the strength to resist, wanting nothing more than to turn around and take her to the ground, the way he had last night. He wanted to shove himself into her until he felt the white-hot, blissed-out feeling of being home again, of being right where he belonged, a part of her, those graceful limbs wrapped around him, her mouth pressed hot and damp to the side of his throat.

God. He was going to combust or do himself bodily harm.

"Brody?"

"I'm fine," he managed to grit through his clenched teeth, sounding like a bastard. He could imagine her flinching at his tone, that tender flair of concern in her eyes dimming beneath the force of his anger.

"This isn't going to work, is it?" she whispered. "How are we supposed to—"

The sound of a fist pounding on his front door saved him from having to hear what she'd been about to say. "Carter, open up!" Cian called out. Turning off the faucet, Brody grabbed the hand towel off the front of the stove as he moved past her, into the living room. Yanking open the front door, he found his partner standing on the porch, the scent of the cleanser they'd used to remove Pippa's blood still tangy and sharp in the air.

"Isn't it a little early in the day for you?" he rasped, eyeing his partner with a wary gaze.

Cian took a slow drag on his cigarette, eyes heavy beneath his brows. "Duty calls," the Irishman muttered.

Damn it. He didn't like the sound of that. "What's going on?"

"Mason got the call from Dylan this morning," Cian grunted. "They're making the vote on Jillian in just under an hour."

Chapter 14

Once Michaela had learned Brody was going to Shadow Peak, she'd asked if he could drop her off at Eric's while he was in town, so that she could spend time with Max. Feeling guilty over the way he'd walked out on her in the night, Brody had reluctantly agreed, though it went against the fierce burn of possession in his gut to leave her in the protection of the Lycan.

She'd rushed to get ready, and they'd left the house not fifteen minutes later, taking his truck, with Cian riding along in the backseat. Now, as Brody steered the Ford up the private road that led to Shadow Peak, there was a devil sitting on his shoulder, whispering in his ear that he was making a huge mistake—that something wasn't right. He chalked it up to being on edge, and yet he couldn't shake the uncomfortable feeling that he should turn around, take Michaela home and never let her out of his sight.

The rain started falling in a torrential downpour halfway there, slowing them down, so that they were already late by the time he pulled in front of Eric's house. After listening to his stern warning to remain inside with Eric and Max until he came back for her, she got out and waved goodbye, and Cian moved to the front seat while Brody waited for her to get safely into the house before driving away.

When they were underway again, he reached for his back pocket and pulled out the list of names he'd printed up that morning. Unable to sleep, he'd been working on his laptop at sunrise, when he'd received an e-mail from Monroe with the names he'd requested. Brody had glanced over them, but nothing had caught his attention. Still, he'd printed it up, planning to run it by the rest of the Runners as soon as he got the chance. Handing the list to Cian, he was about to tell him to take a look at it, when his cell phone started buzzing on his hip. Glancing at the number, his gut tightened when he saw the call was coming from Eric's house.

"What's wrong?" he grunted into the mouthpiece, at the same time he steered the Ford into a parking place on the side of the road and flicked off the windshield wipers, thankful that the violent burst of rain was already letting up.

It was Michaela calling with some unsettling news. Eric knew nothing about Jillian's hearing and was under the impression that a committee meeting was on the morning's docket instead.

"Eric's on the committee and is expected to attend, but he doesn't plan to leave Max and Elliot. Doesn't it seem strange that they would hold a committee meeting at the same time they're taking a vote on Jillian?"

"Yeah, that's weird," he murmured, slanting a worried look

toward Cian, who was watching him with a concerned expression on his dark face.

"Where are you now?" she asked.

"We've just parked on Second Avenue, one street over from Main Street and the Town Hall. We're heading over right now."

"Okay. Just promise me that you'll be careful. I don't want to sound paranoid, but I have…" She hesitated, then said, "I have a really bad feeling about this, Brody."

"Me, too," he grunted, raking the fingers of his free hand back through his hair. "I should've left you in the goddamn Alley. Whatever the hell happens, you stay there with Eric. Understood?"

"I won't leave," she assured him. "Just figure out what's happening and then get back here."

"I mean it, Doucet. Do *not* leave that house."

"I won't," she promised, and then she hung up.

"What's going on?" Cian rasped, pulling out a cigarette.

Brody filled him in as they climbed out of the truck, unease moving them swiftly down the road, their long legs eating up the sidewalk with rapid strides. "Seems weird they'd schedule the meeting to coincide with Jillian's hearing."

"This doesn't feel right," Cian murmured, scowling as he took a long drag on his smoke.

"We need to find the others, because I have a bad feeling we've been told what was needed to get us here," he muttered, at the same time a stark, resonating howl echoed in the distance. Both men stopped in their tracks.

"It's a bloody setup," Cian grunted.

They shared a dark look, then started running toward the Town Hall.

* * *

Replacing the phone in the cradle attached to Eric's kitchen wall, Michaela chewed on the corner of her mouth, struggling to calm her emotions. But it was a wasted effort. They'd been at full tilt for too long, ever since the shattering hours she'd spent in Brody's arms the night before. Hours that had stripped her down, leaving her shaky, as jittery as an addict going through withdrawal.

She'd channeled all her energy into the hope that Brody would finally open up to her when she opened her body to him, but she'd been wrong. Despite the blistering intimacy they'd shared, in the end, he'd walked away from her, just as Ross had done. The effect, however, was so much more devastating, because while she'd cared for Ross—she was passionately, head over heels in love with Brody Carter.

She felt foolish, but she couldn't escape the sharp burn of worry piercing her chest, terrified that something was going to happen to him—that his life was in danger. "I got Brody," she murmured, looking toward Eric as he walked into the kitchen. "He's going to check out what's going on at the Town Hall and then get back here."

Eric nodded as he leaned back against the counter, brawny arms crossed over his chest. "Max should be down in a minute. He and Elliot are just finishing up with one of his training exercises."

Curious about her brother's training, Michaela started to ask for details, when a long, sinister howl suddenly sounded from the front of the house. Eric stiffened, pulling his dark brows together into a deep vee over the metallic gray of his eyes. "Son of a bitch," he hissed, turning and heading for the living room, while Michaela ran after him.

"What was that?" she gasped.

Peering around the front blinds, Eric cursed a guttural string of words under his breath. "Max! Elliot!" he shouted. "Get down here!"

Another howl came from outside, so close it sounded like the animal was in Eric's front yard. "What the hell is that?" she asked again, her voice growing shrill with fear.

"Rogues," Eric grunted, still staring out the window. "About five of them in the street. Looks like some of Sheffield's groupies, but I don't see Dustin." Slanting her a dark look over his shoulder, he said, "This isn't good, Michaela. I want you to go in the back bedroom and stay there. Whatever you hear, do not come out. I'll call Brody, but the boys and I should be able to hold them off till the Runners can get over here."

"What do you think they want?" she asked unsteadily, unable to believe this was happening. Her chest grew tight, making it difficult to breathe.

Before Eric could answer, a guttural voice shouted, "All we want's the girl, Drake! If you don't want any trouble, send her out!"

"Well, that answers that," she muttered, at the same time as her brother and Elliot came racing down the stairs. Eric immediately began firing instructions at the young men. Michaela stood silently by the wall, listening, until Eric turned toward her.

"Get the hell out of here," he barked. "Right now."

She ran to Max and gave him a quick hug and kiss, whispering, "Be careful!"

Then she headed for the back of the house. By the time she'd reached the bedroom, she could hear the fighting in the front, the sharp sounds of shattering glass and breaking wood. Were the rogues coming in through the windows? Breaking down the front door? Unless a miracle happened, they were all going to die—because of her.

And they'd seemed a bit short on miracles lately.

Pacing from one side of the room to the other, Michaela listened as the sounds of fighting grew louder, wondering why it was taking so long for help to get there. Had something happened to Brody and the others? Should she try to call him, in case Eric hadn't been able to get through? Rushing for the phone sitting on the bedside table, she'd just picked it up, when she felt chills break out along her arms, slithering across the back of her neck. Closing her eyes, she threw out the soft, diaphanous web of her power, and could *feel* Dustin Sheffield. He was on the left-hand side of the house, creeping slowly toward the far window.

Michaela knew he was powerful enough to break through the window with ease—and by the time the others got to her, she'd already be dead. Rushing to the bedroom door, she cracked it open a careful fraction, wondering if she could make a run for it, but the hallway was blocked by the massive, fur-covered body of a golden werewolf fighting Eric.

Closing the door, she glanced at the window on her right, and could see beneath the partly lifted blinds that the sky was slowly darkening with another ominous wave of storm clouds. Soon, it would start raining again, and Brody had explained to her that rain hampered a Lycan's sense of smell, making it difficult for them to track their prey.

If she slipped out the window, maybe she could outrun Dustin until the rain came down, covering her trail. It wasn't much of a plan, but it was better than staying in that bedroom and waiting for him to break in and kill her.

Sensing that Dustin was preparing to crash through the blind-covered window on the other side of the room, Michaela ran to the one on her right, pushed it open, and climbed out, surprised to discover that Eric's yard bordered the edge of the forest. With adrenaline pouring swiftly through her veins, she set off into the woods at full speed, thankful for the sneakers that covered her feet. Though she moved as quickly as she could, it wasn't long before a stitch began twisting in her side, slowing her down. Gritting her teeth, she forced herself to keep moving, knowing that if she stopped, he'd catch her—and then he would kill her.

She would die. Pure and simple.

Michaela had always believed she'd experience a moment of clarity when this time came, facing her death, but only two truths filled her mind. She was going to miss her brother—and she wished she'd told Brody that she loved him.

Praying for the growing storm which had yet to break, she kept running, certain that Sheffield had already picked up on her scent and given chase. She'd no sooner finished the thought, when she sensed someone closing in on her. *Dustin.* As she used her power to read him, Michaela could feel the anticipation rushing swiftly through his veins, the heavy weight of lust and hunger in his gut for the moment when he'd take her down. She thought she heard him off to her left, then her right a moment later, and her stomach heaved as she realized what was happening. He was playing with her, the way a lion cub might tease its prey before finally making the kill.

But Dustin Sheffield was no cub—and Michaela refused to be his plaything.

Jumping over a fallen log, she struggled to keep her balance, when he suddenly burst onto her path, coming out from the dense foliage to her left. She skidded to a jarring, jolting stop, and he smiled at her, his face and body still human, though his hands were anything but, sporting long, deadly claws. "Well, hello there," he drawled.

Taking a step back, she hissed, "Stay away from me."

"No can do, little Cajun. While Drake is busy turning the Runners into mincemeat, I thought we could enjoy a little private playtime." He stalked closer, running his tongue over his bottom lip, mouth curled in a malicious smile, while his eyes glowed like golden embers of fire. "I've been looking forward to this, Michaela. You have no idea how much."

"It was you, wasn't it?" she whispered, taking another step back…and then another. "You're the one who's been watching me?"

His low laugh was obscene, slipping down her spine like cold, wet slime, making her shiver. "So he's had his eye on you, eh? I wondered about that. Drake wasn't happy about you being in the mountains, worried what that little gift of yours might allow you to pick up from him."

"From who? Drake?"

"No, the one your Runner has been hunting," he told her. "The one with a taste for cute little blondes."

"Who is it?"

"Oh, I can't go spoiling the surprise," he crooned, matching each step she took until her back came up against a tree. "And we have more important things to keep us busy. Why don't you use that power of yours and tell me what they are?" Reaching out, he trailed his claws down the front of her sweater, the tip of the middle one just catching on her left nipple, making her cry out in pain. "Come on, Michaela," he drawled. "Something tells me you'll get it right on the first guess."

Trembling, she said, "You'll have to kill me before I let you rape me."

"And what makes you think that'd be a problem for me?" he asked with a slow, cruel smile, chuckling under his breath, the sound as sinister as it was soft. In a startlingly swift move, he took her to the ground, catching her wrists in one clawed hand, imprisoning them over her head. Then he pressed his denim-covered erection against her at the same time the shape of his face transformed, a long, fang-filled muzzle stretching out his jawbones, popping and cracking into position, and she screamed. Screamed louder than she'd ever screamed in her entire life.

"Don't worry," he purred in a tone that all but dripped with venom. "You won't die. At least not yet. After I have my fun with you, I have orders to take you back to Drake." His deadly mouth twisted into some kind of grotesque imitation of a grin, while his eyes burned with malevolent pleasure. "He's got special plans for you, little Cajun. You're gonna be a present to all of those who've served him. A kind of 'job well done' bonus. Too bad you won't survive it. Oh, maybe the first few, but after that, you'll bleed out before the others can get to you."

"You're sick," she whispered.

"We'll see how sick you think I am when I'm done with you," he murmured, a low, guttural laugh vibrating deep within his chest, while he ran his claws lightly down the right side of her face. He scratched her skin just enough to break the surface, so that blood welled hotly from the stinging slice, and she sobbed from the pain.

Still grinding himself against her, Dustin leaned down and

licked the shallow cuts, his tongue rough and warm against her face, and Michaela cried out, struggling against his hold, as he hummed, "Mmm. You're a tasty little thing, aren't you?"

He reared back then, his knees straddling her thighs, and with his free hand, the fingers still elongated into gnarled, claw-tipped weapons, he reached for the fly of her jeans. "No…no…no," she chanted, twisting her upper body every possible way that she could, but he was too strong, the hold he had on her imprisoned wrists impossible to break. Terror consumed her, smothering her to the point that she couldn't breathe, could no longer even scream, nothing but a broken stream of dry, choking whimpers breaking out of her.

And then suddenly, Dustin was rearing backward, being pulled through the air, and Michaela blinked against the incredible sight of Dylan Riggs holding the rogue by the scruff of his neck. Scrambling to her knees, she watched in shock as Dylan, who was still in his human form, with only his hands shifted into claws, slammed Dustin face-first against a nearby tree, then turned him, pinning the younger Lycan against the thick trunk. Dustin snarled in outrage, and before she could draw in enough air to scream, the Elder's head transformed into the shape of his wolf, and he killed the rogue Lycan with a single vicious bite.

Nausea overwhelmed her, but Michaela fought against it as she watched Dylan step back, releasing Dustin's body, which slumped lifelessly to the ground. The Elder's head shifted back into that of a man and he turned to look at her with piercing eyes that glowed an unearthly hue, as if lit from within. Shock made her stumble backward, a cry breaking out of her mouth as she found herself bombarded by a horrific wave of hatred and despair that emanated from him, the blackness seething inside him overwhelming her with a torrent of gruesome images and fractured emotions.

She was reading Dylan Riggs, and she suddenly understood why she'd felt so uncomfortable around him, so on edge.

Oh God. Dylan is the one...the one Brody has been hunting!

"You can read me now, can't you?" he asked, staring at her with tortured eyes that revealed both horror and pain.

She nodded, too shocked to speak.

"I was almost hoping you *would* be able to tell, Michaela," he stated in a soft rasp, a wry smile tipping the corner of his mouth. "That you'd be able to read me, the way they say you can sometimes do. That's why I've been watching you. Wondering if you'd see what I was hiding. Half hoping you'd expose me and bring this nightmare to an end. But you didn't pick up on me. Not in the clearing on the night of Max's ceremony, and not even—"

"In the woods, when we found the body," she whispered, taking another instinctive step back as he moved closer, keeping one eye warily focused on the claws he'd yet to shift back into human hands. "And last night as I was walking with Brody to his cabin."

"That's right."

"I picked up on you," she admitted, "but something was jamming the signal. All I heard was static. But I...I can read you now, Dylan. You're hurting because you...killed someone you cared about."

"Her name was Jessie," he told her, his words soft, barely more than a whisper. "Jessie Bonness. She was a human, like you. Blond and blue-eyed, the most beautiful thing I've ever seen."

"What happened?"

Shaking his head, he said, "I kept our affair a secret from the pack, but I'd been trying to work up the courage to tell her the truth about me for months. I knew I'd have to give up my position on the League if she agreed to marry me, but I was willing to do it, if it meant having her in my life. My only concern was how she would react to the truth about what I am. And then one night I went down to the city to see her, and she told me she was pregnant."

He broke off his explanation, staring at the leaf-covered floor of the forest, lost in the memory. After a moment, he took a deep breath and went on. "I knew I couldn't put it off any longer. So I told her…everything. She didn't believe me, and we argued. She called me crazy, so I shifted just my hand for her to see, and she reared away from me in horror, her features twisted with disgust, as if I was some kind of monster." A low, bitter sound lost somewhere between a sob and a laugh jerked from his throat, and he raised his gaze back to her. "I loved Jessie, she was pregnant with my child, and all she could do was scream at me, calling me names, telling me I was an animal. At first, there was nothing inside of me but the most excruciating, hollow sense of pain, of loss—and then she told me that she'd rather die than ever have me touch her again, and something inside of me snapped. Suddenly, that hollow feeling was gone, replaced by the most intense, vile wave of hatred I'd ever experienced. And in that moment, my beast awakened, lashing out at her in its fury, and I…"

His throat worked as he swallowed, brow drenched with sweat, tears streaming from his eyes, running through the blood on his face. "I didn't mean for it to happen, but I killed her. It was like watching something in a movie, as if it wasn't

really me doing those horrible things to her body. But it was."
He shuddered, his voice lowering as he said, "And my beast,
it'd found a taste for something it liked—an outlet for all the
primitive rage roiling in its blood over the loss of its mate. And
she was, you know. My mate. I knew it the first moment I
scented her skin. Jessie walked by me in a bookstore down in
Covington, and I damn near tripped over my feet as I turned
to chase her down."

"But why the others?" she asked, wondering if Brody
would track her down in time to save her. Though Dylan had
rescued her from Dustin, Michaela still didn't trust him.

The corner of his mouth quirked with another smile, and
it was clear the Elder was no longer sane. "Like I said," he
told her, "the beast had found a way to ease its heartache."

Disgust thickened her voice as she croaked, "By eating the
hearts out of those innocent girls?"

"I don't expect you to understand," he said quietly. "Hell, I
hardly understand myself. But as that blackness inside of me
grew, I lost more and more control, until I became the monster
humans depict us to be in their horror folklore. And my wolf
liked it. It enjoyed becoming the monster Jessie accused me of
being."

"Drake somehow found out, didn't he? And he blackmailed
you into helping him."

"Yes, on both counts," he admitted, while thunder boomed
in the distance, the scent of rain growing stronger as the next
storm finally prepared to roll in. "After reading about the
legend, Stefan had been waiting to find a weak link in the
League, needing an Elder he could force to help him. Hoping
to catch one of us in a compromising position, he'd been
having each member of the League followed. Suspicious

about my trips down to Covington, he'd assigned Anthony Simmons to follow me, and got what he'd been looking for. The night I killed Jessie, Simmons was watching through her bedroom window. On Drake's orders, he covered up the murder. Then Stefan told me that I would be working with him—telling me that I just needed to learn to focus my rage and control my beast, but it…it just kept wanting to kill again. And so I kept finding those girls, all blond and blue-eyed, reminding me of Jessie. And each time my wolf relished the sweet reenactment of its revenge, as if it were killing her all over again."

"Why not just tell Drake no?" Michaela pressed, aware that no more than a handful of steps separated them, knowing he'd have her down in a second if she tried to run.

"He threatened to send Dustin after my sister, fully aware that I'd have nowhere to turn for help so long as he held that information against me. He'll stop at nothing to get what he wants, which is revenge against the League and full control of the pack. And he's going to get it, Michaela. Nothing can stop him now."

"What do you mean?" she demanded, recalling with terror Dustin's claim about the attack on the Runners.

"Drake drew the Runners to Shadow Peak on purpose today, knowing they'd come to support Jillian. It's all a setup. Today's his final bid for power. With my help, he's already pulled the wolves from those townspeople who showed up for the committee meeting. Once he had them in his control, he ordered half of them to turn on the League itself."

"He assassinated them?" she asked, stunned.

"All of them. After that, we pulled the wolves from the other half, who were outside with the Runners." His gaze dropped to the ground, shifting uneasily before he continued in a broken rasp. "Without the power of the moon, the Runners will be unable to fully shift."

"You just left them there to die?" she whispered, almost taking a step forward, wanting to scratch and claw at him. "How could you do that?"

"I didn't have a choice!" he seethed, lifting his gaze to her tear-streaked face. "He'll kill Jenny if I don't do exactly as he says."

Terrified for Brody and the others, she struggled for a way to appeal to the man who was trapped within the insanity of his beast. "It's not too late to do the right thing, Dylan. You can still help them."

A hoarse crack of laughter burst from his throat. "Why would I want to do that?"

"Damn it, they're your friends!" she cried. "You can't just let them die!"

"No," he rasped, his dry laughter fading. "They're not my friends. Not now. Not anymore. If they survive, it will be their job to track me down and kill me. I can't…can't let that happen. I have to find a way to protect Jenny. That's why I came after Dustin."

"Isn't there any way to stop it? To put an end to what's happening?"

"They would have to kill Drake," he said after a moment. "That's their only hope. Once he dies, the feral wolves will change back."

"Then come back with me," she pleaded, knowing the Runners would need all the help they could get. "Please, Dylan."

"No," he grated, backing away from her, and she knew he was going to run. "You can't go back to town, Michaela. You'll die."

"Then I'll die," she screamed at him, her voice cracking with fury. "But at least I'll go knowing that I did everything I could to help the people I care about!"

He stared at her a moment longer, his eyes growing deeper, face pale beneath the crimson stain of Dustin's blood. Then he turned and walked away. Wiping at the tears spilling down her cheeks, Michaela started back toward town, moving as quickly as possible, ignoring her aches and pains, praying only that she would make it in time.

After racing toward the Town Hall at the sound of the first howl, Brody and Cian had found the other Runners already engaged in battle, facing off against an overwhelming number of fully shifted werewolves. The nightmare, it seemed, that the Runners had been waiting for had finally arrived, unfolding across the morning like the terrifying pages of a horror novel, complete with blood and gore and a maniacal madman.

"What the hell's going on?" he'd shouted at Mason, who was striking claws with a honey-colored wolf.

"We got here and found a crowd gathered outside on the steps," the Runner had shouted back at him. "Said they were supposed to be here for a committee meeting, but that Drake had told half of them to wait outside, then locked the doors. Next thing we knew, they started changing and attacked us. We were able to get Torrance and Jillian out of here, but Drake has the other Elders trapped inside!"

Together, he and Cian had joined the battle, the Runners hoping to fight their way into the Hall and rescue the League before Drake killed them. Brody had fought alongside his friends until Eric had called and told him about the attack on his house. He'd left the others fighting, and headed for

Eric's in his truck, going hell-bent for leather, but by the time he'd gotten there, Michaela was gone…as were the rogues—except for the two that lay dead in the living room, killed during the fight.

When they'd found Dustin Sheffield's thick scent outside one of the bedroom windows, Brody had realized she'd probably had to run for her life. He'd nearly choked on the great rising wave of fear that overwhelmed him, terrified he wasn't going to get to her in time. He'd told a blood-spattered Eric to take Max and Elliot to Jillian's—and then he'd immediately taken off after Michaela.

Running as fast as he could, Brody's legs now powered him through the damp forest, the air growing heavier as thunder rumbled in the sky, heralding the coming storm, while he followed the lush trace of her scent. He could scent Dustin as well, the rogue's musk ripe with lust, and his insides twisted with rage.

A broken, snarled stream of swearwords tumbled from his lips, his heart hammering within his chest to a painful, panic-filled rhythm. And then suddenly, he could hear someone ahead of him, moving directly in his path, Michaela's scent growing thicker…richer, and then she was there, emerging from between two towering trees. She cried out when she saw him, throwing herself into his arms, their combined momentum crashing them against one another.

"Brody!" she gasped, running her hands over his shoulders and arms as she stared up at him with wide, tear-drenched eyes. "Oh God, Brody, you're alive!"

"Doucet," he grated, his throat tight with emotion, unable to believe he'd found her—or that *she'd* found *him,* since she'd run right into him. Now that he had her in his arms, he wanted to throttle her for scaring the hell out of him, at the same time he wanted to kiss her senseless. And since he'd have rather chewed off his own arm than harm her, the kiss won out.

Wrapping one arm around her waist, Brody cradled the back of her head with the other, her hair cool and damp against the heat of his skin. "I will not lose you," he growled against her mouth, sharing her breath…and then he claimed possession, pouring everything he had into his kiss. She tasted like sunshine, honeyed and warm, her flavor rolling through him like a miracle—like something that belonged to him and no other. She clutched at handfuls of his hair, trying to crawl her way up his body, her tongue stroking his, making him so hot he was amazed steam didn't sizzle off his skin as the sky cracked open and a deluge of rain poured down on them, the raindrops sharp and cold against their faces.

Forcing himself to break away from the heaven of her mouth, Brody grabbed her shoulders, staring into the deep, fathomless depths of her eyes. "I almost died when I got back to Eric's and found you were gone," he rasped, his breathing choppy, while his body shook with a mixture of anger and piercing relief.

"I'm sorry," she panted, "but I sensed Dustin getting ready to break into the bedroom where I was hiding and knew I had to run. Is Max safe?"

"Eric's taken him to Jillian. He's fine, just a little scratched up. You're the one I'm worried about," he growled, one hand hovering over the scratches that Dustin had left down the side of her face, afraid to touch her lest he cause her more pain. "Are you okay? Where's Sheffield now?"

She shuddered as if something slimy had crawled over her skin. "Back…there."

"Son of a bitch." Staring at her torn clothes, he could feel his rage punching against the inside of his body, pressing against his skin, as if it would break out of him in a vicious, violent demand for revenge. "Did he touch you?" he asked in a soft, seething rasp.

She shook her head, pale face drenched with tears. "No, he…he was going to, but Dylan stopped him."

"Riggs was there?" he grunted, shocked. He'd assumed Dylan was inside the Town Hall with the other Elders, either as a prisoner…or as Drake's accomplice. "And he let you run off on your own?"

Taking a deep breath, she said, "Dylan killed Dustin. When it was over, I thought he was going to bring me back to you, but it didn't take long for me to realize that something was wrong."

The back of his neck prickled. "What do you mean?"

Clutching handfuls of his damp T-shirt, she explained. "Dylan's the one, Brody. Drake was blackmailing him. That's why he was cooperating with Stefan. But that's not all. He's the one you've been hunting. The one killing the girls."

A sharp, guttural curse fell from his lips, his head spinning as he absorbed her words. She went on to quickly relate what had happened, telling him about Jessica Bonness, the human Dylan claimed to have fallen in love with, and Brody was shocked to realize he recognized the name from the list Monroe had sent him.

"Goddamn it," he finally snarled.

"You're going to have to take me with you."

He knew she was right, but the idea of taking her into danger infuriated him. "You will stay where I tell you, Doucet. No running. No interfering. You got it?"

"I will, I promise."

Grasping her hand, he threaded their fingers together. "Come on," he growled, pulling her along behind him. "We don't have any time to lose."

By the time they made it back to Main Street, chaos and death covered the streets in a gruesome, crimson wash of blood. Brody parked his truck on the side of the road, ordering her to stay inside, and to drive like a demon if anyone came within ten feet of the vehicle. She understood what it had cost him to take her back into town with him, but she also knew he didn't have any choice. He had to come back and help the others. It was a part of who he was—one of the things that made him so remarkable. The rain had mellowed once again to a gentle mist, and Michaela was able to watch Brody through the front windshield as he fought his way toward the center of the action, where the Runners were still battling their way into the Town Hall, Eric Drake fighting at their side.

"It's too late," she could hear Brody shouting, his voice raised so that he could be heard over the chaos. "The League is already dead!"

Mason turned toward him, his expression furious as he listened to Brody, and she knew that he was explaining about Dylan, while danger loomed around them. Again, she could hear Brody shouting, "I'm telling you, man, Dylan's the one!"

Mason shoved him hard, then, nearly sprawling Brody in the middle of the street. "I told you that was enough of that shit!"

Taking down a gray werewolf, Jeremy turned and lunged between them, shoving them apart, at the same time Brody shouted, "I'm telling you the truth, Mase. He confessed to Doucet. Told her everything. Said the only way to put an end to this is to take down Drake."

"Goddamn it," Mason roared. "If you're lying, I'm taking you apart myself."

"Oh, but he isn't lying," a cold voice suddenly called out, and her gaze scanned their surroundings as Michaela searched for the source.

The Runners looked up to see Stefan Drake standing just outside the now-open door at the same time Michaela did, a cruel reptilian smile of triumph creasing his lean face. At his back, werewolves filed out of the Hall, one after another, their jaws dripping with blood. "With the help of your dear friend, I've taken out the League, and you Runners will be next. I'll gain control of the Silvercrest, and my rogues will maintain order. Anyone who doesn't like the new establishment will, of course, be dealt with accordingly."

"You sound awfully cocky for someone who hasn't won yet," she heard Jeremy call out.

"It's only a matter of time," Drake laughed. "The second I give the word, you and your pathetic friends are going to be torn to pieces. There'll be too many of them for you to fight at once, no matter how bloody good you are at killing."

With her breath held tight in her chest, Michaela watched in horror as the first wolves threw themselves from the top step, taking the Runners to the ground. She sat frozen in fear, until she saw Drake moving down the stairs. He didn't even have to fight his way through the gory battle; a small group of the feral wolves he controlled moved with him for protection. She wondered what he was up to, until she realized he was stalking closer and closer to where Brody now stood fighting at the edge of the group.

As if moving through a thick, hazy fog, Michaela found herself opening the door and climbing out of the truck, her steps gradually picking up speed, drawing her nearer to the bloodthirsty fighting. She felt…compelled, positive that something awful was going to happen. She had no claws or fangs, or powers like Jillian's that could help her in a fight. All she had was the love that burned in her heart, propelling her forward. Her skin felt tight, hot, while a cold wave of terror swept through her insides.

Brody was engaged in deadly battle with a black-furred werewolf, their claws clashing against one another. He lunged to his side when the Lycan made a move for his gut, then stepped back as the wolf advanced and separated him from the rest of the Runners, herding him toward the steps that Drake was slowly descending. As the Elder's hands transformed into sinister claws she realized what Drake meant to do.

Reacting purely on instinct, Michaela began running right into the heart of the battle, straight toward the man she loved.

Chapter 15

A strange sense of finality spread over Brody's flesh, as if death were stroking his skin, as his opponent maneuvered him to the edge of the conflict and away from the others. He knew he needed to take him down, and fast, before he was attacked by one of the wolves on the stairs behind him. Striking out with a powerful side kick, he slammed his boot into the Lycan's jaw, breaking it, at the same time as a high-pitched cry of outrage sounded behind him. Spinning, he found Michaela diving between him and Stefan Drake, who was lunging at him from the steps leading up to the Town Hall.

With only a split second to react, Brody wrapped his arms around her and reared backward, dragging her with him, but he wasn't fast enough. She screamed, jolting in his arms as Drake's claws sliced into her abdomen, their backward momentum as Brody crashed onto the ground the only thing that kept her from being ripped in two. A great roaring wave of fury filled his head, broken and raw. He knew he'd made the horrific sound, though he couldn't feel the cry breaking out of him. All he could feel was rage as he watched the Elder stalk forward, the tips of his claws stained with Michaela's blood.

"She's mine now!" Drake snarled, while his pale eyes burned with maniacal triumph and he lunged forward, going for the kill. Brody shouted for Cian, but knew his partner couldn't get to them fast enough. Sprawled on his back, with Michaela's injured body draped lifelessly over him, Brody felt the cold chill of inevitability seep into him as he realized he couldn't move quickly enough to save her. Like an evil specter, Drake descended closer, his malevolent gaze fixed on Michaela's throat as his jaw expanded and his fangs speared through his gums. Brody clutched Michaela in his arms and rolled, shielding her with his body and protecting her throat as he tumbled her beneath his frame. And then, just as Drake reached them, something slammed the Elder's body to the side, the powerful force moving so rapidly that Brody couldn't be sure what it was.

Brushing the long, windblown strands of Michaela's hair out of his face, he turned his head to see Dylan Riggs rolling over the bloodied road with Drake, locked in battle. It was clear that despite Drake's power, Dylan had the upper hand. As if sensing that fact, Drake opened his mouth, calling out to the feral wolves still battling the Runners and Eric. "Take him down!" the Elder screamed. "I want Riggs dead!"

Like puppets on a string, the wolves instantly ceased their battles and moved toward the two fighting Elders wrestling in the middle of the road. Dylan pinned Drake's body beneath his as they locked claws, their bodies human but for the shape of their hands and heads. Like zombies robbed of their free will, the Lycans threw themselves at the Elders, one after another, until the two were lost in a snarling, writhing pile of bodies.

"Mother of God," he heard his partner rasp as the Irishman crouched beside him. Blood oozed from a nasty gash on Cian's temple, dripping down the side of his face in a thin, meandering trail.

"Help me sit up," Brody croaked, trying to be as gentle as possible with Michaela's limp form while Cian supported his back and helped him into position. From the corner of his eye, he watched Eric and the Runners move toward them, the group as battered and bloodied as Brody felt.

"They're both going to end up dead," Mason snarled, and Wyatt grunted in agreement.

Stunned, the weary group stared in shock, unable to believe what they were witnessing. It was a gruesome, violent sight, until suddenly the roiling mountain of bodies grew eerily still. Like a caving mound of sand, the mountain fell as the Lycans began stumbling away from the pile, changing fluidly back into their human shapes. They swayed on their feet, clutching their heads, many falling to their knees, confused and disoriented. Some burst into tears, while others just stood in the middle of the street, staring at their blood-covered bodies with horrified looks of astonishment.

As they staggered away, one by one, the two Elders were finally revealed. Cian made a sharp, hissing sound through his teeth, while Mason swore under his breath. Drake's body had been torn into mangled pieces, while Dylan lay on his back beneath him. Somehow, he'd managed to roll Drake on top of him when the feral wolves had closed in, and though his chest lifted with short, shallow breaths, he was obviously dying from his injuries.

"Dylan," Mason rasped, kneeling beside the broken, bloodied body of his friend. Dylan's flesh was torn in more places than not, vicious bite marks on the side of his throat, down his arms, his abdomen. "Hold on, man. We'll get you to Jillian."

"No," Dylan argued weakly, his voice a hoarse thread of sound. "I need to...talk."

"It can wait," Mason grunted.

"Can't..." Dylan gasped, his breath rattling in his chest. "I've lied to you, Mase. And misled you. I told you I was in Alaska at the time that you were finding those first dead girls. I lied to throw you off my track. I was hiding out on the other side of the mountain, trying to get my head together."

"Christ," Mason grated, his shock at learning that his friend was the brutal killer they'd been hunting, as well as Drake's accomplice, evident in the hollow sound of his voice. "They were yours? All but the redhead that Simmons killed?"

"Yeah," Dylan croaked, his face nothing more than a ravaged mask of pain.

"For God's sake, why?" Mason demanded.

"Ask Michaela. She'll...explain. Told her...everything. I'm...I'm sorry, Mase," he said softly. "I was going to run...but...I'm glad I came back."

The Elder drew in his final breath, and his head listed to the side. Mason leaned down and closed his eyes, then turned back toward the place where Brody sat in agonized silence, clutching Michaela against his chest, her body cradled across his lap.

"Where's Jillian?" Brody hissed, rocking her gently in his

arms, painfully aware that her life was slipping away with every second that passed by.

"I've already called her. She's on her way," Jeremy told him. But it was obvious the Runner feared his wife was going to be too late.

Brody didn't know how many minutes passed before Cian knelt down beside him again, but it felt like hours, the time stretched out and drawn like a body on the rack. He'd pressed his left hand against Michaela's blood-soaked sweater, across her wounded abdomen, still rocking her gently back and forth, devastated by the knowledge he was losing her. It twisted through him like a lethal blade, as if it were his own life spilling out over his fingers in a warm, wet flow.

"Brody, man, you need to loosen your hold on her."

"No," he croaked, his own voice unrecognizable, ravaged by grief. "I can't let go."

"You've got to," Cian told him, placing his hand on Brody's shoulder, "or Jillian won't be able to get to her injury."

"She's dying," he rasped, his vision blurred by tears for the first time since he was a boy, as he pressed his lips to her temple, her skin cool and infinitely soft against his mouth. He blinked impatiently at the hot tears that wouldn't stop falling. And then he could see Jillian settling on her knees in front of him, her gentle voice telling him to loosen his hold through the roar of noise buzzing in his ears—loud and disorienting—but he couldn't do it. His body wouldn't follow the command of his mind.

"Listen, man. She's going to be okay," Cian assured him, his deep voice cut with compassion. "Just let Jillian do her thing. She's going to make it, Brody."

Taking a slow, trembling breath, he reached deep and

finally found the strength to relax his muscles, easing his hold on her, and she fell softly away from his chest, still cradled within his arms.

With gentle movements, Jillian lifted Michaela's gray sweater away from her stomach, pushing up the bloodstained material to reveal the horrifying evidence of her wounds. His gut clenched, heart stuttering, breath suspended, unable to comprehend why she'd done it, putting herself between him and Drake the way she had.

Saving his life.

Michaela gave a soft, nearly inaudible groan and turned her face toward him, nuzzling his bicep, when Jillian placed her hands directly over the raw, vicious claw marks that had ripped open her skin.

Time seemed suspended as Jillian knelt there on the blood-covered ground, eyes closed, blond hair concealing her face while she whispered quietly under her breath, her skin glowing a warm, vibrant shade of gold, as if lit with heat from within. No one spoke a word as they waited for the Spirit Walker's power to work its magic on Michaela's tender flesh.

Carefully shifting her head into the crook of his arm, Brody leaned down, pressed his mouth against the tender shell of Michaela's ear, and whispered his secrets to her, the emotion pouring out of him in a broken, rambling stream of words.

He only wished that he'd had the guts to say them sooner…when she could have heard them.

Walking through the front door of his cabin the following morning, Brody couldn't help but notice the increase in his heart rate at the thought of seeing Michaela. She'd still been sleeping peacefully when he'd left at daybreak, going with the other Runners back up to Shadow Peak to help deal with the lingering confusion and chaos that would take weeks, if not months, to sort out.

When he'd gotten Michaela back to his cabin the previous afternoon, he'd laid her in his bed, tucking the covers up around her chin, handling her as if she were made of spun glass. Making his way into the kitchen, he'd found the others waiting for him, Torrance and Reyes sitting at the table with a shattered looking Mason, while Cian and Wyatt had propped themselves up against the counters, their ankles crossed in front of them. Reyes's right arm had been in a sling, bandages in various shapes and sizes covering the others, since Jillian would've been drained if she'd healed each of their injuries. She'd handled the severe ones, but most were left to heal the old-fashioned way, over time.

They'd discussed Drake's plan, marveling at how all the pieces had fit together in the end. The Elder had finally gotten the revenge he'd wanted against the League for failing to order his wife's assassination, and if things had worked the way he'd intended, he would have gained ultimate control of the pack. The move would have allowed him to rule the Silvercrest with a prejudiced hand, one that would have ushered in a reign of terror, they suspected, for both Lycans and humans alike.

In its own twisted way, his plan had been horrifically brilliant. By using the townspeople to murder the League, Drake had not only found the means of gaining the power he coveted, but he'd done it in a way that would have played on the guilt of those who'd made the kills, even though the feral wolves had been under Drake's control at the time. And with his contingent of rogues already in place, he'd had the means of keeping in line anyone who disagreed with the new leadership, like his own personal, diabolical SS.

Eventually, everyone had headed home, and Brody had made his way back to Michaela. Unable to resist, he'd lain down beside her, needing to be close to her, holding her in his arms, reassuring himself that she was okay. That they'd survived the nightmare.

As he'd slid under the covers, hope had begun to burn in his chest as he thought of what she'd done that day. Why had she put herself in front of him that way? What did it signify? He was so afraid to believe, and yet he couldn't stop the foreign, sweet churning of excitement, of hope, burning like a warm, dazzling glow in his chest, expanding out through his body in a gently pulsing wave. As tired as he'd been, he'd felt more alive than ever before, looking forward to the morning— to the moment when she'd awaken and they could talk.

Now, as he wandered through the cabin, making his way toward the bedroom, he rubbed at that pulsing spark of heat in the center of his chest, a low rumble of laughter breaking out of him as he realized what the odd sensation was.

Happiness.

Wearing a crooked grin, he stepped quietly into the bedroom, in case she was still sleeping. But she wasn't. In fact, the bed was empty. Turning around, he hurried back through the cabin, his heart pounding harder with each breath when he failed to find her anywhere.

Heading for the front door, Brody ripped it open, intending to go straight to Mason's cabin and look for her there, but he was brought up short by Cian, who stood on his doormat, a cigarette hanging precariously from the corner of his mouth. "Let me guess," the Irishman drawled. "You've lost your little lady love."

Brody scowled. "How the hell do you know that?"

"Just ran into Jeremy," Cian murmured, slipping past him into the cabin, making himself at home as he perched on the wide arm of a leather chair. "He said that both Torrance and Jillian are gone. Left notes saying they'd be back tonight and not to worry."

Rubbing his palm against his whiskered jaw, Brody asked, "And what does that have to do with Michaela?"

Cian shook his head with mock sympathy. "You're not thinking straight, boyo. Obviously, all the ladies have wandered off together while we were up in town."

"Goddamn it," he grunted under his breath as realization suddenly dawned, and with it the sickening knowledge that he'd lost her—that she'd left him. "They've taken her home."

"Probably," his partner drawled, pinching his cigarette between his thumb and index finger and taking a slow drag, while keeping his keen gaze focused on Brody. He knew the bastard was studying his reaction, but he couldn't play it cool. Too much was crashing together inside of him. Anger. Hurt. Frustration. Turning to pace toward the far wall, Brody ripped his hands back through his hair, then locked his hands behind his neck, his jaw grinding. All the budding hope that had been burning in his chest since last night turned to ash, charred by the devastating sense of loss flooding through him, and he struggled to hold back the telling, guttural stream of obscenities that poured quietly from his lips.

"I thought so," Cian whispered, narrowing his pale gray gaze. "You sneaky son of a bitch. You've been keeping secrets, boyo."

"What the hell are you talking about?"

"I'm talking about the fact that she's your mate!" Cian growled, tossing the butt of his cigarette in the empty grate as he surged to his feet. "Were you ever planning on telling her?"

Like a verbal set of brakes, the Irishman's words stopped him dead in his tracks. For a moment, he just stood there, panting, every muscle in his body rigid with tension, and then he finally croaked, "Hell no."

"Why not?"

"Open your damn eyes, Cian!" he snarled, pinning his scowling partner with a blistering look of outrage. "In case you didn't notice, she could do a helluva lot better than tying herself to me for the rest of her life!"

"Well, she apparently doesn't share your crappy opinion," Cian snapped, his fury evident in the crisp tones of his speech. "If she did, she wouldn't have nearly gotten herself killed yesterday trying to save your miserable ass. She loves you, man."

Brody made a rude sound in the back of his throat. "If that's true, then why did she leave me?"

"Jaysus, you don't understand anything about women, do you?" Cian grunted, making Brody want to throttle him.

"Don't push me," he growled.

"You need it," his partner shot back. "You need to have your miserable ass kicked, is what you need."

"She left me!" Brody roared, losing complete control of his temper, nearly floored by the caving pain in his chest.

"And did you give her any reason to stay?" Cian demanded. "Did you ever tell her how you feel about her?" Brody's silence was all the answer the Runner needed. "Yeah, that's what I thought," the Irishman sighed, his voice thick with disgust. "Did it ever occur to you that she'd need to know, Brody? That she has her own fears? She can't read your goddamn mind."

His partner was right. She *couldn't* read him.

Hesitantly, he said, "You think I should tell her?"

"If you can find her," Cian snorted with a heavy dose of sarcasm. "Honestly, you're as bad as Mason was before he finally pulled his head out of his ass and married Torrance. From this point on it's mandatory bonding for the lot of you. God knows you guys can't keep track of your women."

"I know where she's gone," he stated in a quiet rasp, his anger swiftly shifting into nervous energy that ramped up his heart rate with stunning force. All that churning chaos was slowly coming together, solidifying into a brilliant, terrifying plan. "She would have gone back home, to her house in Covington."

"Then get off your ass and go get her," Cian drawled, while the corner of his mouth kicked up in a grin, his gray eyes glittering and bright. "Or else I'm going to be stuck listening to you bitch and moan for the rest of my days."

Yeah, that's it. Go get her. Tell her everything. All of it.

Could it really be that simple? Like walking to the edge of a cliff and just flinging himself off in a daring, breathtaking dive, hoping he didn't crash and burn.

Rubbing at his chest, Brody looked inside himself. Was he brave enough to go after the prize? To put his heart on the line and finally tell her everything he'd bottled up inside?

Damn straight he was.

Brody made the drive down to Covington in record time, and just as he'd expected, Jillian's car sat parked in front of Michaela's house. In fact, it was the pack's Spirit Walker who answered the door when he knocked. Before she could say anything, he shoved his shaking hands in his pockets and blurted out, "I need to see Michaela. Alone."

Snuffling a soft giggle under her breath, she smiled and moved aside so that he could enter. Torrance grinned at him, and the two women shared a knowing look as they slipped on their jackets. "We'll give you two some privacy and head back home now," Jillian told him, surprising him with a quick hug.

"Better start getting your excuses ready," he warned them with a wry grin. "Mase and Jeremy are pissed as hell that you left the Alley without telling them."

Jillian laughed, and Torrance rolled her eyes. "They'll get over it. And Mic ran upstairs to grab a quick shower, but she should be getting dressed by now. I think she's gonna be happy to see you." She winked at him then, and they walked out of the house, closing the door behind them. Taking his hands out of his pockets, Brody rubbed his damp palms on his jeans-covered thighs, released a choppy breath, then turned and headed up the stairs.

He found Michaela in the spare bedroom they'd shared before, staring out a window that looked over the backyard. She was wearing stonewashed jeans and a long pink sweater that looked fuzzy and soft as it hugged the womanly perfection of her body. Dappled sunlight painted her skin a warm, golden hue, glinting off the midnight strands of her hair as it fell in long, feminine curls over one shoulder.

She turned, as if sensing his presence, and the second their gazes caught, her dark blue eyes went wide with surprise. "You came," she gasped.

Nodding, he wanted to demand an explanation for why she'd left him. Instead, Brody heard himself say, "There's something I should have told you, Michaela."

Her lush mouth trembled, glossy and soft, and she wrapped her arms around herself, her eyes luminous with tears, so beautiful they took his breath. Quietly, she said, "You don't need to thank me for what happened, Brody."

"Well, there's that, too," he rasped with a tender smile, "but I was thinking more along the lines of—"

"Mon dieu," she suddenly cried, as if only just realizing what he'd said. "You called me Michaela! You *never* call me by my first name."

His smile slipped into a nervous grin. "That's because I've been terrified of getting too close to you, of how I felt about you, but I—"

"You're not stuck with me any longer," she said shakily, cutting him off again. He could see the tenuous hold she had on her emotions slipping, her cheekbones flushed with vibrant color, breath coming in short, shallow pants. "You no longer have to protect me. It's...over, Brody."

"Not quite," he murmured, stepping into the room, the need to touch her like a physical ache within his body.

She blinked, looking uncertain. "What do you mean?"

"We still have unfinished business, sweetheart."

"We do?" she asked in a breathless rush, followed by a whispered, "Did you just call me sweetheart?"

"Sure did," he drawled, wearing a ghost of a smile.

Terrified she was going to wake up and find she'd been dreaming, Michaela watched as Brody stepped closer, then closer still. When he stood before her, he took her face in his hands, carefully avoiding the healing scratches made by Dustin's claws. The touch of his callused skin was hot and slightly rough, his warm, masculine scent filling her head like the rush of a pleasure-giving drug, smooth and rich and sweet. Shaking with nerves and excitement, she stammered, "Wh-what unfinished b-business?"

"The fact that you're my life mate," he rasped, staring deeply into her eyes, the fierce green of his gaze burning with tender intensity. "As well as the fact that I'm madly in love with you."

"You're…what?" Michaela croaked, blinking up at him in amazement, unable to believe she'd heard him correctly.

"I love you." The corner of his mouth lifted in a boyish smile, and as he threaded his fingers through her hair, she could have sworn his eyes glittered with a sheen of tears.

"You love me?" she gasped.

"Completely. Utterly. Irrevocably. Always. And forever," he rumbled, his deep voice so wonderfully sexy, it made her shiver. "And if you ever leave me again, I won't be able to make it without you."

"Oh my God, Brody," she sniffed, her eyes overflowing with the hot, salty wash of tears that burst out of her. "I love you, too."

He caught a teardrop with his thumb, asking, "Then why did you leave me?"

"I wanted to stay so badly. But I…I needed to put this decision in your hands. I was too afraid to hope that anything like this could ever happen, but I knew if we had any kind of chance, then I had to trust my heart and have faith that you would come after me, or else I'd spend the rest of my life always wondering, never knowing if you were with me out of some sense of gratitude or guilt. I didn't want you to feel pressured. I was so scared, but I knew I had to have faith that you'd come for me, if that's what you really wanted."

"I'd like to see you try to keep me away," he murmured in a husky tone roughened by emotion, while he rubbed his thumb against the corner of her mouth. "And the only guilt I've felt is sticking you with someone like me. I know you deserve so much better than me, but I swear I'll love you, that I'll be true to you, till the day I die."

"Brody, I love you so much," she sighed, unable to stop the cathartic flow of tears, "but sometimes you can be so blind. There is *no one* better than you."

A sexy rumble of laughter fell from his lips, his breath warm and soft and sweet against her mouth. "God, you're the blind one, sweetheart. But I'm sure as hell not going to be the one to buy you glasses."

"I don't need them," she sniffed, pressing her palms against his chest, over the thunderous pounding of his heart. "I see you just fine, inside and out."

Arching one russet-colored brow, he said, "I thought you couldn't read me?"

"I don't need powers to know the kind of man you are," she told him with firm conviction.

"Oh yeah? And what kind is that?"

"Brave. Beautiful. Honorable and strong. Rough and tender and everything I could ever want. And mine," she stated with a rich, delicious sense of satisfaction. "All mine."

His hands smoothed their way down her neck, to the curve of her shoulders, before trailing down the length of her back, setting a blaze of need beneath her skin, melting her with desire. "All yours," he rasped. "For as long as you'll want me."

"Then you had best settle in for forever, because once I claim you, I'm never letting you go."

"Claim me?" he drawled, flashing her a slow, wicked smile that made her toes curl. "Sounds kinky."

Michaela laughed, pressing her damp face into the warm hollow of his throat. "I'll do my best to see that it is."

He lifted her face with his fingers beneath her chin and kissed her then, and it was unlike any other kiss she'd ever had. Full of breathless passion and urgent need, and yet, achingly tender, conveying just how desperately he cared about her. She could taste the emotion on his lips, feel it in the tremor of his body against hers.

"I want to be the last wolf watching over you," he growled, taking her to the nearest bed and pulling their clothes from their bodies. When he laid her out over the cool, crisp sheets, he pressed reverent kisses over the healing pink scars that crossed her abdomen, then higher, covering the aching tips of her breasts with his mouth, one by one. "I want that right," he rasped moments later, breathless, his hunger conveyed through the urgency of his touch as he positioned her beneath him, "along with all the others, to be mine and mine alone."

"Always," she whispered as passion consumed them, spinning them in its shimmering, dazzling web. They couldn't touch enough, get close enough.

"Hurry," she urged him, running her palms down the slick heat of his spine, craving his possession with a need that would have frightened her, if he hadn't been there to keep her safe.

He threaded their fingers together, imprisoning her hands on either side of her head, covering her with his heat, with the mouthwatering strength of his hard, beautiful body, so warm and solid and perfectly male. "No," he told her in a husky rasp that made her shiver from the inside out. "This time I *take* my time."

"No way," she argued, arching beneath him, rubbing her body against his, doing everything she could to seduce him to her will. "We have the rest of our lives to take our time. I need you *now,* Brody!"

"Michaela," he groaned, and she loved the sexy way that he said her name, the sound of it on his lips the most provocative thing she'd ever heard. "Don't tempt me right now, sweetheart. I need to hold it together, and you're going to push me past my control."

"And maybe that's what I like. Pushing you to the edge. You don't scare me, Brody. I love every part of you."

"Damn it," he hissed, and she could see the sharp points of his fangs as his lips pulled back over his teeth.

She took a deep, trembling breath, then softly said, "If I were to say that you want to bite me right now, I'd be right, wouldn't I?"

He closed his eyes, his features tight with strain, accentuating the pale lines of his scars, then slowly lifted his lashes. "Yes," he grated, his voice hoarse. "You'd be right."

"Well then, what are you waiting for?" she drawled, loving the heated look of surprise that flared in his eyes. "Go ahead and stake your claim, Brody. In case it escaped your notice, I'm not telling you no."

He stared down at her, his breath rushing through his slightly parted lips—and then he smiled, slow and sweet and beautiful. "Trust me, baby. I noticed."

"I want it, too," she confessed, meaning every word. "I want you to do it, Brody."

The corner of his mouth twitched as he rumbled, "Christ, woman, you could tempt a saint."

"Oh yeah?" she laughed. "And what about a devil?"

"Him, too," he grunted. "But I'm not going to put you through that right now. I love you too much, Michaela. No matter how badly I want it, we're waiting till you're strong enough."

"I'm strong enough now," she argued, rubbing herself against the hot, thick heat of his rigid cock as it pressed heavily against her stomach, huge and hard and hungry. She wanted him so badly she could have screamed, desire coiling through her like a smoldering spark that only he could ignite.

His hair fell around his face like a crimson veil, thick and beautiful as he shook his head, growling, "No."

"Oh yeah," she murmured in a seductive tone. "Just see if I'm not. And I have to warn you that I won't let you hide from me anymore, Brody. I'm going to want everything from you. Everything."

"You can have anything from me," he promised in a deep, graveled voice roughened by need, his eyes darkened by hunger. And then, there at the edges of his irises, she could see the warm glow begin to break through, his wolf awakening within his big, beautiful body. "Whatever you want, Michaela. I'll give you everything that I am, that I'll ever be." He shifted lower and pushed inside of her then in a thick, delicious thrust, giving her every inch of him, his muscles flexing…rippling as he rode her, driving deeper…harder, her body so wet, she was more than ready for him. "I can't get deep enough in you," he growled. "I want in your heart, in your mind, in your very soul. I want to own them. Claim them."

"Yours," she told him with a husky cry, writhing beneath him as he pressed his mouth against the side of her throat, his hair soft against her face and shoulders, like silk. His fangs pricked against her skin in a deliciously erotic caress, and Michaela knew it wouldn't be long before he could no longer fight the blistering need to bite her.

And to her endless delight, by the time the moon had climbed its way into the evening sky, he'd finally done just that.

Epilogue

Three months later…

Curled up on the swing in front of the house in Covington, Michaela enjoyed the beauty of the sunset while Brody put dinner on in the kitchen. He'd sent her outside with a chilled glass of Pinot, telling her to simply relax and enjoy her wine. They'd spent a beautiful weekend in the city, but tomorrow they would head back up to the Alley, to their cabin and their friends.

It still amazed her, the changes that the last three months had brought to their lives and to the pack, since the deaths of Stefan Drake and Dylan Riggs. In a shocking move to improve relations between the Bloodrunners and the Silvercrest, Eric Drake had organized an interim government based on free election—one in which the Runners would play a significant role, handling all elements of security for the pack and the town. In fact, her brother and Elliot now shared an apartment in Shadow Peak, and were both set to begin their Bloodrunning training by summertime.

And while it had taken another week of searching, the Runners had finally found the mountain hideout for Drake's teenage rogues, many of whom had been forced to turn. Most of them had refused to give in and ended up dying in battle. There were some rogues, though, who had come home in tears, emotionally scarred, but with the help of Jillian and her mother, Constance, who had offered her assistance, they were slowly finding peace. Their guilt, however, for the things they had done would live with them forever.

There had also been talk, thanks to Eric, of rewriting the Bloodrunners Law so that full-privileged membership was a right available to all Runners automatically, though the men had grumbled about it, claiming it wasn't necessary. Despite the fact that relations between the Runners and pack were slowly improving, Michaela knew it was going to be a long while before past animosities and resentments were forgotten. The pack lay on the verge of a new era—the arcane, rigid ways of the past giving way to the freer, open-minded path of the future. As Eric would often say, the Lycans had evolved, and it was time their societal rules and structures evolved with them, though they knew it wouldn't be an easy road. Still, it was a fascinating time, like watching the birth of a civilization.

But the most miraculous change of all was in the man who held her heart. Michaela had never dreamed that Brody could lower his shields to let her in the way he had, and yet, he'd opened himself to her completely. She knew, because from the moment their blood bond had been made, she'd been able to "read" him—and what she saw in her mate made her feel like the luckiest, most cherished, most beloved woman in the entire world. And best of all was the happiness she could feel burning inside him. At her urging, he'd even made contact with his grandmother, putting the pain of his past behind him and learning to forgive.

Abigail had even come to their wedding the month before, and enjoyed herself immensely, sharing a special dance with her grandson that had brought tears to Michaela's eyes. But then, she'd been teary eyed that entire day, so full of love and happiness, it had been impossible to hold it all inside. Max had given her away, and a great roaring cheer had gone up from the guests when Brody had devilishly bent her back over his arm as he'd kissed her, the touch of his mouth against hers the sweetest, most poignant moment of her life. He'd whispered a husky "I love you" against her lips, and she'd melted from the possessive, joy-filled look on his handsome face.

As if summoned by her thoughts, the screen door opened and Brody stepped out onto the front porch. Their next-door neighbors, the Hendersons, were in their front yard gardening, and they waved when they caught sight of the tall Runner. Unlike before, when he would have shied away from all humans, he held his head high, his thick auburn hair pulled back from his ruggedly beautiful face in a sinfully sexy ponytail, and gave the elderly neighbors a friendly wave in return. Feeling overcome with emotion, Michaela smiled at him, beckoning him closer with her finger. A powerful look of love and hunger darkened his deep green eyes, and his mouth curled in a devil's grin as he moved toward her, saying, "You just made one of my favorite daydreams come true."

She laughed softly, and when he reached the swing, he

leaned over her, placing a hot, delicious kiss against her mouth, making her melt as easily as he always did.

They spent the last minutes of twilight cuddling there on the swing, content just to be in each other's arms. As the sun finally dipped beneath the horizon, Brody pressed his mouth to hers, and whispered, "I love you so much, Michaela. All I want is to spend the rest of my life with you, making you happy, giving you everything your heart desires, making all your dreams come true."

With the soft, lavender twilight surrounding them, Michaela curled her arms around his shoulders with soul-deep pleasure, gave him an impish smile, and said, "Speaking of dreams, I've been wanting to tell you about this one I had on the night you first kissed me. There was this field, filled with flowers, and you and I were playing with a beautiful baby girl…"

* * * * *

Be sure to watch for more scintillating romances from Rhyannon Byrd, coming to both Silhouette Nocturne and HQN Books in spring 2009.

THOROUGHBRED LEGACY
*The stakes are high when it comes to love,
horse racing, family secrets
and broken promises.*

*A new exciting Harlequin continuity series coming soon!
Led by* New York Times *bestselling author Elizabeth Bevarly*
FLIRTING WITH TROUBLE

Here's a preview!

THE DOOR CLOSED behind them, throwing them into darkness and leaving them utterly alone. And the next thing Daniel knew, he heard himself saying, "Marnie, I'm sorry about the way things turned out in Del Mar."

She said nothing at first, only strode across the room and stared out the window beside him. Although he couldn't see her well in the darkness—he still hadn't switched on a light…but then, neither had she—he imagined her expression was a little preoccupied, a little anxious, a little confused.

Finally, very softly, she said, "Are you?"

He nodded, then, worried she wouldn't be able to see the gesture, added, "Yeah. I am. I should have said goodbye to you."

"Yes, you should have."

Actually, he thought, there were a lot of things he should have done in Del Mar. He'd had *a lot* riding on the Pacific Classic, and even more on his entry, Little Joe, but after meeting Marnie, the Pacific Classic had been the last thing on Daniel's mind. His loss at Del Mar had pretty much ended his career before it had even begun, and he'd had to start all over again, rebuilding from nothing.

He simply had not then and did not now have room in his life for a woman as potent as Marnie Roberts. He was a horseman first and foremost. From the time he was a schoolboy, he'd known what he wanted to do with his life—be the best possible trainer he could be.

He had to make sure Marnie understood—and he understood, too—why things had ended the way they had eight years ago. He just wished he could find the words to do that. Hell, he wished he could find the *thoughts* to do that.

"You made me forget things, Marnie, things that I really needed to remember. And that scared the hell out of me. Little Joe should have won the Classic. He was by far the best horse entered in that race. But I didn't give him the attention he needed and deserved that week, because all I could think about was you. Hell, when I woke up that morning all I wanted to do was lie there and look at you, and then wake you up and make love to you again. If I hadn't left when I did— the way I did—I might still be lying there in that bed with you, thinking about nothing else."

"And would that be so terrible?" she asked.

"Of course not," he told her. "But that wasn't why I was in Del Mar," he repeated. "I was in Del Mar to win a race. That was my job. And my work was the most important thing to me."

She said nothing for a moment, only studied his face in the darkness as if looking for the answer to a very important question. Finally she asked, "And what's the most important thing to you now, Daniel?"

Wasn't the answer to that obvious? "My work," he answered automatically.

She nodded slowly. "Of course," she said softly. "That is, after all, what you do best."

Her comment, too, puzzled him. She made it sound as if being good at what he did was a bad thing.

She bit her lip thoughtfully, her eyes fixed on his, glimmering in the scant moonlight that was filtering through the window. And damned if Daniel didn't find himself wanting to pull her into his arms and kiss her. But as much as it might have felt as if no time had passed since Del Mar, there were eight years between now and then. And eight years was a long time in the best of circumstances. For Daniel and Marnie, it was virtually a lifetime.

So Daniel turned and started for the door, then halted. He couldn't just walk away and leave things as they were, unsettled. He'd done that eight years ago and regretted it.

"It *was* good to see you again, Marnie," he said softly. And since he was being honest, he added, "I hope we see each other again."

She didn't say anything in response, only stood silhouetted against the window with her arms wrapped around her in a way that made him wonder whether she was doing it because she was cold, or if she just needed something—someone—to hold on to. In either case, Daniel understood. There was an emptiness clinging to him that he suspected would be there for a long time.

* * * * *

THOROUGHBRED LEGACY
coming soon wherever books are sold!

Thoroughbred Legacy

Launching in June 2008

A dramatic new 12-book continuity that embodies the American Dream.

Meet the Prestons, owners of Quest Stables, a successful horse-racing and breeding empire. But the lives, loves and reputations of this hardworking family are put at risk when a breeding scandal unfolds.

Flirting with Trouble

by *New York Times* bestselling author

ELIZABETH BEVARLY

Eight years ago, publicist Marnie Roberts spent seven days of bliss with Australian horse trainer Daniel Whittleson. But just as quickly, he disappeared. Now Marnie is heading to Australia to finally confront the man she's never been able to forget.

The stakes are high when it comes to love, horse racing, family secrets and broken promises.

A new exciting Harlequin continuity series coming soon!

www.eHarlequin.com

HT38984R

Silhouette Desire

Cole's Red-Hot Pursuit

Cole Westmoreland is a man who gets what he wants. And he wants independent and sultry Patrina Forman! She resists him—until a Montana blizzard traps them together. For three delicious nights, Cole indulges Patrina with his brand of seduction. When the sun comes out, Cole and Patrina are left to wonder—will this be the end of the passion that storms between them?

Look for

COLE'S RED-HOT PURSUIT

by USA TODAY bestselling author

BRENDA JACKSON

Available in June 2008 wherever you buy books.

Always Powerful, Passionate and Provocative.

REQUEST YOUR FREE BOOKS!

2 FREE NOVELS PLUS 2 FREE GIFTS!

Silhouette®

n o c t u r n e™

Dramatic and Sensual Tales of Paranormal Romance.

YES! Please send me 2 FREE Silhouette® Nocturne™ novels and my 2 FREE gifts (gifts are worth about $10). After receiving them, if I don't wish to receive any more books, I can return the shipping statement marked "cancel." If I don't cancel, I will receive 4 brand-new novels every other month and be billed just $4.47 per book in the U.S. or $4.99 per book in Canada, plus 25¢ shipping and handling per book plus applicable taxes, if any*. That's a savings of about 15% off the cover price! I understand that accepting the 2 free books and gifts places me under no obligation to buy anything. I can always return a shipment and cancel at any time. Even if I never buy another book from Silhouette, the two free books and gifts are mine to keep forever.

238 SDN ELS4   338 SDN ELXG

Name	(PLEASE PRINT)

Address	Apt. #

City	State/Prov.	Zip/Postal Code

Signature (if under 18, a parent or guardian must sign)

Mail to the **Silhouette Reader Service:**
IN U.S.A.: P.O. Box 1867, Buffalo, NY 14240-1867
IN CANADA: P.O. Box 609, Fort Erie, Ontario L2A 5X3

Not valid to current subscribers of Silhouette Nocturne books.

Want to try two free books from another line?
Call 1-800-873-8635 or visit www.morefreebooks.com.

* Terms and prices subject to change without notice. N.Y. residents add applicable sales tax. Canadian residents will be charged applicable provincial taxes and GST. This offer is limited to one order per household. All orders subject to approval. Credit or debit balances in a customer's account(s) may be offset by any other outstanding balance owed by or to the customer. Please allow 4 to 6 weeks for delivery. Offer available while quantities last.

Your Privacy: Silhouette is committed to protecting your privacy. Our Privacy Policy is available online at www.eHarlequin.com or upon request from the Reader Service. From time to time we make our lists of customers available to reputable third parties who may have a product or service of interest to you. If you would prefer we not share your name and address, please check here. ☐

SN08

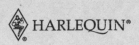

nocturne™

COMING NEXT MONTH

#41 WILD HUNT • Lori Devoti
Unbound

Sound the horns and let loose the hellhounds!
Venge Leidolf travels the nine worlds looking for
ways to grow stronger—only to be truly tested by
Geysa Brynhild. Together, the natural enemies—
hellhound and Valkyrie—brave the great hellhound hunt,
only to be overcome by forces neither can control.

#42 DARK DECEIVER • Pamela Palmer
The Esri

Kaderil the Dark is the most feared immortal in
Esria—and he plans to invade the human realm. In
Autumn McGinn he disovers the means to claim victory,
if only she'll betray her people. Torn between duty and
conscience, can Kaderil overcome his sinister desires—or
will he find redemption in Autumn's vibrant embrace?

SNCNM0508